HOT CHOCOLATE FOR THE UNICORN

HOT CHOCOLATE FOR THE UNICORN

AND OTHER FLIGHTS OF FANCY

MARY E. LOWD

CONTENTS

1

HOT CHOCOLATE FOR THE UNICORN

THE CURVED neck and stretched wings of the black Dragon dwarf the figure of the doe-like white Unicorn. They make an unlikely picture behind the glass panel and aluminum frame of my sliding glass kitchen door. As always, quite the sight to see. I ask them in.

Scaled claws and downed hooves step through the door. The Dragon slashes his tail, impetuous at being kept so long. The Unicorn paws the linoleum floor and bows his horn. "An honor, as always," he says.

I slide the glass door shut behind them, careful that all the tails are on the right side.

"Is the water ready?" the Unicorn asks.

"Not yet." I walk around the counters to the electric stove feeling the Unicorn close behind, his breath on my shoulder. The Dragon stays away from the kitchen, where cupboards and countertops would cramp his wings. He lingers instead, looking at pictures on the wall. Grumbling to himself.

My tea kettle sits on the Formica counter in the customary spot, nestled between the sink and the toaster. I fill it with water and put it on the stove. The Unicorn shuffles his hooves in restless excitement as I open the cupboard with the mugs. "You know which one I want," he says, "right?"

He always picks the mug with a picture of geese wearing bonnets, drawn by Beatrix Potter.

The kettle whistles, piercingly, and I pour the steaming water. As always, I make ginger tea for the Dragon, lemon tea for myself, and hot chocolate for the Unicorn. I place the mugs on a tray and carry them into the living room where we settle on the floor. My friends are ill-suited to sitting at tables. Chairs don't fit them well.

The Unicorn folds his hooves neatly beneath him, and the dragon crouches, all angles, with his wings half folded and his sinuous limbs bent like compressed springs. Entirely alert. I place their hot beverages before them on the living room rug.

"Shall I tell a story now?" I ask.

"Let's play a board game," says the Dragon. He takes his mug, my largest, in his great talon. He dwarfs the tiny mug and has to drink from it daintily. A giant sipping tea from a thimble.

"I'd like a story," the Unicorn says. He's been blowing on his hot chocolate to cool it. He stretches his snowy neck, leaning his nose down to taste the dark liquid.

"You always want a story," the Dragon snarls. The Unicorn shies away from him, but he's not really scared. The Unicorn and Dragon are the best of friends. My best friends.

"I'll tell stories first," I say. "Then we'll play chess," I tell the Dragon.

The Dragon rolls his massive, round, green eyes heavenward, but he holds his forked tongue. He can wait. Dragons can be both patient and impatient.

I tell stories to the Unicorn until he falls asleep, head resting on hooves, nostrils flaring gently with deep regular breaths, and the shining tip of his horn barely gracing the carpeted floor. His sides heave with a sigh, and I know he's dreaming about the worlds in my stories: a world with an ocean whose smallest drop can turn you into a rabbit; a world where glittering, faceted cat statues are cut from gemstones and come to life; a world where otters fly water-filled spaceships.

"Shall we play chess now?" the Dragon asks, his voice a soft hiss so as to not wake the Unicorn.

I agree, and we're deep in a game when the phone rings. "Just a minute," I say as I go to the old style corded wall phone to answer it.

The call is from my boss. He wants to be sure that I remember to bring in the files for our meeting tomorrow. I hate it when he calls me at home, but it's true that otherwise I would have forgotten. I get the files and place them on the end table by the front door where I can't possibly miss them. Now I won't forget.

I go back to the living room and see my spiral note-book on the floor open to a freshly scribbled page; the copy of *Historical Chess Games* that I checked out from the library is propped up next to my chess board; and there are three mugs—one filled with lemon tea, and two empty on the floor.

"Dammit! This was easier as a child," I say.

I close my eyes and remember my friends. My imaginary friends. They're insubstantial, transparent, shadows of the vivid beings they once were. When I was young, the world was filled with fantastical creatures, and they all centered around me. Ponies galloped through my back-yard; cats with wings flew above me, following wherever I went. I never had to think about them. They were just there. An everyday part of my life.

Now, I work in an office, and I come home to an empty house at night. But I'll be damned if I let them fade out of my life like the song. My Dragon will not be Puff. My Unicorn will not be forgotten.

I open my eyes, and the Dragon says, "It's your turn already. *Move.*"

So easy. And, yet, so easily lost.

I sit down and finish the game with him. When it's over, I place a hand on the Unicorn's rump. He wakes up at the touch and says, "Is it time to go?"

I nod, and I show my friends back to the sliding glass door in the kitchen. "Come back soon," I say as the fear-some black Dragon disappears into the dark of the backyard at night. The small Unicorn walking by his side, glowing and white, is visible much longer.

I close the door and return to the living room. I tuck the notebook and chess book carefully under a throw pillow on the couch. Then, I put the mugs away. Mine in the dishwasher. The other two, I return to the cupboard.

2

<hr>

A PEARL FOR AMELIE

THE LETTER WAS SEALED and stamped but had never been sent. Amelie almost passed it over entirely while going through her aunt's old boxes of science articles and research notes. It was addressed to a professor at the University of Crosshatch, Maryland. Amelie didn't think her aunt had ever worked there, but Aunt Jill had traveled a lot. She'd studied giraffes in Africa and wild horses in the Gobi Desert. She'd worked her way across Europe studying the few remaining bison, all kept in zoos. It seemed like there was nowhere Aunt Jill hadn't been, so Amelie couldn't be sure

Amelie ran her hands over the aged paper and felt a small lump in the corner of the envelope. In the end, though, it was the handwritten address that saved the letter from being dumped, unopened on the discard pile with years worth of vet bills (something was going to have to be done with Aunt Jill's pet pygmy goats, Fred and

Ginger), paperwork, and the other detritus left behind at the end of Aunt Jill's long life.

Amelie could picture Aunt Jill's freckled hands scribbling out the address in that loopy scrawl, and for a flash of a moment, Amelie felt connected to Aunt Jill again, across all these years.

She opened the letter and tilted the envelope. A single white pearl rolled into the palm of her hand. Amelie put the pearl aside carefully in her pocket and pulled out the letter.

The paper inside was frail with age, and the handwritten lines were tight, squeezed up against all the edges, filling every inch of the page. The careful, cursive style spoke of an earlier time, but Amelie could read it. Aunt Jill had insisted she learn, even though cursive hadn't been taught in the schools for years.

July 10, 1959

Dear Professor Kohensart,

I hardly know if I should write this letter to you—let alone send it when I've finished. My studies have taken an unexpected turn here in the Florida Keys. I came to the Keys on a three year grant, nearly two years ago, to study an endangered species of deer, a subspecies of the white-tailed deer, that lives only on these islands.

My grant supplied me with the funds for lodging in a small cabin on No Name Key and the assistance of one graduate student. I selected a young woman, Kara, from one of my upper division courses—the only other woman in my department. We came to our cabin on No Name Key with our bags filled with camping gear. As the entire island is unattached to the electrical power grid, everything in our cabin had to be powered by a small, diesel generator.

We began our work at the tail end of summer. Kara and I followed the Key Deer, watching the different herds, naming and identifying the individuals so we could track their changes and behavior. In the evenings, we talked and played backgammon by the dim, flickering light of a kerosene lamp in our cabin.

Summer waned into fall, and the warm rains warned us that it would be an El Niño winter. In order to increase our observations before the winter set in, I assigned Kara a herd of Key Deer on the coastline, and I kept track of a herd further inland. The long, lonely hours with nothing but deer through binoculars to keep you company and a notepad to tell your thoughts to would be enough to leave anyone feeling a little edgy. And Kara was already troubled.

Kara had recently separated from her husband, and she spoke of him frequently during our backgammon chats. She clearly still loved the man and was tortured by the scandal she'd caused by leaving him. I assumed that they'd fought over her desire to pursue her studies. I believed that she felt the same calling to science that I did.

Every night, before we played backgammon, I looked

over Kara's notes from the day, and we discussed the changes in our herds. The peculiarities in her observations started out small: she spotted an albino deer. It was odd that she hadn't noticed the deer earlier, but albinism among deer is not unheard of. Several days later, she saw the albino deer again. This time, she insisted it was the same deer as one she'd been observing earlier in the month, a deer she called Chaplin. Kara was a fan of the moving pictures, and she named many of the deer in her herd after movie stars: Chaplin, Keaton, Garbo, Hepburn, and Astaire.

An albino deer is an oddity; a normal deer whose fur turned suddenly white? I was forced to begin questioning Kara's reliability.

The next week, Kara told me that Chaplin had lost his antlers. Normally, Key Deer don't shed their antlers until February or March. This was much too early. On the other hand, perhaps this development lent credence to Kara's earlier claims. Perhaps Chaplin was a very sick deer.

Finally, on a particularly rainy night, Kara told me that Chaplin had begun to grow a new antler—a single, pearly spiral in the center of his forehead. I suggested that the rain must have obscured her vision. Kara insisted it had not.

Wondering if my graduate student had lost her mind, I told Kara that I wanted to come observe Chaplin with her the next day. I needed to know if any of her observations could be trusted or if I'd wasted two months of funding on a graduate student who was unreliable. Was she delusional? Incompetent? Or purposely interfering with my research?

Whichever it was, I knew I couldn't use her work anymore. She wasn't performing serious research. She was making up tales of unicorns.

Kara played the next several games of backgammon in silence. When she spoke, she pleaded for me not to interfere with the coastal herd. She could hardly deny her advisor the chance to monitor her research. However, she argued passionately that my presence might spook Chaplin at a critical time, disrupting the natural behavior of the herd. She knew that her findings sounded strange and hard to believe, but she assured me they were accurate and begged me not to make a choice I would regret, destroying both my research and hers.

I was taken aback. I didn't know exactly what I was dealing with, but I tried to think through the possibilities.

If, in all unlikelihood, Kara had discovered a strange, rare illness among the Key Deer, then she was right: changing our routines now could disturb the gentle creatures, affecting their behavior. If, however, Kara's work was corrupted by malice, insanity, or incompetence, then a few extra days wouldn't substantially change the situation. And, finally, if Kara had gone mad, did I really want to antagonize her?

I promised Kara to wait at least a few days, pending her evening reports, before I interfered in her observations of the coastal herd.

Remarkably enough, for the next week, Kara's evening reports no longer mentioned the snow white deer with a spiraling horn. When I questioned Chaplin's sudden disappearance, Kara answered lightly that she hadn't seen him. The next day, when I read over her notes, a single line stood out:

"deer with pale fur near the water—reflection off the ocean makes the light brown fur appear white—Chaplin?—can't make out the antlers—the sound of a cracking branch—gone now"

After that a clear pattern developed. Any time I mentioned Chaplin, he appeared in Kara's notes the following day, sounding increasingly sickly. Otherwise, he was gone.

I knew I needed to do something about Kara, but I had never fired a graduate student before. I didn't want to shatter her dreams of earning a PhD and condemn her to the unwanted life of a housewife. I also didn't want to waste my limited funds and endanger my own career. Fortunately, Kara handled the problem for me.

Without warning one morning, Kara told me she'd decided to reconcile with her husband. She intended to leave the graduate program and go home to him immediately.

Neither of us had been into the town to pick up supplies and check the post office for nearly a week, and there was no telephone in our cabin. So, I was unsure what had prompted her sudden change of plans, but I was relieved to have my problem solved for me. I wished Kara luck, helped her pack, and gladly walked her to the road off the island.

With Kara out of my way, I immediately changed my routine and began observing the deer along the coastline. Within two weeks, I'd spotted all of the deer she'd named, except Chaplin.

Would he have hidden from me forever? I think he might have, if he'd had the choice, but—I told you it was an El Niño winter—the rains came suddenly. I was wading through a marsh at the edge of the ocean. The day was almost warm, but the skies opened up with a torrent. Heavy, large droplets filled the air, splattered over me, and left me stumbling, blinded. I tripped, twisted my ankle, and fell into the water. I must have hit my head on a piece of wood, because I blacked out. The next thing I remember...

I'm a scientist, but none of this sounds like science. I can't publish it. No one will believe it. They'll say I'm a crazy woman, and women don't belong in the sciences. Maybe Kara was crazy. Maybe I am, too. Or maybe it's a secret of the old world—a secret not mine to tell—a secret the world means to be kept.

The next thing I remember, I floated above the water in a bubble, buoying me up and protecting me from the rain. The edges of the bubble shimmered and buzzed like millions of minuscule, iridescent wings. Against my prone back and arms, the pressure of the bubble tingled like my limbs had fallen asleep.

The bubble floated me away from the marsh and set

me down at the edge of the forest. Then, the shimmering surface distorted, flew apart, and formed a miniature tornado mixed with the falling rain. The tornado twisted wildly along the tree line, moving away from me. I watched it go, and when it drew my eye to an albino deer with a single, twisting horn in the middle of his forehead, I wasn't even surprised.

The mouth of the tornado lifted from the ground to the tip of Chaplin's horn. Then the twisting, shimmering disturbance diminished and disappeared. A moment later, Chaplin disappeared too, a ghostlike figure hidden behind the pouring rain and the branches of the forest.

After trudging back to my cabin in the rain with an aching head, I might have dismissed it all as an hallucination. But, in the creases of my jacket, I found the crushed bodies of minuscule insects the like of which I hadn't seen on the island before. I'm not an expert on insects, but they looked like cicadas, only much smaller and nearly translucent. I gathered the tiny exoskeletons in the palm of my hand. As I tilted my hand, their iridescent wings shimmered in the kerosene lamp light.

I had neither the proper equipment nor training to study the insects on No Name Key, but I carefully preserved them to share with the entomology department when I returned to my university.

Over the next few months, my work suffered. I'd lost my assistant, and then I lost my focus. I ordered entomology books to be shipped to me from the university library, and I pored over them late into the nights, straining to read them by lamplight.

The habits and behavior of the No Name deer no longer held any interest for me—except for one, and I'd spend days tracking him only to lose him after a single, short sighting. It was as if he purposely eluded me. Perhaps he did. I don't know how much the changes in Chaplin's physiology affected his brain and intelligence.

I did learn about his life cycle.

Here I come to the part of my story that pushes it beyond the implausible tale of a deer with a strange disorder causing it to superficially imitate the physiology of a—a *unicorn*—and into the impossible flight of fancy of a woman out of her mind.

I shall never trust my judgment or own senses again.

I tracked Chaplin every day until one day I caught up with him on a sandy beach. He was not alone. I was not alone. Waist-deep in the waves, a woman covered with her own long, wet hair held her bare arms out to Chaplin. He came to her, stepping gingerly through the surf. She must have been kneeling for the water only brushed the small deer's belly as it crested by the time he reached her. He lowered his head and touched the tip of his pearly horn to her extended hand.

The air began to shimmer around them, growing outward from the tip of his horn. Tiny cicadas buzzed through the air around me, brushing me with their wings. Then the swarm withdrew, back to Chaplin's horn.

"You've been following my unicorn," the woman in the

water said. Sunlight reflected from the water, glaring all around her. Chaplin's white fur had never looked so bright.

"I've been studying him." My voice faltered. "I've never seen anything like him. I just want to understand."

The woman quirked an eyebrow. "You don't have a wish that you're hoping to make?"

I shook my head.

"I believe you," she said. She beckoned for me to approach.

I walked up to the water's edge. Chaplin stood his ground instead of bolting for the woods. I would never have an opportunity like this again, so I waded into the surf, paying no mind to drenching my clothes. Knee deep in the water, I knelt down beside Chaplin and the strange woman of the water.

"You can touch him," she said.

I put my hand tentatively against Chaplin's side, felt his white fur and the rhythm of his breath. All these months studying the Key Deer, and I hadn't until that moment touched one of them. He showed no sign of alarm, so I moved my hand upward. I stroked his neck, let him nuzzle my palm with his nose, and then petted his long ears.

Finally, with a deep breath, I braved to touch his horn. It looked smooth like a pearl, but it felt bumpy, spiraled with ridges. Up close, it made me think of the sea shells of ladder horn snails. It was open at the top where I'd seen the cicadas come out.

"The insects," I said, "they come out of his horn. It's a symbiotic relationship, yes?"

The woman nodded. "The queen burrows into the forehead of a deer—or similar animal. Then she builds her home."

"The horn."

"I'm here to harvest the eggs." She opened her hand, showing me a cluster of what looked like pearls in her palm. "Their life cycle is long. These eggs won't need hosts for decades."

"You said something about wishes..." I felt like a fool as soon as I said it. Here I was, studying the most fascinating symbiotic relationship I'd ever seen, and I let myself get carried away by a superficial similarity to ancient mythology.

The woman's face hardened. "Humans have slaughtered unicorns in the past, believing they granted wishes."

"It's a myth, of course," I said. "It must be. I'm sorry I brought it up."

The woman seemed placated by my apology, but something about the way she'd said *humans* had sounded strange to me, as if she didn't think she was one of us.

I asked if I could examine one of the eggs, and, after some thought, the woman agreed. With three fingers, I reached into her palm and—making a choice that shall haunt me and cause me to question my own character as a human being until the day I die—carefully took two of the eggs, making it seem as though I'd only taken one.

Professor Kohensart, that second egg is included in the

envelope with this letter. I don't trust myself with it any longer. Part of me wants to cut it open with a microtome knife and examine it under a microscope. Part of me...

Let me tell you the rest.

After I returned the other pearl, the woman didn't stand to walk away. I don't think—I'm not sure—but I don't think she was kneeling. I think—I can't even write what I think. Insects that are symbiotic with deer are far fetched enough. Must I write words like *unicorn* and *mermaid*?

Suffice it to say, I think the woman swam away from our meeting.

Then, a few weeks ago, on my vacation home from the Keys, I met with my former graduate student Kara. She wouldn't talk to me about what had happened to her on No Name Key, but she told me the real reason that she'd separated from her husband two years earlier. Apparently, Kara and her husband had wanted children, but they'd had no luck. The pain of wishing for something she couldn't have had driven her away from him.

Yet, merely a year after inexplicably abandoning her studies with me on No Name Key to return to her marriage, Kara was the proud mother of a newborn baby named Charlie. She told me that Charlie was a wish come true.

Professor Kohensart, I know that anecdotes like these have no place in serious biological study. But what am I to think? Could the insect queen and her swarm of minuscule cicadas in Chaplin's horn have somehow affected a change in Kara's body to alter her barrenness? Was a swarm of insects truly strong enough to lift me and carry me out of the marsh? How can I even wonder at things so entirely ridiculous? If I do wonder, then must I also wonder what else that insect queen could do?

How am I to continue as a scientist?

I must know if I can trust my own senses, but my studies of the crushed cicada bodies that I preserved have taught me nothing. Perhaps with your expertise, Professor Kohensart, you can learn something from the enclosed egg. As the foremost expert on cicadas, there is no one more qualified.

You will tell me whether I'm sane or have lost my mind on No Name Key. That is how I will continue. I eagerly await your response.

SIGNED,

Jillian R. Anders, Ph.D.

AMELIE PUT down her Aunt Jill's unsent letter. The memory of Aunt Jill's voice echoed in her mind. Amelie remembered sitting on her lap as a child, listening to the stories of her many expeditions, and the many graduate students she'd advised. Amelie had never heard of Kara before, but Aunt Jill had worked with many other aspiring women scientists.

Somehow, Aunt Jill had found a way to remain a scientist without sending this letter.

Amelie took the pearl from her pocket. She placed it in her palm and pushed it around with a single finger from her other hand. It looked like an ordinary pearl at first, but the longer she stared at it, the more it seemed to swell and shrink, almost imperceptibly, almost as if it were breathing.

Decades had passed since Aunt Jill had sealed the pearl into that letter. If the story were true, it would hatch soon. It would need a host.

Amelie went to the window of her Aunt Jill's study and looked out at the pet pygmy goats, Fred and Ginger, munching on the lawn. They were funny animals. Amelie's mom had wondered why Aunt Jill had chosen goats, instead of a more normal pet like a cat or a dog. But Amelie thought it perfectly natural—a goat was an ungulate, like the giraffes, horses, bison... and *deer* that Aunt Jill had studied.

Amelie didn't know whether pygmy goats were similar enough to Key Deer to be appropriate hosts, and she didn't know whether the pearl was really a cicada egg. Or if it would ever hatch. She supposed that she ought to have it studied. If Aunt Jill's story were true, it could be a treasure of science, and she'd never known Aunt Jill's stories to be untrue.

On the other hand, the egg might also be a living thing, almost ready to hatch. It would be wrong to hurt it. Aunt Jill may not have sent the letter to Professor Kohensart partly to protect her reputation, but Amelie knew her well enough to believe there had been another reason. Aunt Jill studied animals. She didn't dissect them.

Amelie slipped the pearl back into her pocket. She would keep it. She would need to look up the ordinances for keeping pet goats in the city, but she would find a way to keep Fred and Ginger, too. It's what Aunt Jill would have wanted.

Then if the egg did hatch... Well... Amelie thought that Ginger would make an adorably funny unicorn.

3

———

THE DRAGON'S MASK

Bark broke from the trunk of the sharillow trees in large, curved chunks, littering the forest floor along with their fallen leaves. Storakka sifted through the pieces at the base of the biggest tree she could find, her talons running over the slightly curved sheaves of wood, rough on one side and smooth on the other. Finally she found an oval one she liked, about the same size as a human face.

Storakka's own dragon face twisted into a fearsomely happy smile at the sight of the brown oval held in her talons. She took the piece of bark to the edge of the forest where several of her kin-folk had charred the trees, found a nice piece of blackened twig, and drew a simple, smiling face onto the oval.

An older, more powerful dragon might have been able to cast the spell Storakka had in mind without a physical focus for it, but she didn't have that kind of power or skill.

Storakka spread her wings, took to the sky, and flew to the nearest lake, deep in the middle of the sharillow forest. She landed at the lake's edge, held up the mask she'd crafted from bark and a simple drawing, and cast the glamour. She watched her reflection in the water—green scales sparkling in the summer sunlight—fade away and be replaced by the image of a human woman, wearing a simple cloak and gown, with a plain, oval face.

The face moved whenever Storakka moved the mask. The woman stood on tiptoes when she held it up high, looking toward the sky, then knelt down low when she moved it close to the ground. The illusory image followed the physical focus of the bark mask. It was perfect. Finally, Storakka would be able to use her magical abilities to enter the human town beside the forest, instead of only watching it from afar. She would be able to meet and mingle with humans. Her heart thudded in her broad, scaly chest. This was what she had dreamed of for years, only now possible because she'd learned an invisibility spell to accompany the glamour.

Storakka flew toward the village shielded from sight by her invisibility spell. She kept low to the ground and landed far enough away from the outskirts that no one would see her glamour puppet appear as if from nowhere. She walked into the village on three of her four legs, using a funny, hobbling gait, so she could keep the mask held at an appropriate height. The glamour of a human woman needed to seem like she was walking normally.

Perhaps if Storakka enjoyed her visit to the human village and wanted to come again, she would figure out how to wear the mask strapped around her long neck so she wouldn't have to hold it all the time.

Humans waved and smiled at Storakka's human glamour as she entered the village. The dragon softened her naturally booming voice to a low, gentle whisper and nervously returned the humans' greetings. She was half sure her voice would give her away, and she'd find herself flying out of the village with flaming arrows sailing through the air after her.

But none of the humans noticed anything odd about the newcomer to their village. And eventually, after strolling the roads at the outskirts of town for some time, Storakka got up the courage to ask a human for directions to the village market. Sure, she had seen it from the sky before, but she found herself all twisted about and lost, trying to navigate the town she'd seen from the sky whilst down here in the middle of it.

The woman who Storakka asked for directions offered to walk with her to the market.

"What should I call you?" the woman asked as they walked together.

"My name is Stora—" Storakka couldn't finish saying her own name. It was too clearly the name of a dragon. She had not planned for this. Her heart raced, and she feared the woman would hear it.

"Story? That's pretty. I'm Faye."

But the woman didn't hear the racing of a dragon's heart; she simply saw the face of a potential new friend.

Storakka and Faye walked together, and the dragon listened while the human told her all about the town—the local gossip, her own dreams of traveling across the countryside someday, and which stalls in the market had the best treats to buy.

Storakka would need to bring money next time she visited. She pictured the paltry hoard of gold in her cave back in the mountains. She didn't care for hoarding gold much, but it's what dragons do. So, she'd done it. And while her hoard was paltry compared to that of other dragons, it would surely be enough to buy herself a few sugary treats in a human market. But she'd need a better way to store it than spread across the floor of a cave. Some kind of pocket. Perhaps a satchel.

Storakka noticed a selection of cloth and leather satchels hanging from the top of one of the market stalls and stopped to stare at them.

"You like those?" Faye asked.

Storakka moved the oval mask in her talon, causing the glamour of Story to shrug. "I wish I had one to fill with my gold."

"Your gold?" Faye asked.

"I didn't bring any with me..."

Storakka looked down at the human who had befriended her. Faye chewed her lip, stared at the mask in Storakka's talon, and crinkled the skin around her eyes.

She seemed to be thinking. Judging the glamour of Story very carefully.

Storakka looked around the market and saw other humans looking at each other—less intently, perhaps, than Faye stared at Story—but still, they looked directly at each other, staring into each other's eyes, looking at each other's faces.

Storakka wondered what it would be like for a human to look at her face that way, look into her real eyes and not the imaginary ones conjured by the focus of a piece of sharillow wood.

"You've run away from home, haven't you?" Faye said.

"Maybe," Storakka conceded.

"You have a rich family... but you don't feel like you belong, and you had to run away?"

All the dragons Storakka knew were very rich. Faye's interpretation was not entirely wrong. She waggled the piece of wood, making Story nod in agreement.

Faye reached a hand out and took hold of one of the glamour's hands. Storakka's talon itched, wondering how it must feel to touch the hand of this woman who was being so kind to her. She would never know. All she could do was watch.

"I don't feel like I belong either," Faye said. "Come with me. I know a beautiful hollow in the woods where we can hide and talk. And you can tell me everything. We'll figure something out. A plan for you."

Storakka felt a shiver over her scales, like the coldness

of a waterfall splashing over her back. Excited and uncertain. She felt so close to this human woman, and yet so very far away. But she agreed to come, and Faye led her through the market, buying a few treats for a picnic as they went.

Finally Faye led the disguised dragon back to the edge of town and into the forest. Storakka had to hobble all the way, though she watched her illusory human shadow walk with ease.

The hollow was one Storakka recognized. An enchanted grove. Few humans would ever be able to find it, as it was the place where a unicorn had once died, leaving behind a protection spell for the woodland creatures she'd loved. It was beautiful, brim-full with buttercups and foxgloves—yellow and purple, peeking from between the swooping fronds of ferns. And thousands upon thousands of tiny white flowers, shaped like stars, dotted the mossy ground.

Faye settled on the grass, and Storakka found a comfortable way to squat beside her, holding the bark mask at the right height.

The human and dragon talked for hours. They shared the kind of secrets that you only tell when drunk on the heady potential of a new relationship. The kind of secrets that only come out after you've stayed up all night, discussing philosophy and meaning under the silver light of the moon.

As morning dawned, Storakka explained that she must return home before she was missed, but Faye urged her to meet her at the hollow again in a few night's time.

And so they planned to continue their conversation then.

Weeks passed, and the two friends met under the waning and then waxing moon in the unicorn's hollow more and more often. At first, Faye always brought a picnic, but Storakka never dared to try the delectable treats laid out on a blanket for them. She didn't see a way to do so without breaking her glamour and revealing herself. Faye never pressured her, and eventually stopped bothering to bring them.

What Faye did bring was stories of the human village and her own struggles to fit in there.

Storakka watched Faye clasp her ghostly glamour's hands as the two of them grew closer. She watched Faye's eyes light up and sparkle as they connected over the ways they felt like outsiders among their own people. She watched Faye smile—shyly at first and then like the sun itself—at the face she'd created but that wasn't truly her own.

Sometimes the dragon and human met at the outskirts of town instead of the unicorn's hollow and walked through the village together, whispering secrets and seeing sights. Storakka began to develop a limp from walking three-legged so often, but she tried not to mind.

The dragon started to feel jealous of her own creation. Why couldn't she *be* the mask? Why did she have to be a dragon?

And yet... dragons weren't all bad. In her time, Storakka had used her strong wings to fly from one end of the continent to the other. Her hard, metallic scales protected her from the elements, meaning she could curl up on a mountainside in the middle of a thunderous rainstorm and still sleep comfortably. She used the fire she could conjure with her breath to roast dead deer before eating them. And although, she certainly *could* use that same fire as a weapon, she never, ever had.

Wouldn't a clever human like Faye understand that a dragon wasn't inherently bad? Wouldn't the hours they'd spent talking and sharing count for something—a built trust? Mightn't Faye be able to see that many of Storakka's dragon traits which humans feared were also strengths?

As the sun broke over the horizon and filtered through the branches of the sharillow trees in brilliant, golden beams one morning, Storakka decided to take a chance.

"I... want to show you something," Storakka said.

"Okay," Faye agreed, smiling warmly at the bark mask. Storakka wanted the warmth of that smile for herself, not for it to be wasted on a piece of useless wood.

"It might scare you," Storakka warned.

Faye shrugged. "You? Scare me? You're my best friend. I've never felt closer to another person. And I've never met anyone else as much like me. So whatever it is, I want to see."

Storakka drew in a deep breath and let it fill her lungs, the air roiling around inside of her, filling her with the potential to breathe fire. But she had no intention of breathing fire. She was going to do something much harder. Much scarier. And she needed to feel the fire inside of herself to gain the courage.

She was brave. And so was Faye.

But their friendship... was nothing if she had to hold up a mask for Faye to look at, week after week. Storakka had enjoyed her time with Faye, but she couldn't play this game anymore. She wanted something real.

Storakka let the fire inside her cool, and slowly breathed out, trying to release all her fear along with the air.

Then, for the first time in front of Faye, she let her glamours dissipate.

The image of Story disappeared, and Storakka's scaly, scintillating, emerald green body emerged from the cloak of shadows and misdirection she'd worn.

Faye's gaze fell on a massive dragon, contorted into an awkward position, holding an oval of sharillow bark with a smiley face drawn on it in simple black charcoal

But all she saw—all her brain had time to process before she began screaming—was a dragon.

As Faye screamed, she threw herself at the ground, cowering and shaking, and hiding her face.

Abashed and horrified, Storakka cast her glamours again. "I'm sorry," she said, holding the oval mask farther away, trying to give Faye a respectful space. "So sorry." Her apologies burbled out of her like a well-spring, pure and sweet, completely natural and uncontrollable.

But the aftertaste the apologies left curdled in Storakka's throat and belly, making her hate herself for being a dragon. And she couldn't help being a dragon.

She didn't know who was more wrong—herself for lying to and deceiving her friend, or her friend for only loving her conditionally. Only loving her if her body was the right shape—small, smooth-skinned, wingless, and human.

The two women of wildly different species fell into an awkward silence as Storakka's apologies withered away and Faye's frightened sobs dried up.

Faye lifted herself from the ground, twisting around to see her friend again. She smiled at what she saw:

A human woman, wearing a simple cloak and gown, with a plain, oval face. Her friend, Story.

Rubbing the back of her wrist across her eyes, smudging away the tears of fright, Faye said, "You told me about your magic... but... I didn't..." Her words halted, and the dragon could almost see the gears turning in Faye's head, the work being done to create a story she could live with. A story that felt safe. "I didn't realize what a powerful witch you are. You must have very strong magic to make yourself look so completely like a dragon. It startled me."

Faye was offering Storakka a way out. A way to cover up what had been revealed and go back to the way things were.

Storakka had never felt so deeply misunderstood in her entire life. She had always been an odd dragon—too peaceful, too fond of human things, too much uninterested in gathering wealth and hoarding it. And obviously, she was not really a human. But Faye had seemed to see beyond all that. Beyond the mask and the species to the person underneath. Not dragon. Not pretend human. Just a curious and hopeful mind. A mind who had thought she'd found a friend. A real friend.

"You should warn me next time before you do that, okay?" Faye said, still shaking from the sudden fear of seeing her friend's true face but trying to turn the shaking into laughter. An invented, fake sort of merriment.

"I..." Storakka had so many things she wanted to say. So many ways she wanted to defend herself and dragons. They weren't all bad. She wasn't bad. At least, she didn't think so. But the words turned to ashes in her mouth as soon as she thought them, before they could be said. If she said them out loud, the defensive anger in them would burn too much like fire. And the force of her feelings would melt Faye's pretty story about her being a witch away.

Faye would understand Storakka was a dragon—a real, true dragon—for sure.

And then she might start screaming again.

And Storakka could not handle Faye screaming at the sight of her. Not again.

In all the decades of Storakka's life—not fitting and not belonging and not knowing what was wrong with her —that moment had been the worst, and she couldn't face it happening again.

Looking at Faye, still quaking from a single sighting of

her true face, Storakka knew it would do no good to defend herself or dragons. "Of course. I should have warned you." She laughed, a rough sound—more of a sob, disguised as a laugh than a sound of true merriment. The perfect match for Faye's falsified laughter meant to cover her fear.

"I hadn't realized my illusion had gotten so strong. The last time I showed it to anyone, they only laughed." Technically, not a lie. Storakka had shown her human glamour to another dragon once, and the beastly oaf had rolled on his back, wings flapping and belly shaking with helpless mirth at the ridiculousness of a dragon wanting to fit in with humans.

Perhaps the beastly oaf had been right.

Storakka waggled the piece of bark with her human face drawn on it, as if the face were shaking its head sadly. She felt sad, and she wanted her puppet self to show it.

Faye smiled tentatively, settling into this new reality they were creating together out of lies, a reality where what she'd seen—a true dragon's face, staring into hers from only inches away, begging to be seen, understood, and maybe loved—was only an illusion. "Well, it's gotten really good. I think you could fool anyone with that illusion." Her smile got stronger, truer, and suddenly she laughed for real. "Sorry," she said, "I was just imagining the trouble we could cause with such an illusion!"

Storakka shifted uncomfortably and forced herself to hold the bark oval steady and stay her own forked tongue while her friend told her about all the pranks they could pull by showing such an ugly, scary dragon illusion to other humans.

With each insult of her true face, the air in Storakka's lungs soured, growing ashier and ashier, until it felt like her own fire was burning her from the inside out.

"I don't think I like pranks very much," Storakka said.

The two friends struggled with an uneasy awkwardness between them for the rest of the night, and Storakka bought herself some time to adjust to the evening's disappointment by pleading that her rich family had grown suspicious, and she couldn't afford to sneak out for another few weeks.

When they did meet again in the unicorn's hollow, Faye acted as though nothing strange had happened at their last visit. Everything could have gone back to normal.

But Storakka could feel the two of them growing farther and farther apart with every interchange, each step down the conversational path that had started with her lie—agreeing she was not a dragon but a witch. Somehow, this new lie seemed to be so much worse than the original lie—pretending to be a human.

And Storakka felt their friendship becoming more and more divorced from reality with every word, no matter how inconsequential it seemed. She couldn't take it. Fitting herself inside a fake friendship hurt more than a clean, clear, straightforward rejection possibly could. Because at least a rejection ends. There seemed to be no end to the pain of fitting herself inside the box she'd built for herself.

And so Storakka decided to stop walking down the path of lies. She didn't want to see where it led. Even if it was the only path she could walk along with Faye.

"I'm sorry," the dragon said, painfully aware of her own, hidden dragon-nature and stumbling over her own words. She didn't want to be saying them. But she had to. "I lied to you. I deceived you. But we would never have had this time together if..." No, she would not defend her lies. She said simply, "I'm sorry."

Faye looked startled and confused by her friend's interruption and confession. "What do you mean?"

Storakka turned the bark mask away from Faye, and then she turned her own scaly back as well. She didn't want Faye looking at a fake face while she said what she needed to say. And she couldn't say it while looking at Faye. The fear of what she was losing—which was nothing, because Faye didn't know her, but also everything, because Faye was the only person who had ever really known her—was just too much.

This might be the last night she had with Faye, and she couldn't end it by watching Faye's face crumple in disappointment and horror at the revelation of her deception.

"My name is not Story, and I am not a human, nor a witch. My name is Storakka. And I am a dragon, just like I showed you before. Everything else I've said was true, and I think... our friendship is the most important treasure I've ever seen. I think, it might even be more than friendship. If you can still care for me... knowing I'm a dragon..." Her voice choked off, like a fire dying. "I will return here at the full moon. If you're too scared of dragons, all dragons... even me... to come. I'll understand."

Storakka hated that she would understand her best friend rejecting her. And yet, she would. Dragons could be scary.

Storakka dropped her glamours again. Spread her wings. And flew away into the starry night, trying so very hard not to think about the gasp she'd heard when the glamours fell for their second and final time.

Was it fear again?

Or could it be... awe?

Could Faye see Storakka as something beautiful? Storakka thought Faye was beautiful.

She didn't know if Faye could see the real her and still like her. She didn't know if she wanted to know. It might have been easier to reject Faye herself than to have given Faye the power to reject her. And either way, she would have to wait until the full moon to find out. That would give Faye time to adjust. Time to decide whether she could accept Storakka for who she truly was... Or whether their friendship would be destroyed, because Storakka's self lived inside the body of a dragon. Was inextricably tied with the body of a dragon.

As her wings flapped, and she felt air flow over and under them while the air inside her boiled with the potential to burn, Storakka accepted for the first time that her body wasn't merely something she was trapped inside of.

It was her. Part and parcel. Wings, scales, and mind—all one piece.

And although other dragons burned down fields and villages, ate humans, and terrorized the whole of human society, she wasn't one of those dragons. But she was a dragon. And she didn't want to change that. So maybe, there was no space in the world for the flickering embers of connection she'd felt to Faye. And maybe, although she'd loved seeing the human village so much during her few visits there, it simply hurt too much to ever go to it again.

Maybe she needed to accept her place.

And yet, the flickering ember continued to smolder in her heart. A touch of hope.

The hope burned painfully, but it wouldn't go out and leave her in peace.

For long days, Storakka awaited the full moon, draped miserably over her paltry pile of gold in her dank cave, staring at the wooden oval with its scrawled face, wondering what made it so much better than her own face. So much easier to like and possibly love. She was the very picture of depression, but dragon-style. And yet, even in her sadness, she had to appreciate the way that the kink in her neck finally relaxed, now that she wasn't always hunching herself over the glamour of Story. She hadn't realized how much pain the limping and hunching to fit herself behind the glamour had been causing her, until it finally went away.

When the night of the full moon finally came,

Storakka burned the bark mask with her fire, leaving it charred and ruined at the mouth of her cave. Discarded. Destroyed. She didn't want to be tempted to bring it with her, say she'd lied, and try using it again. And she was tempted. But lying about herself had only hurt her.

It took everything in Storakka to fly to the unicorn's hollow without turning back. She had made this flight so many times before, but this time was different. This time might be the last. Her heart clenched at the sight of the sharillow grove—the trees and their long shadows made her heart jump, each one looking like it could be Faye, disguised by the cloak of darkness. And with each jump, she admonished her heart, telling it to stay calm and hard, braced for Faye to not be there.

Or to be there—*because she was there, and Storakka's heart was so confused by the sight of her friend, it didn't even think to jump again*—but filled with recriminations, or worse, leading the charge of a hidden army who would chase the evil, lying dragon away with arrows and screams.

Reluctantly, Storakka landed on the far side of the hollow, folded her wings primly behind her, and waited with her eyes cast downward. She couldn't bear to watch. So she stared at the dirt and tried to imagine it was a glittering pile of gold and that gold under her talons could ever make her as happy as Faye's friendship had.

The human woman approached the dragon. Her footsteps were heavy, suggesting she carried a burden of some sort slung over her back. When she stood directly before

Storakka, Faye said, "I've heard of a place—across the ocean—where humans and dragons live side by side. Do you think..."

The pause stretched out long enough for Storakka's brain to fill in the blanks with so many different options, but most of them were ways that Faye must be trying to soften her rejection by sending Storakka away, offering a substitute for her own friendship. But Storakka didn't want a panoply of potential friendships with hypothetical humans across the ocean. She didn't want to fly around the world alone. She wanted Faye.

"Do you think," Faye repeated, "you could fly us there? Together? I want to run away with you."

Storakka raised her eyes, heart leaping, filled to the brim with new hope, more hope than she'd ever felt before. A whole new life suddenly stretched out in front of her—a life she actually wanted to live—brightening all the coming days in her sight of them.

Faye stood before her, a large sack slung over her back, heavy and bulging at the seams. It looked like it could hold all of a human's belongings. She was truly offering to leave this place—her village, this entire continent—and seek out a world where humans and dragons could be accepted as friends.

Faye held out a small leather satchel in her hands and said, "I got you something to put some of your gold in. I remembered you liked it, the first time we walked through the village together."

Storakka's heart swelled, and she reached out, ever so

delicately, with one of her talons to grab the tiny gift. The leather strap was too short to go over her head, and the pouch would only hold a few human handfuls of gold. A minuscule fraction of her paltry hoard. And yet, she loved it more than any treasure she'd ever seen before. It was a gift, from her friend. "Thank you. It's perfect."

Faye looked Storakka in the eyes—her real eyes—for the first time, and the intensity was almost too much to bear.

And Storakka loved it.

4

WEREMOOSE

A SHADOW of antlers stretched ominously over the snow. Darkfoot crouched behind a fallen log. White flakes tickled his muzzle, but he dared not shake them off. With its long legs, the moose could easily outrun a young wolf like him. Or kick him in the skull.

If Darkfoot downed a moose alone, though, then his pack would never mock him again.

Giant hooves clomped into view. Legs like four-year-old elm trees bent and passed before him. Darkfoot sprang at the moose from behind, aiming for its massive neck. The moose turned, and its brown-furred head, nearly the size of Darkfoot's whole body, swung at him. Knocked him from the air. Destroyed his plans to prove himself.

Whimpering on the snow-covered ground, Darkfoot expected the moose's giant hooves to trample him. Instead, he felt the dull, stabbing pain of a leaf-eater's teeth on his flank. Panicked, pained, and confused, Darkfoot lost consciousness.

HE AWOKE COVERED IN SNOW, under the dull glow of the winter moon. His pack mates nosed him gently, rousing him to get up. He could see the laughter in their eyes. He'd taken on a full grown moose and lost. He'd taken on a moose alone. He was a fool like they'd always thought he was.

Darkfoot tried his paws and found they held his weight, though his side throbbed in pain. A crescent of tooth marks marred his flank, angry with blood. He licked his fur clean. Then, dejected and limping, Darkfoot followed his pack mates home.

NIGHT AFTER NIGHT, Darkfoot stayed home to heal while his friends, his brothers and sisters, went on the hunt. The pain in his flank ebbed, but the crescent scar remained. It marked him as separate from the others, a badge of his lunacy.

As the winter moon waned, Darkfoot grew increasingly solitary and strange. His pack mates brought back food for him from their kills, but he barely ate.

On the night of the new moon, his pack downed a moose. The flesh tasted wrong on his tongue. The flavor lingered like guilt over a broken taboo. From that day on, Darkfoot wouldn't eat meat at all. Instead, he munched on the winter berries down by the river and, stranger still, gnawed on the twiggy branches of young oak trees and the fallen needles of pine. His pack thought he would surely starve.

Darkfoot, however, felt a new strength growing inside him and found new comfort in his solitude. His legs felt long and powerful; his shoulders broad and heavy; and a sense of majesty filled him at the slightest turning of his head. His pack saw a mangy, sickly wolf. Darkfoot knew better. Darkfoot saw the shadow of what he was becoming stretched across the snow before him.

Darkfoot saw the shadow of antlers.

5

CYCLOPS ON SAFARI

THE LITTLE BOY pressed his nose up against the minivan window, twisting himself up under his seatbelt. He strained his one eye, trying to peer all the way across the golden field littered with shiny white unicorns, gamboling and playing, their manes rippling in the wind. Danny was sure that if his parents would just let him roll down the window so he could stick his head out, he'd be able to make out a *moose* in the forest edge beyond. Instead, all he could see was stupid unicorns.

"Daaad," he whined, "drive closer to the trees."

"We're supposed to stay on the road," his dad answered from the front seat.

Danny's whining, though, caused his mother to look back from the passenger seat in the front to check on him. "Sit up straight," she said. "Your seatbelt won't do you any good twisted up like that." Although, she knew it didn't really matter with how slow they were driving on this safari track. For months, Danny had begged and begged and begged to be taken on a drive-thru safari for his birthday. Now that they were here, all he could do was whine about moose.

In the backseat, Danny slumped down, not even bothering to look out the window any more. He pulled his beloved mythology book out of the seat pocket in front of him and flipped to the page about the magical mystical moose.

Danny traced his finger along the majestic curves of the moose's broad antlers. So elegant. So amazing. He peeked out the window again and sneered at the pathetic unicorn horns. Those simple spikes were nothing to the beautiful branching of a moose's antlers.

Danny closed his eye and started singing the song he'd learned in school about moose. His mother sighed.

Several rounds of the song later, his mother interrupted him: "Danny, we're past the unicorn fields now. Don't you want to see the faeries?"

Danny didn't want to see the faeries, but he opened his eye and looked out the window anyway. Dainty sprites with iridescent wings and silver tresses flew among the trees and danced tiny waltzes in the middle of toadstool rings. At least, they were driving through the trees now, but Danny still didn't see any moose.

Danny groaned. "Come on!" he said. "Isn't there anything interesting here?"

Danny's dad grunted in the front seat, an angry inarticulate sound, but his mother said, with a tired patience, "Like what, honey? What were you hoping to see?"

Danny held up his book, open to the gorgeous drawing of the moose, his favorite picture in the whole world.

Danny's mother looked confused. "Moose aren't real, honey. That's a mythology book."

"But I've read about them! People have seen them in forests!"

"Well, sure," his mother said, "People think they've seen them. But, they were probably just looking at a dirty unicorn with its horn tangled up in some branches. You don't think an animal could really walk around with such ridiculously huge horns on its head?"

Danny was mad and felt like crying. He'd come all this way to see a moose, and now his mother was telling him they didn't exist? He flipped to another page in the book, hoping to make some amends out of this trip. "What about this one?" he said. He flipped to the picture of the bushy-tailed squirrels. Maybe the trip wouldn't be a complete loss if he could just see one of them.

But his mother shook her head.

"What?" he cried. "How could someone imagine up a creature as funny and cute as them?!"

"Well," his mother began in her I'm-about-to-give-you-a-really-boring-lecture-on-something-I-think-is-interesting tone of voice, "There have actually been studies done on how most 'squirrel' sightings happen in the dead of winter, when faeries are all wearing their long, fuzzy, cold-weather coats."

She rambled on for a while about how faeries gathered tufts of shed yeti fur to make their coats, but Danny wasn't listening. He'd gone back to looking at the pictures in his mythology book, dreaming about a better world.

When he got to the last page, Danny placed his index and middle finger on the two eyes of the creature labeled *human*. He knew what his birthday wish would be this year, when they got back home and he blew out the candles on his cake. He would wish he could live in a fabulous world with moose and squirrels, have two eyes instead of his one, and be a human.

6

THE CAROUSEL OF SPIRITS

THE CAROUSEL TURNED, and Artie watched the ponies go by. He shifted his weight as he sat on the green, metal frame bench. It was one of many around the edges of the giant, window-walled room that housed the carousel. Artie was beginning to think that he should upgrade the benches. These ones looked nice, but they weren't easy on an old man's back.

Not that the children and their young parents who came to the carousel seemed to mind. Perhaps Artie would simply buy himself a nice cushion and bring it with him when he wanted to sit and watch his ponies.

Each of the ponies had a fancy name, painted in careful, cursive letters on a placard hanging above it. *Silverina Starspire. Tigerella Jungle Queen. Tuffington Cupsworth.* Artie had made up each name himself and painted the letters by hand. But, he thought of them all by simpler names. *Silly Girl. Tiger. Worthy.*

Silly Girl with her flowing white locks and silver horn was always popular with the children. So was Tiger. The bold orange blazes that cut stripes across her black mare's body attracted boys and girls with adventure in their hearts. Artie liked to watch and see which children picked which of his ponies. Many children simply took the closest steed, but some had their hearts set on a particular one. He'd watched one girl ride the carousel five times one day, standing back in the line and waiting for an entire go if Froggy—the green pony with freckles and yellow hair—was already taken.

Artie's favorites were the children who picked Worthy. It didn't happen often because Worthy was a simple horse, the first Artie had ever carved. Brown eyes, brown body, and a curly brown mane. If Artie saw a child pick Worthy —truly pick him, not just ride him because he was the only horse left—he made a point of seeking out the child's parent afterwards with a pair of free tickets. He wondered sometimes if he should fancy Worthy up—paint his mane a brighter color or give him a unicorn's horn. But Artie couldn't do it. Worthy would have to make do.

As Artie watched the carousel today, he thought about where on the wheel he could fit in a new pony—which of the old ponies that he hadn't replaced yet with a carving of his own would be next to go. For he could tell it was time to carve another horse.

He'd noticed the gray shimmer, like smoke or a cloud, in the corner of the carousel room a few weeks ago. He didn't approach it or try to look at it straight on, but he cast the gray shimmer occasional glances. It moved around, mostly hiding under the benches. Over time, its shape had grown clearer and Artie could finally tell what it was.

The ghost of a sea otter.

Artie kept an eye on the little fellow for the rest of the afternoon. When the evening light slanted over the sea and cast long shadows through the wall of windows, Artie closed the carousel up. He sent home his two employees— a pair of local high school kids, one to sell the tickets and another to control the carousel. They could clean up tomorrow.

Alone in the large window-walled room, except for all the horse statues and the shimmering gray otter spirit, Artie said, "I'm going to my workshop now. I'll leave the doors open, though, so I expect I'll see you soon."

The otter spirit loped after Artie. Its ethereal back bunched up, and its wide tail swayed from side to side. The door to the carousel room stood open behind them.

Salt breeze from the beach blew into the still room while evening darkened to night outside. When the first star appeared in the purple sky, the stillness in the room changed. Wooden bodies that had stood stiff all day shifted, flexing muscles, drawing in breaths through carved nostrils. Each of the ponies took its own time, stretching out legs that had posed in frozen prances, and stepping down from the wheel of the carousel. They left strange empty spaces on the carousel between the old ponies which Artie hadn't carved and which yet stood still as statues, and they left gaps in the gold metal poles that were their anchors during the day.

The ponies spilled out of the carousel room, prancing in their carnival colors on the sand of the nighttime beach. Two of them, though, headed straight for Artie's workshop.

Blocks of wood in various sizes were spread around Artie's worktable, but he hadn't begun carving. The chisels were lined up in a row, untouched. The tool in his hand was a colored pencil. An entire rainbow of the pencils were strewn around the sheet of paper in front of him. On the sheet, he'd drawn a pony with a purple, green, and yellow striped mane; a white body with little red polka dots and large orange ones; and a golden saddle with a silver bridle. The pony's front legs reared up, and it held its head at a jaunty angle.

"Colorful," a melodic voice intoned over Artie's shoulder.

The old man turned to see Silly Girl with her shining white fur standing beside him. Warm breath from her nostrils puffed at his neck. Artie reached a hand up and stroked her muzzle. "Indeed," he said. "Sea otters have always made me think of clowns. Something about their foolish manners, and their wide noses."

"You should give it a neck ruff then," Silly Girl said. "Clowns wear those."

"I like that," Artie said, smiling. He turned back to the drawing and sketched in a black neck ruff with purple stars.

While Artie carefully filled in all the corners of the stars, Silly Girl turned to look at the sea otter spirit. The gray otter shape had been touching noses with Worthy. When it saw Silly Girl pointing her horn its way, though, it bobbed its head and turned in a quick circle, almost dissolving from its otter shape back to an amorphous cloud.

"You'll be the most fancy one of us, Otter," Silly Girl said, her voice sounding imperious.

"Jealous?" Artie asked, not yet looking up from his sketch.

"No," Silly Girl said, but she clearly meant *yes*.

"Don't worry, Silly Girl," Artie said. "You're still my only talking companion." He knew she feared the day that another human ghost would find its way to him and join the ranks of the ponies on his carousel.

Silly Girl had been an important woman during her human life. A politician or lawyer. At least, that's what Artie gathered from her somewhat muddled memories. By the time she'd found him, Artie figured she'd already been a ghost for several decades. And her accent suggested she'd traveled a long way to find him, probably all the way across the country. Her deep southern accent and antiquated mannerisms faded with time. Her air of confidence had not. She was the only unicorn and clear leader of the ponies on his carousel.

"Will you take Otter to meet the others?" Artie said to Silly Girl. "I think he's ready now." Artie didn't know if the otter ghost was male or female, but he knew that the carousel could use another stallion. So, Otter would be male in his new life. If that was a change, he'd get used to it. All of the ponies, except for Horse, had had adjustments to make in getting used to their new bodies.

Artie tried to make it as easy as possible for his ponies, giving them bodies that he felt suited them. He made Eagle a pegasus; he'd given Tiger her familiar stripes; Froggy was green and freckled; and Worthy had exactly the coloring of the chocolate lab who'd been Artie's best friend until the day he had passed away. However, none of his ponies had been horses in their previous lives except Horse. So, none of them looked as comfortable—as much at home—in their pony bodies as Horse did.

Artie watched as Silly Girl walked over to Otter. She stepped lightly, holding her head bowed. The otter ran to the back of the room and turned in circles, afraid of her approach, but Silly Girl's horn glowed, an almost imperceptible change in its silver shine, and the otter's fear seemed to subside. Artie couldn't tell exactly what magic Silly Girl held in her horn. She liked to keep some secrets from him. But he suspected she could talk to the other ponies—mind to mind—and even the ghosts before they became ponies.

"Come on, Otter," she said. "We'll start with Bunny and Rabbit. I don't think they'll scare you as much as Tiger does."

"Wait," Artie said, before the shining white unicorn could lead the hazy gray otter shape out of the workshop.

He picked up his drawing and held it out for the otter to see. "Do you like it?" Artie asked.

The otter's expression didn't change, but Silly Girl said, "Don't be so insecure. Of course, he likes it. Now get to work so Otter doesn't have to stay a ghost any longer than absolutely necessary."

Silly Girl had told Artie about how cold and nauseous she'd felt during her entire time as a ghost. It was a terrible experience, and she wouldn't wish an extra minute of it on anyone. Even a pony who was going to be more "colorful" and "fancy" than her. She had a good heart.

Worthy stayed in the workshop with Artie. The old man arranged blocks of wood on his worktable, deciding which pieces he would carve into which parts of Otter's anatomy. Meanwhile, Worthy leaned his warm, heavy body against Artie. "Good boy," Artie said. "We can go for a ride later." He always went for a ride with Worthy before going to bed for the night. He knew the ponies stayed up later than him, but an old man needs his sleep. Already yawning, Artie changed his mind. "Know what, Worthy? I can work on this tomorrow. Let's go for our ride now."

Outside of the workshop, Artie climbed up onto Worthy's back and settled into the simple, black saddle. He could see Silly Girl, Rabbit, and Bunny already on the beach.

Silly Girl's horn was glowing in the night, and Rabbit and Bunny were prancing. He couldn't make out the ghost shape of Otter in the dark, but he thought Rabbit and

Bunny must be playing with him. Silly Girl was right to introduce Otter to them first.

Artie rode Worthy along the beach, right at the edge of the waves. Artie remembered when he and Worthy would play fetch here. He would throw the tennis ball into the surf, and Worthy would chase after it, bringing the soggy green ball back to him, held in a gentle mouth. Man and dog. Now they rode together. Man and horse. It was different, but Worthy was still his best friend.

"You brought all these friends to me," Artie said, patting Worthy on the neck. "I would never have known to build carousel horses for them if it weren't for you." Artie thanked God and luck every night that, in his grief over Worthy those many years ago, he'd carved a carousel horse and painted it with Worthy's coloring. Whatever mystery of nature and divinity had caused Worthy's ghost to enter and animate that wooden body had changed everything about Artie's life.

Worthy and Artie rode to the rocky outcropping that ended their stretch of beach before turning back. At the end of the ride, Artie said goodnight to his ponies and settled down to sleep on the cot in the back of his workshop. He returned home less and less these days, preferring to sleep in his workshop.

After he finished building Otter's new body, perhaps his next project would be to make his workshop a more comfortable apartment. It already had a small bathroom with a sink and toilet, but a shower and better kitchen facilities than the single hotplate would be nice.

Artie heard the hoof falls and whinnies of his ponies blend with the sound of the waves on the beach as he fell asleep. Sometimes Silly Girl sang a lullaby about the bayou, but he could never be sure if it was only a dream.

When the morning light woke Artie, he climbed up from his cot and stumbled, still clumsy with sleep, to the open door of the carousel room. Tiger, Bunny, Rabbit, Froggy, Eagle, Horse, Worthy, Silly Girl and all the others stood as still as statues on the tented wheel. They were statues. All day long.

Artie shook his head. His life was hard to believe sometimes, but the gray shadow of Otter, hiding in the corner, served as proof. Cold and nauseous and waiting. "Come on, Otter," Artie said. "The carousel won't open for hours yet. Let's go work on your body." *Besides,* he thought, *you'll spend plenty of days here at the wheel once you inhabit it. For now, you can spend the day with me.*

Artie worked day and night, chipping away at the pieces of hard maple wood that turned into hooves and legs, muzzle and ears, strong back and flipping tail. Curling wood chips littered the floor, and the smell of sawdust mingled with sea salt in the air. None of the pieces came out exactly as Artie planned them. Sometimes the wood grain fought with his tools, and he had to adjust his plans, hiding his mistakes or marveling in the beauty that his tools uncovered, pre-existing in the wood.

As the weeks wore on, the heat of summer began to cool into early fall. Artie felt the ache in his hands grow as they tired from daily sawing, chipping, sanding, and re-sanding. When all the pieces were done, though, he fit them together with dowels and glue. Finally, piece by piece, they came together, forming the hollow horse-shape that would eventually become Otter.

The plainly wooden horse stood in Artie's workshop for a week while he waited for his hands to recover. He would need a steady hand to paint it.

When he was ready, Artie brought out an extra bright light to shine on the wooden horse. He could carve, at least partly, by feel, but he had to paint by sight. The brightly colored paints he used were oil based. The gold for the saddle, however, was actual gold leaf in sheets as thin as a human hair. The silver for the bridle wasn't real silver as that would tarnish too easily. Instead, it was made from aluminum.

It took less physical effort to paint the horse than it had to carve it, but the painstaking detail and Artie's aging eyes made it the hardest part.

When the final coat of paint dried, Otter's body was the most beautiful carousel horse Artie had ever carved. Of course, he thought that about each of his ponies when he really looked at them.

Eagle liked to watch Artie do the painting. So, it was her and Worthy at his side on the day when he finally declared Otter's body finished. "What do you think?" he asked, standing back from his masterpiece. The newly carved carnival clown pony reared in its frozen pose in front of them. The polka dots and stripes in the mane were so much more colorful in real life than they'd been in Artie's sketch. His chest swelled with pride.

Worthy butted his head against Artie's arm, affectionately approving. Eagle stamped her front hoof, stretched out her wings, and reared her hooves into the air herself.

"I'm glad you approve," Artie said. "Shall we find Otter?" But, of course, that wasn't necessary. The shadow of ghostly gray that was Otter's ethereal form already sat in the doorway of the workshop. Artie didn't know how, but the ghosts always knew when their bodies were done. Perhaps the same force that drew them to his carousel called them to their wooden forms.

Artie hoped one day that he would feel that call. The unicorn body that he'd carved for himself was already waiting, obscured behind a slat of wood, in the back of his workshop. He didn't know what caused some animals—and people—to turn into ghosts when they died. And he didn't know why some of them came to him. But, if he had anything to say about the organization of the universe, when he was called to leave this human body some day, he would take a gray ghostly form—like Otter now held and like each of his ponies had come to him in—and he would return to his carousel.

Artie closed his eyes thinking about it, and, when he opened them again, the stiff shape of the clown pony had relaxed and put its front hooves down. With soft white fur and cheerful polka dot spots, Otter came over to Artie and nuzzled his new muzzle against the old man's face. Artie laughed and smiled. "How do you do that?" he asked. "I've made so many of you, and, still, I can't believe when another one comes to life." He put one hand on each side of Otter's long equine face and looked him steadily in his liquid brown eyes. "Are you happy, Otter? Will you come to life again and again? Every night?"

The melodic voice of Silly Girl spoke from behind them, "Are you worrying again? You're not crazy, unless I am."

"You, Silly Girl," Artie said, "are a carnival unicorn who thinks she used to be a woman from Louisiana. I don't think you should be claiming to know what crazy is."

"Fair enough," Silly Girl said, but when Artie turned to look at her, she tossed her mane in a way that left no uncertainty: she stood by what she had said.

"Well, Otter," Artie said, "we have a tradition here. When a new pony joins the wheel, we all ride down the beach together. Would you be kind enough to let me up on your back?"

Otter whinnied and threw his head back. His ears flicked, and he lifted his hooves in a dancing step.

"He's still getting used to his new body," Silly Girl said.

Artie nodded, and he waited for Otter to settle down. When his hooves stilled, Artie took Otter's silver bridle in his hand and led the new pony out of the workshop and down to the sand. All the other ponies followed.

During the weeks that Artie had spent building Otter's body, they'd all gotten to know the spirit that was now inside. But this was their first introduction to the cheerful, goofy, polka dotted pony who would join them on their wheel tomorrow.

Rabbit and Bunny came up to him first. They bumped their noses against his and shared a snort of warm breath. Then Tiger pranced her way over, somehow managing to communicate a jungle cat's stealthy prowl, even while sporting equine legs. She held her distance, eyeing Otter, but she seemed to approve. His colors were as bold as hers, albeit in a different style.

The ponies pawed the sand with their hooves and bobbed their heads. Artie was sure they could communicate with each other somehow, possibly through the simple understanding that while they had all come here different they were all the same in one important way. They were all ponies of the same carousel.

When Silly Girl told Artie they were all ready, he mounted Otter. He felt Otter's body shift beneath him, and, instead of urging Otter to take off down the beach, Artie let his new pony find his own footing. He walked to the water's edge and let the wavelets there break against his hooves. Salt water slid over the sand beneath him.

"It must be different to feel the sea against a horse's hooves than it was to float in it as an otter." Artie's voice was quiet, but he could tell Otter had heard him. "I know that Eagle still wishes she could fly," Artie said. "I imagine, if I'm ever lucky enough some day to join you, that there will be things that I'll miss too."

Artie sat on Otter's back, stroking his long neck and rainbow striped mane. The moon shone down and reflected in the glassy waves. Otter's white face reflected there too.

Artie looked down the shore and saw the other ponies waiting for them, dancing in the shining wet sand and sea foam. Artie combed his fingers through the green, yellow, and purple hair of Otter's mane. He'd made the best body he could for Otter; now it was up to Otter to find peace with it. "Shall we go?" he asked, squeezing his knees gently against Otter's sides.

Otter whinnied, and, finally, his reverie was done.

Artie and Otter cantered down the beach toward the others, and Otter's legs stepped high. He raised his nose, and shook his mane. He pranced and danced like the clown Artie had made him into—like the clown Artie had guessed he already was.

Eagle reared and flapped her wings at him. Rabbit, Bunny, and Froggy hopped around him in lighthearted gaiety. When they all set off down the beach, Worthy rode close by Otter's side. And, although Artie couldn't be sure over the sound of the wind in his ears, he thought he heard Silly Girl singing a song.

An entire carousel's worth of ponies rode together down the moonlit beach, and, tomorrow, they'd ride all day together again, in circles filled with smiling and laughing children.

7

THE UNICORN KEEPER

AMALIOONA PRANCES INTO THE STABLES, her tufted hooves gleaming. They are the same sparkling shade of white as a hillside of snow in the sun. They are dainty, perfect unicorn hooves. How is it, then, that she always seems to clumsily knock over the slop bucket—no matter where I put it—and kick up the fresh hay into a veritable dust storm?

Sneezing from the whirling dust, I try to sweep the golden hay back into a comfortable pile for her bed and mop up the dingy water from the bucket.

"Did she have a good time at the carnival?" I ask the trapeze artist who has walked my unicorn home. They do high wire tricks together—nothing stops a show like a unicorn on a unicycle on a trapeze.

"The best!" the trapeze artist exclaims before waving goodbye to Amalioona. Not to me. I'm just the unicorn's keeper. Who would pay attention to me when there's a shining, bright unicorn around?

I sigh and prepare Amalioona's evening meal—a crystal bowl filled with lavender buds, rose petals, and four leaf clovers. Only the four leaf ones. Three-leafed clovers don't taste right. She won't eat them.

Amalioona lowers her head toward the crystal bowl and, like always, manages to scrape my shoulder and chin with the dagger-sharp tip of her clear-as-ice horn. I wear bandages constantly. Of course, the obvious solution is to put Amalioona's flowery salad in a trough. Or even to secure the crystal bowl on a pedestal.

But Amalioona's a hand-fed unicorn. I found her as a tiny fawn, small enough to tuck under my arm and carry home, wrapped in my baggy jacket with me. Now she stands as tall as I do, but she's never outgrown the way I babied her as a foal. Why should she? If I try to lay down limits, she stops eating and her ethereal glow—silver like moonlight—fades to a sickly, flickering shade—gray like a staticky television screen.

And I'm to blame. And everyone around me steps in: "What's wrong with her? Aren't you feeding her right? Make her better! Make her better RIGHT NOW."

And because there'd be nothing worse than being the person who killed the unicorn—the brilliant, beautiful unicorn who stars in the carnival and visits children's birthday parties and volunteers at the library where disadvantaged kids practice reading to her—I always fold. Amalioona gets what she wants.

Amalioona snuffles out the last of the clovers from the crystal bowl, and then she snuffles my hand, gripping the bowl's side. Her lips are warm and soft and being kissed by a unicorn feels like a blessing.

But then she prances off to her golden pile of hay, managing somehow to kick me in the knee with her perfect hoof on the way. The pain is sharp, but quickly dulls to an ache.

I watch her curl up in the hay. Her side heaves gently with her breathing. She closes her eyes and falls asleep. Her sleep radiates from her like the warmth of sunlight. You could almost feel rested just from watching her sleep. That would almost be enough.

I love her more than anything.

It is an honor to spend my days searching out four leaf clovers for her.

I limp a little as I make my way out of the stable, empty crystal bowl clutched in my hands, waiting to be filled again.

8

FERAL UNICORN

As I brought the mug of fresh-brewed coffee to my lips, the steaming liquid froze solid. Startled by the sudden coldness in my hand, I dropped the mug. The handle broke off when it hit the linoleum floor. To make matters worse, the magic wore off almost instantly, and the mug-shaped block of coffee-ice promptly melted, puddling on the floor.

For weeks, ever since Angelo's horn came in, I'd been finding small works of mischief around the house—summer strawberries, fresh-picked from the garden, ruined by frost; icicles blocking up the faucets; and hot drinks that simply wouldn't stay hot. This was the first time it had happened to something while I was looking at it.

I turned toward the kitchen doorway and saw the small fawn-like creature standing there, barely larger than my largest cat. The snowy whiteness of his fur and the pearlescent shine of his horn bespoke purity, but I could swear the bastard was glaring at me. He disappeared before I could move, running off to hide behind the sofa. We barely saw him anymore, only found the traces of his mischief.

"Stupid unicorn," I grumbled, grabbing a fistful of paper towels and kneeling on the floor in my pajamas. I wiped up the mess on the linoleum, thinking about how I'd have to brew a whole new cup of coffee in the French press. It made good coffee, but it took longer than the instant stuff I used to have. That wasn't a problem before, but, with a four-month-old baby, every minute counted. I didn't know how long I'd have before Noah woke up. Chances were good I'd have to either skip the coffee or miss out on my five minute shower today.

The more I thought about it, the more angry I got. My husband was out of town, and I couldn't stand the idea of a whole week of cleaning up after unicorn pranks on my own.

"Libby!" I called to my eight-year-old daughter who was reading comic books in the other room. "Where's that golden bridle Grandma gave us?"

"The one for Angelo?" she called back. "I was using it with my stuffed toys. I think Muff-Muff is wearing it."

I rolled my eyes. "Enchanted bridles aren't toys. Could you go get it?"

A minute later, Libby appeared in the kitchen doorway, dangling the golden ropes of the bridle and kicking at the floor. "Does this mean we're giving Angelo to Grandma?" she asked.

"He'll be happier there," I said. My mom had experience with mystical pets, and Angelo would get along better with her miniature dragon, Smug, than with my cats. They didn't like him at all.

"You don't think Gabriel and Angelo will miss each other?" Libby asked.

We'd found the twin foals more than a year ago in a hollow under the thorn bush that grew along the edge of our backyard. Back then, they'd been small enough to fit into the palms of my cupped hands. My mom and I had caught them, and Mom had cast a spell on their feral mother to make her infertile. The last thing we needed was a neighborhood overrun with feral unicorns. The foals were young enough, though, that I'd decided to tame them and keep them as indoor-only pets. They'd have a better life that way than out on the streets.

It had been working out well enough until their horns came in...

"I don't know, Libby. If they miss each other, then we can always take Gabriel to live with Grandma, too." Besides, I couldn't be completely sure all the mischief was Angelo's work until he was gone. Though, Gabriel certainly got along better with the cats.

"But then we won't have any pet unicorns!" Libby stomped her foot and threw the golden bridle on the floor.

I frowned at her and said, "You know better than to act

like that. Now will you help me catch Angelo before Noah wakes up?"

Libby and I chased Angelo around the house still dressed in our pajamas. He hid behind one piece of furniture after the other. Once Libby thought she'd cornered him in the gap between the washer and dryer, only to find it was actually Gabriel. He shied away from us, too. We could only tell them apart by Gabriel's slight dappling of white spots on white, visible only from certain angles, and a softer look in his eyes.

Finally, we chased Angelo upstairs into Noah's room, the smallest in the house. I sent Libby away, shushing her, and closed the door behind me. Angelo was trapped now. I'd put the golden bridle on him, call my mom, and then we could drive over to visit her—and give her this godforsaken unicorn—after I took my shower and got Noah up.

I peeked in the crib and saw Noah sleeping peacefully, rolled up in a swaddling blanket like a little burrito. If I was quiet, maybe this wouldn't even wake him up.

The space under the crib was filled with boxes of hand-me-down baby clothes, and the only other piece of furniture in the room was a combination changing table and dresser by the window. It sat flat on the floor, so Angelo had squeezed himself into the narrow space between it and the wall. I approached him slowly with the bridle held out in front of me, crooning quiet words to soothe him.

"Good unicorn. Easy unicorn. Stay where you are, Angelo." I knelt down by the dresser to get closer.

Angelo pawed the carpeted floor with his tiny, cloven hooves and reared back on his hind legs. He looked more like a wild animal than one of my pets, but I told myself it was just a show. I'd sheltered him, cared for him, and fed him for more than a year. When he was foal without a horn, I'd held him on my lap and stroked his fur.

My mom had told me the bridle would take Angelo's frost magic away and make him docile, at least for a few hours. After that, the enchantment would begin to wear off. All I had to do was get it on him. How bad could it be? Even if he iced my hands, the cold would disappear as soon as the bridle was on.

I took a deep breath and reached my left hand toward him. He cowered as far in the corner as he could squeeze himself. His flank quivered when I touched him. I started to reach in to the narrow space with my right hand, holding the bridle, but Angelo reared back again, kicking at my left hand with his front hooves. He kicked hard, and his tiny, cloven hooves were surprisingly sharp. My hand seared with pain, but I had to get that bridle on him.

"Hold still," I growled, trying to steady his struggling body with my increasingly battered hand. I brought the bridle forward. Angelo swung his head, aiming his horn, and ran my right hand through.

I gasped in pain and shock at the sight of his pearly horn emerging from the back of my hand. I pulled my hand away, sliding it off Angelo's horn. It hurt so badly that I screamed out.

Noah cried, and Libby called from the other side of the door. "Are you okay, Mom?"

Somehow I'd backed myself across the room, away from the wild creature in my baby's bedroom. A trail of blood followed me across the carpet, and I realized my hand was bleeding everywhere. My pajamas were soaked red. I couldn't face the idea of trying to capture Angelo again. I'd have to leave him trapped in here and deal with him later. For now, I had to pick up Noah.

Libby wasn't tall enough to reach into the crib, and I couldn't leave the baby in here with Angelo. If he froze my coffee to annoy me when I let him be, and he did this to me when I didn't, then who knew what he might do now that I'd made him mad?

"Bring me a towel!" I called through the closed door.

"Are you okay?" Libby called back.

"Towel!"

I wrapped the towel around my hand as soon as Libby brought it to me, twisting it tight to staunch the blood. "Now get back out, and close the door," I said. "I'll get the baby."

As I reached into the crib, I realized my other hand was bleeding too from all the little, crescent hoof prints. I started crying, but I couldn't take the time to bandage my hands properly, just wipe them as much as possible with the towel. I scooped up the screaming baby whose arched body relaxed as soon as he felt arms holding him. Once outside the nursery with the door shut behind me, I said, "Libby, please hold your brother."

She was crying, but she took him. Scattered dots of blood on his swaddling blanket matched the bleeding hoof-marks on my left hand.

First thing first: I got my cell phone from my bedroom and fought my shaking hands to call my mom. My fingers smeared blood on the display screen.

I sat down on my bed, feeling faint. I switched the cell to speaker phone while it rang and set it on my knee. I held my hands uselessly in front of me, watching the blood coil down my wrists.

"Hello, Janie," my mother said.

"Mom!" The words poured out of me in a rush: "That unicorn is not a pet! He's wild! All he does is glare at me and hide behind furniture and play frost tricks on me. I don't think he's let a human hand touch him since his horn came in. And now he's stabbed my hand! There's blood everywhere." A sob shook my voice. "He can't stay here anymore. What if he decided to freeze the baby? He's trapped in the baby's room. Can you come over and help me? He can't stay. I have to get him out of my house today."

There was a pause at the other end.

"Mom?" I sobbed.

"I'll be over in ten minutes," she said and hung up.

Ten minutes was too long to sit and stare at my hands bleeding, but I didn't know how I was going to bandage them myself. I went into the bathroom and turned on the sink with my elbow. I rinsed off as much blood as I could, then I dried my hands quickly on the already blood-soaked towel. By moving fast and repeatedly dabbing the towel at the beads of blood that formed on my hands, I managed to get out the first aid kit and scatter an array of bandages on the bathroom floor without getting too much blood on the bathroom cabinet. I knelt down and started matching different sized bandages to the various hoof wounds on my left hand. Once I had the blood mostly stopped on one hand, it got easier.

My right hand was swollen and growing stiff. I wrapped gauze as tightly as I could around the stigmata-like gouge in my palm.

When I looked up, I saw Libby standing in the bathroom door, bouncing Noah and watching me. "I wish this hadn't happened," she said.

"I wish that too." I didn't say, *Too bad unicorns don't grant wishes.*

My mom arrived wearing a ridiculous looking wizard's hat from an old Halloween costume over her bouffant hairdo and one of the garlic braids that she gets at the farmer's market draped around her neck. She held a bouquet of purple-dyed daisies that she'd probably bought at the grocery store on the way over.

"Isn't garlic for vampires?" I asked.

"It's a general purpose ward," she answered, looking at me sternly over her bifocals. She went straight into my kitchen and got out the olive oil. "You don't mind?" she asked.

"What are you going to do with it?"

"Anti-frost spell," she answered opening the bottle. She

dipped her finger in and smeared the oil on her forehead and cheeks while chanting. Then she asked, "Where's the bridle?"

"I dropped it in Noah's room."

"And Angelo's shut in there?"

"Yes."

I followed my mother dumbly up to Noah's room. When she got to the door, I panicked and said, "Wait!"

She turned to look at me. I didn't understand her spells, but she seemed so sure of herself. So prepared. Maybe I wouldn't be in this situation if I'd taken magic lessons from her like she wanted.

"Never mind," I said, wringing the towel that I was still holding in my hands. "Be careful."

She went into the nursery and closed the door behind her. I couldn't stand waiting outside, not knowing how it was going, so I cracked the door open, not enough for Angelo to squeeze through if he tried to escape but enough for me to see my mom scattering the purple daisies, dancing and singing. Once all the daisies were on the floor, she approached the corner where Angelo hid. I saw her crouch down, and I listened to the voice that had lulled me to sleep as a child.

Clearly, I'd handled the situation all wrong. I should have called my mother over in the first place. Then, my hand wouldn't hurt. We'd already be drinking tea and watching Angelo get acquainted with Smug.

Then she screamed.

I should never have let my mother go in that room with a

feral unicorn. She kept screaming. What had he done to her?

My mother came running out, no eyebrows and her hair on fire. I threw my blood soaked towel over her head, knocking off her wizard's hat and inadvertently knocking her down too.

We sat on the floor in the hallway outside the nursery together. My mother's hair was no longer on fire, but she'd turned her ankle, and the burns on her face where she'd smeared the olive oil looked bad.

"That little jerk set me on fire," she said. "Since when can a unicorn have both frost and fire magic?"

"Can he still attack us out here?" I asked, looking worriedly at the door.

"Unicorns can't cast spells on things they can't see," Mom said, touching her face gingerly and wincing. "Line-of-sight magic."

"Are you okay?" I asked.

"I don't know."

I looked her over, trying to figure out what to do. Her face was red and cracked. I didn't know how to treat burn wounds. "Let's make sure you're okay," I said. I got up and called out in a loud voice, "Libby, get dressed! We're taking Grandma to urgent care."

I threw exercise clothes on and found enough supplies to dress Noah in the baby bag in the living room. Thank goodness. I only hoped Angelo wouldn't set the house on fire while we were gone.

There was hardly any wait at the urgent care. I guess

that's the advantage of getting attacked by a unicorn early in the morning. My mother, daughter, baby and I crowded into the little examination room with the doctor. My mom sat on the examination table; Libby took the one chair; and I stood in the corner, bouncing Noah, leaving the wheeled stool for the doctor even though he stood too.

"Second degree," he announced after examining my mom's burns. "I'll dress the wounds, give you something for the pain, and you'll be fine."

"I'm working on a healing spell that would clear something like this right up," my mom said.

"Uh huh." The doctor got supplies out of a drawer, spread a shiny salve over my mom's wounds, and set to work bandaging them. When he was done my mother looked a little like a half-wrapped mummy.

"You're the second person I've seen today for a mystical animal attack," the doctor said. "The last guy had deep scratches all down his arm from his pet griffin. If you ask me, mystical animals should be outlawed as pets."

I knew my mom loved her dragon, but, right then, I couldn't disagree with the doctor. Though, I wondered how many people he saw for attacks from cats, dogs, raccoons. Any animal with claws can scratch.

"You should look at my daughter's hands, too," Mom said.

"I'm fine," I said, but, when I tried to close my hand, I realized it had grown too stiff to bend.

I passed Noah to my mom, and the doctor looked at my hands.

"You're lucky," he said. "No bone or nerve damage. If that horn were any thicker around, I'd be sending you to a hand surgeon. As it is, you'll have to be very careful to make sure it doesn't get infected."

We took the prescriptions the doctor gave us to the closest pharmacy. My mom waited in the car with Noah; Libby and I went in. While the pharmacist prepared our drugs, Libby hopscotched around the colored tiles of the floor, and I tried to figure out what to do about Angelo when we got home.

We couldn't get the golden bridle on him. That was clear. I could leave him shut in Noah's room until he starved, but that would be horrible. Besides, Noah wouldn't let any of us sleep if I messed with his bedtime routine. Maybe there was someone I could call. There had to be professionals who dealt with situations like this. *Who you gonna call? Unicorn-busters!*

When we got home, Mom set Libby up with a movie and settled in the rocking chair to sing to the baby. I looked up the number for animal control on my computer.

I didn't like the idea of having Angelo removed like a wild animal that had invaded my home. What if they insisted on putting him down? But I tried calling anyway. The phone tree I reached gave me options for reporting animal abuse, complaining about loud barking, advice for the proper care and feeding of mystical animals, registering a new pet... Nothing seemed right. None of it sounded like it would lead me to an actual human. I hung up.

After another minute of thought, I decided to call the vet who'd seen Angelo and Gabriel when we first caught them.

"Wellspring Animal Hospital. This is Dianne. How can I help you?"

"Hi, Dianne," I said. "I'm calling you because I don't know what else to do. I have this unicorn who I brought to see Dr. Eiler as a foal, and ever since his horn came in he's been playing frost tricks on me. Today, he ran my hand through with his horn, and he set my mom on fire. I had to take her to the doctor."

There was silence on the other end of the phone, so I kept telling my story.

"I've trapped him in the smallest room in the house, but I can't let him out. I have a four-month-old baby who'd be completely defenseless, and now that Angelo's mad... I don't know what I'm expecting, but the vet's who you call when you have trouble with animals. So, I thought... Do you have any ideas?"

After a moment, Dianne said, "Have you tried opening the window?"

"Angelo's an indoor-only—" I stumbled over the word *pet* and ended up saying *unicorn.*

"It sounds like he can take care of himself."

"That's true." I didn't know if Angelo would be willing to go out the window. He was used to living in a warm house with bowls of fresh oats fixed with heavy cream, brown sugar, and mint leaves. Living on the streets would be a much harder life. Yet, he seemed to hate living with me. "I'll give it a try," I said. "Thanks."

The window wouldn't be latched since it was summer, and it would be easy enough to pop off the screen from the outside. Noah's room was on the second story, but I got the ladder out of the garage and climbed up on the roof rather than risking going in that nursery with Angelo again.

When I popped the window screen out, I saw feathered fingers of frost on the glass panes behind it. Angelo had been casting his magic at the window. Was he trying to get out? Looking into the nursery, I noticed a few singes on the carpet, but those could be from when he attacked my mother. The rest of the room looked perfectly normal. I couldn't see Angelo at this angle which meant he couldn't see me.

I pushed up the window and quickly got out of the way. I felt terribly exposed, standing on the slanted shingles of my roof. I wanted to go down the ladder and get the hell out of there, but then how would I know if Angelo had gone? I waited with my heart racing.

A snowy equine head graced with a mane like a tiny waterfall emerged tentatively from the window. I wished I'd brought a shield or weapon to defend myself. Maybe one of my mother's spells. Angelo stood on the window ledge, looking all around. When his head turned far enough to see me, our eyes locked. As fast as a shadow disappears when the sun comes out, Angelo moved from the window ledge to the edge of the roof.

He gave me one last look, triumph burning in his eyes, before jumping down from the roof. *I escaped*, his look said. *You trapped me, but I outsmarted you.* I wondered if I'd ever see him again.

I climbed in through the window and gladly shut it on the world of wild animals outside. The screen could be put back later. I sat on the bloodstained, singed carpet of my baby's room for a while, cradling my swollen, injured hands and figuring out what I'd say when I went downstairs. I hoped Libby and my mom wouldn't be too disappointed. They couldn't really believe that Angelo belonged in either of our houses after this morning.

I must have sat there for a while, because Libby's movie was almost over when I came down. Libby was stretched out on the couch, and Mom was still in the rocking chair. Libby paused the movie, and they both looked at me.

"Well?" Mom asked.

"Angelo's an outdoor unicorn now."

"I think that's best," Mom said.

"Can we still fix bowls of oats for him and put them outside?" Libby asked.

After all the trouble that Angelo had caused, I felt like he could forage for mint leaves on his own. There were plenty of nice gardens around. "Maybe," I said.

Libby's face quivered, and she cried, "I miss Angelo!"

Until today, Libby hadn't interacted with Angelo for

months. I closed my eyes and said with as much patience as I could find, "We still have Gabriel. They're practically the same." Except, of course, one of them turned out to be evil. I hoped it was only the one.

Exhausted, we all watched movies for the rest of the afternoon. My mom helped scrub the blood out of the carpet in Noah's room before she went home. She pressed a small bunch of lavender and mistletoe sprigs into my hand when we said goodbye. "Treats for Gabriel," she said. "Unicorns love mistletoe. Don't let the cats or baby get it though. If you're not mystical, it's poisonous."

"Right."

"And if he gives you any trouble, I'm willing to take him. Do you know if he has the same kind of magics as Angelo?"

I shook my head. "I've barely seen him since his horn came in. I think Angelo was pulling all the pranks, but it's impossible to be sure. I guess I'll find out soon."

"Hmm." Mom frowned. "If he has frost magic—and only frost magic—the bridle will work on him. If he turns out to have some other kind of magic, let me know, and I'll re-enchant the bridle."

I couldn't imagine trying to put an enchanted bridle on a unicorn ever again. I'd rather open another window. But it would be different with a unicorn who was really my pet, a unicorn who wasn't feral, wouldn't it? The question was: was Gabriel my pet?

All evening, I jumped at shadows, expecting objects to freeze in my hands or the water in the faucet to dry up, blocked by an icicle. I kept an eye out for Gabriel, but all I saw were my cats. I could have been imagining it, but they looked grateful to have Angelo gone.

Once the kids were down for the night, I could finally relax. I took the bandages off my hands. The left hand didn't look too bad, but my right hand was still so swollen around my stigmata that I could barely curl my fingers. I'd assumed the wound would be getting better by now with all the medicine the doctor had given me, but it was worse. The gouge was bloody and oozed with puss. I washed it like the doctor had instructed and then re-dressed it, wrapping the gauze tight and trying to ignore the throbbing.

I crawled into a bed littered, as always, with cats. I began to drift off, then I felt a new weight at the foot of the bed. I opened my eyes and saw a pale shadow so much like Angelo it made my heart jump.

I forced myself to stay calm and reached for the sprigs of lavender and mistletoe that I'd tucked into the drawer in the bedside table. Gabriel lowered his head and nuzzled one of my cats, a grumpy calico who I'd seen hiss and spit at Angelo only a few days ago. The calico purred.

I pulled off a few leaves of mistletoe and lavender flowers, placed them on my good palm, and held out my hand. Slowly, one step at a time, Gabriel walked up the bed. I could feel his hoofs, a delicate weight, through my quilt. It terrified me how much he looked like Angelo, but he seemed equally terrified. I held perfectly still.

Gabriel ate the leaves and flowers from my palm. Then

he lay down beside me just like he was one of the cats. I waited awhile, practically holding my breath, then I reached my right hand out, slowly, to pet him. Gabriel startled when my hand touched him. He turned his head, pressed his nose, whickering, against the bandages. I felt a warmth in my hand, and I stiffened, readying myself to fight a fire magic unicorn.

The warmth ebbed, and the throbbing pain in my hand subsided. Moving slowly, so as not to upset Gabriel, I unwrapped the bandage on my hand again. The oozing gouge had closed into a white scar. The swelling was going down by the second.

"You have healing magic," I said.

Gabriel stared at me with soft eyes. I stroked his dappled white body with my newly healed hand. Hidden under his fur, Gabriel's neck was covered in raised lines, healed scratches, and half moon scars.

"You've been fighting," I said. "Who have you been fighting?" I didn't think my cats would do this, and the half moon scars matched the cloven hoof marks on my left hand. Had Angelo been attacking his own brother?

I would not miss that feral unicorn.

This unicorn did not seem feral. He laid his head down on the quilt. His hooves were already folded beneath him. I stroked his neck. Slowly, so as not to spook him, I worked my way up to scritching his ears and running my fingers through his forelock. Finally I touched his horn, the heart of his magic. On his brother it was a dangerous weapon. On Gabriel, it was simply a part of this tiny animal's body. It was like Gabriel had an evil twin outside, roaming the neighborhood, probably freezing songbirds and squirrels.

This morning, I'd had two unicorns, but, with the way they'd hidden behind furniture, darting out of any room I entered, it felt like I'd had none. Now, nestled on the bed beside me, as if he were one of my cats, was a lovely, tiny, unicorn. I'd lost a pet today, but it felt like I'd gained one.

9

BLACK SWANS

I WATCH THE LAKE, peaceful and serene; white swans float on it with the graceful delicacy and stillness of ice sculptures or many-tiered, fondant-covered wedding cakes.

Then the black swans come. One after another. Crashing into the water, wings spread wide and flapping.

Progress has begun.

THE BLACK SWANS send ripples across the water, flustering the white swans, pressing them out of their laconic drowse. A nap that had taken over their lives, making life nothing but a dream.

The black swans land on the mirrored surface, fold their wings, and take their place.

* * *

NOTHING WILL BE the same now.

One black swan might be strange, but it can be ignored. A whole flock of them? They change the way the lake is seen.

Children will draw swans using black crayons now, filling them in with scribbles. Their swooping, curved necks will blend into the darkness of night.

* * *

WE'LL THINK of swans as the complement of ravens—both dark-feathered: one beauties; the others clever. A dichotomy; a metaphor. Black feathers on both. Black feathers are best.

The white ones look pale and bleached now. A line drawing, which a child artist forgot to fill in.

* * *

WHY ARE you afraid of the black swans? They're only swans, floating on the surface of a lake, gleaming with the depth of nebulas in their feathers.

We've traded wedding cakes for nebulas. That cannot be a loss worth mourning.

Cake is nice. The sky is better.

10

THE THIRD WISH

THE SHORE BUBBLED and frothed under Bryen's sotto voce chanting. His hands trembled, conducting currents in the air, and he squinted his eyes tight.

"Knock it off!" Charles yelled at his brother. "How will I ever get a fish to bite if you keep that up?" He kept preparing the boat as he grumbled. "Bunch of rubbish," he said. "Scares all the decent fish away."

Bryen finished his spell, and a gentle wave slid along the sand, pushing all the "treasure" it could find. Boots and bottles, shiny shells, and colorful broken glass. The same haul Bryen made every time. He slogged through the soggy sand, leaving round boot prints, as he picked through the rubble.

A final check and the boat was ready to push off. Charles called to his brother, "Let's get a move on," but Bryen was stooped down, holding a black and gold object.

He brushed wet sand from it, tracing his fingers around the vase's mouth.

"Look what I found!" Bryen called.

"Great. You can put flowers in it and take it to your elf mother," Charles said, cruelly. They both knew Bryen's mother died birthing him. "Would you get in the boat already? We'll have to get well out to sea if we want to catch anything after that stupid trick of yours."

Bryen's face was still turned toward the sandy vase. He placed his fingers over its gold etched patterns. He felt a power in it. "Maybe I will take it to my mother," he said. Then, "Maybe I'll put it by her grave."

Charles looked at him strangely. "That's a long hike, brother. Get in the boat." But, Charles could sense that Bryen wouldn't come. He'd be fishing alone today. And why? Because Bryen found a vase in the drink. "Is there something special about that vase?"

"There might be…" Bryen looked up and grinned. "I'll ask my mother when I get to her." His magic was always more powerful where his mother was buried.

Charles snorted to show disdain, but he felt burning jealousy. Well, Bryen could play his elf-magic games. For him, there was fishing to be done. And, Bryen's limited magic had never gotten him far anyway. Charles pushed the boat off to sea, while his brother began his long hike into the woods.

For the next two days, Charles stewed at sea. He cast his line but caught few fish. Without Bryen's charms, these waters weren't fruitful. Charles had heard the charms many times before, and he tried mimicking Bryen's chant. To no avail. Charles had no magical training, and he had no elf-blood in his veins. He cursed his half-brother.

On the third night, Charles felt a rumbling in the earth as he slept. He threw on his robe and rushed out of his hut by the sea. In the distance, Charles could just barely see a shape blacking out the stars where nothing used to be. The shape was up the coast and inland, the direction Bryen took to his mother's tomb. Even with the strong light of the newly waning moon, Charles couldn't make it out. Perhaps Bryen would bring him news of the dark shape when he returned.

Still, Charles stood for a long time on the beach, peering into the distance. What kept him staring was this: the shape seemed to be growing

In the morning light, Charles could see what he hadn't seen in the dark of night. Stone by flying stone, a castle was building itself deep in the forest. Charles stayed home from fishing that day—he wouldn't catch much without Bryen anyway—to watch the castle grow. Towers, turrets, ramparts, parapets. The pieces assembled themselves like a giant puzzle.

By the evening star, a flag flew, independent like a bird, to the highest tower and perched to unfurl in the wind. It was green cloth bearing Bryen's elven symbol intertwined with a picture of a rose. What powerful magic was in that vase?

The answer came to Charles the next day. While he

crouched on the shore, untangling fishing line, he heard a rustle in the bushes. He turned around and saw a man emerge. The man wore a green tabard; he had come from the magic castle.

"Do you bring news of my brother?" Charles asked.

"I do," answered the man. "I am his page, and he sent me to bid you join him in yonder castle."

"How does Bryen come to have a castle? Three days ago he left here carrying nothing but a tide-strewn vase."

The page stood calmly, looking at Charles. "There was a genie in the vase," he said. "The genie offered my Lord three wishes."

"And the castle was Bryen's first wish?"

The page verified Charles' guess with silence and a nod. He was a quiet man, with a stillness in his eyes. The longer Charles looked at him, the stranger the page seemed. "Where are you from?" Charles asked. "How do you come to be a page for my brother?" This man was of no genealogy that Charles knew: his skin had a greenish cast; his hair was wide and flat like grass; his hands were tough and sharp at the knuckles.

"My lord's second wish," the page said.

"For a page?"

"For a court to fill his castle. Will you come with me? My lord bids me accompany you to the castle, if you will."

"What about the third wish?" Charles asked.

"My lord has not spent it. Will you come?"

"Tell Bryen I'll think about it." And after a moment he added, "If Bryen really wants me, he can use that third wish to make me come." And he sent the page on his way.

Days passed by, and Charles grew used to fishing alone. He trudged into town to sell his fish, and he watched the castle on the horizon. He was looking for a sign that Bryen had spent his third wish. He searched his soul for a sign too—but he did not feel an inexorable calling to join his brother. Of course, he did not expect his brother to expend his third wish on him... Nor would a wish necessarily be visible in the sky.

When the page paid his second visit, Charles immediately asked the question: "Has Bryen spent his third wish? Are you here to force me to the castle?"

The page's petal-pink lips broke into a gentle smile. "My lord does wish for your presence, but he would not force you to come."

Charles heard the page's words, but he twisted them around in his brain until they meant something quite different: *Bryen does not think you are worth wasting a wish on.*

"I am a fisherman, and there are fish to be caught. Tell my brother I will stay here."

The page lowered his head in obeisance. "My lord was afraid you would answer thus. It will sadden him. However, before I return to the castle, let me bestow on you this gift."

The page held out his hand, filled with sparkling, colorful baubles. Charles took the gift and looked at the page with questioning eyes.

"Baits for your hook," the page answered. "My lord imbued them with the fishing charms he used to cast for you."

Charles thanked the page, but the words turned sour in his mouth. Bryen possessed his own magic; why did fate give him a genie too? As Charles watched the page recede into the forest, he resolved to begin studying magic.

He sold the fishing charms at an exorbitant rate and used the money to buy books of spells. He studied the books at night, poring over the pages in his hut. While he fished, he recited the chants over and over in his mind. He practiced the hand motions. His diligence slowly paid off.

The next time the page came, Charles refused his gift and told him to tell Bryen, "I've learned a little magic of my own." To prove it, he fluttered his hands, muttered a few words, and the page's tabard changed: Bryen's elven symbol and rose were replaced by a simple embroidery of a fishing pole. "Show that to my brother. Remind him where he came from."

Years passed by, and the page came less often.

Charles' magic increased, until the nearby villagers hailed him as their fisherman-sorcerer. His spells were simple: fishing charms, spells to make heavy boots feel light, weak love potions... exactly the kind of spells that simple townspeople craved, paid well for, and were impressed by.

Yet, Charles was discontent. Every time he looked over the forest at the castle on the horizon, he felt his hard-earned magic dwarfed by the magic that luck had given Bryen.

How had Bryen spent his third wish? Had he spent it? Perhaps, if Charles went to his brother, then Bryen would gift the wish to him...

But Charles was middle-aged now, with a stiffness in his back, and he was set in his ways. He was used to fishing in the morning, trudging to town in the afternoon, and studying his magic books at night. So he did not go to his brother.

One day, the page came again. In fact, it was not the page—it was a new page, but he wore the same tabard and had the same strange coloring: that greenish cast to the skin. His features were a little different: vine-like hair, that curled at the ends; a suppleness in his limbs; and long, long fingers.

The page said, "My lord, your brother, is ill."

The words took a long time to sink into Charles' brain. It had been many years since his last communiqué from Bryen, but his brother was half-elf and would not have aged as much or as gracelessly as him. "What ails him?" Charles asked.

"The royal physician does not know, but methinks it is heartsickness."

Charles laughed derisively. "What could make my brother heartsick? Whatever it is, let him use his last wish to make it better."

"I do not think he can..." The page suddenly looked

abashed. "But, it is not my place to be speaking so. Will you come to the castle?"

"Is he dying?"

"No sir."

"Then he's simply calling depression illness in an attempt to manipulate me to come. It won't work. I have fishing to do and spells to work for the villagers. Tell Bryen he'll have to do better if he really wants me to come."

But, before the page left, Charles added, "Bring me news if my brother gets worse."

No news came for many months, and Charles convinced himself that his brother had never really been sick.

As time passed by, Charles felt his aging bones more and more. He sat on a simple chair in front of his hut at night, and he watched in the distance as the torches lit up along the castle parapets. Ornate and elegant became warm and secure, a particularly enticing combination compared to the hut's growing chill. Perhaps Charles would join his brother, if a page came again. It would be nice to live in a castle. It would even be nice to see Bryen again.

When the page finally paid another visit, he was harried, hurried, and out of breath. "My lord... your brother... is ill," he said between huffs of air.

Charles looked at the page strangely, but he said, "It will take a few days for me to tie up my loose ends in town."

"You will come?!"

"I can find my way alone. I don't need you to stay and lead me."

"But you will come?!" The page was relieved when Charles agreed. "Come quickly," he admonished, but Charles replied, "I will come when I can."

Since Charles didn't believe his brother was ill, he felt no sense of urgency. A spell book he'd ordered would arrive with the next caravan to town, and he'd promised to work a few charms for controlling the local shepherd's unruly sheep. Then, it rained, and he didn't want to travel in the rain. It was little things that kept him, but he could always make the journey tomorrow.

Then an evening came when the castle didn't light up with the darkening sky. Charles was afraid. He knew in his heart that he'd missed his chance. He wanted to believe it was another ploy to make him come. But he knew better, and he suspected his brother was dead. If only he had listened to the page...

Though the next day was cold and drizzly, Charles packed his knapsack and began his journey to the castle. He hiked all day, barely stopping to rest. By evening, he arrived at the front gate of the castle, but no one was there to let him in. There was no bell to ring. No guard standing inside, ready to take a message. Just a giant, locked, wrought iron gate.

Charles hollered and rattled his walking stick against the iron crossings, but no one came. Eventually, he seated himself on the dusty ground to one side of the entrance and leaned his back against the rocky wall. He would have to make his own way in. He knew the right spell, but it would take all his concentration, all his strength. And he had been walking all day.

So, he rested awhile, drawing patterns in the dust with his finger. He noticed a cut pine-branch lying beside him, and he used it as a broom to clear away the patterns when he wanted to start anew.

How odd that the branch should be so convenient, when all the trees were cleared for at least twenty feet in front of the castle. Charles looked over and noticed that another branch lay on the other side of the gate. The two of them lay right where he would have expected guards to stand.

As ready as he would be, Charles rose to his feet and began to chant. He trembled his fingers with the words, swirling the air into currents that magnified with the chant. He tensed his body, in physical concentration, until his muscles were wracked with pain. But, the spell worked, and the air flowed around him, pulling him gently up and over the castle wall. He collapsed in a cold sweat as he landed, cursing the weakness of his magic. Surely, a truly great sorcerer could fly without so much difficulty.

Finally inside Bryen's castle, Charles began a shaky search for his brother or any news of him. He walked the grounds, the halls, and through echoing rooms draped with tapestries. He found no people but everywhere cut flowers and branches on the floor. Finally he made it to the quarters at the top of the keep. These had clearly been Bryen's. Velvet pillows and silk draperies adorned the bed. Bushels of wilting and drooped flowers filled vases about the room. The furniture was jewel-studded, and the washbasin could have held a horse. It must have taken many servants to fill it with warmed and sudsy water. These were the quarters of a king. Charles felt a stab of envy, and then his face flushed, realizing he'd been such a fool. Bryen had invited him many times. Well, he was here now.

Charles searched among the vases. It didn't take long: the vase that had been belched up by the sea stood out among the others like a lame mule among noble steeds. The black paint was corroded by saltwater, and the gilt ornamentation was chipping. Charles grasped it, reverently, and removed the decaying bouquet.

At his touch, the vase seemed to swell. Its gaping black mouth became a gateway to infinity, and the rest of the room skewed around it. Furniture angled towards the vase, and the empty air bulged, though there was nothing there. Space itself took on a luminescent quality. A scent of fresh flowers wafted over Charles, and he heard a voice in his head but not with his ears:

"You have come to learn of my late master?" the voice boomed.

Years ago, when Bryen had found the vase, the genie did not reveal himself so quickly or so easily. Bryen studied the vase with the guidance of his mother's spirit in the elven burial grove which now lay to the west of the castle's walls. Bryen had to coax the genie out with a ceremonial offering: five white roses, freshly cut under the light of a full moon.

Charles' book-learned magic had not the knack of reading a genie's mind, figuring out what would please him. However, Charles was lucky. He came to the vase with seemingly pure intentions. There was no one else to tell him of his brother's passing, and he fervently hoped the genie would know how it all befell. The genie could not resist such a natural, heartfelt motive.

"Yes," Charles answered. "How did Bryen die?"

Charles could hear the silence in the room, even as the genie spoke in his mind: "Quietly, in that bed." The canopied frame grew in Charles' perception, and he felt his head turn towards it. It was the genie's way of gesturing.

As Charles looked upon the empty bed, the genie filled his eyes with a vision. He saw his brother lying under the rumpled coverlet, and a regally attired woman, as fair as a rose, knelt beside him. "That was your brother's queen."

Charles asked with a touch of bitterness, "Where is she? She couldn't have been very faithful to have fled already."

The genie turned his perception to a single brown-edged rose, cast carelessly on the floor by Bryen's bed. It had once been red, but the bruise of death covered its former color over. It lay where the queen had knelt.

A new vision filled Charles' mind: Bryen, as young as Charles remembered him, standing before the newly built castle. Bryen trimmed cuttings from the trees and picked only the most perfect flowers. At the behest of the genie, under order of Bryen's second wish, the cuttings became soldiers and the flowers maids. Thus was his castle peopled by a court, and that court was bound to him.

The queen-rose was the only bloom taken from the bush that grew over Bryen's elf-mother's grave. "Your brother's choice was short sighted. It was easier to make a queen than find one, but a rose is a rose. She could not bear children. She had no history, no family, no life except for my Lord Bryen. All the court was the same. But, your brother loved them before he realized it, and he found himself ensnared in an unreal world. He hoped you would come and lend it reality, by sharing it."

Charles was dazed. His brother had truly wasted away, wishing only to see him again. "Why did he not use his third wish to summon me?"

"Then you would have become as unreal as the queen."

Charles kept running the past through his mind, trying to find a way to rewrite history without changing his part in it. "He could have come to me," he said. "He could have come himself, instead of sending pages..."

"I think pride runs in your family," came the genie's retort.

Truth stings, and Charles' tentative feelings of regret rolled up and were stowed away behind his umbrage at the truthful charge. "How did Bryen use his third wish? What did he think would save his life better than summoning me?"

"My lord never made a third wish."

Charles was stunned. How could you have three wishes and never use the third? "Can I claim it?" he asked, greed pressing him, and making it hard to breathe at the thought of being granted a genie's wish for himself—or, horrible thought, not being granted it.

The genie's words shattered his hopes: "When my lord died, I used his third wish in his stead to give him a proper burial. His court reverted to their natural form," the genie summoned a vision of all the finely dressed courtiers suddenly whisping back into nothing but cut branches and falling to the floor, "so there was no one else to perform the funeral."

"I would have buried him!" Charles exclaimed. It was outrageous to have his wish stolen for something so humble and, yet, so unobjectionable. Even as he raged, Charles knew it would have been wrong for the genie to leave Bryen lying there, decomposing in his bed, as he waited for a brother who might have never come. "Where is he buried?" Charles asked, his voice become small.

"In the castle courtyard, beneath the yearling willow tree."

"I should go to him."

"Yes, my master."

Charles stopped short. "Master?"

"Of course," the genie affirmed. "When I revealed myself to you, I bound myself to you. You may claim your three wishes whenever you are ready."

The room reeled around Charles. He felt dizzy, and he

couldn't tell if it was the genie's doing or the work of his own stomach making summersaults. *Three wishes.* He had hoped, at best, for only one—the one Bryen hadn't used. Pulling himself together and addressing his ethereal genie, he said, "I will have to think on it."

Charles left the genie's vase where he'd found it, and he headed out to the castle courtyard. He took the wilted queen-rose and gathered other former courtiers on his way. When he found the willow sapling, Charles spread the crinkly dry foliage bundled in his arms in front of the simple tombstone that marked his brother's grave. He sat in the grass, and he leaned against the keep wall. The willow was small, but it would grow. It would make an honorable sentinel over Bryen's eternal sleep.

Charles thought about his brother, and for the first time felt pity for the hard line he'd walked between being elf and being man. Charles had been jealous of Bryen's magic, but that feeling was gone now that he knew he'd become a greater magician than Bryen had ever been. The magic came easier to Bryen, so what? He didn't exercise it, practice it, or fine tune it. His magic was only good for fishing charms and culling driftwood from the sea.

Really, it had been harder for Bryen. Charles lived in the hut by the sea because he disliked the idea of living in town. Bryen lived in the hut not by his own preference but because he knew it was a more comfortable distance for the villagers. Among elves, he would have been slow, bumbling, and ungainly. Among humans, he inspired jealousy, exactly as he had inspired jealousy in his own brother.

Charles felt bad for adding to his brother's hardship. No wonder Bryen had died alone in a castle with only phantasms of his own desire to comfort him. Charles would not make that same mistake. He knew what his first wish would be.

Returned to the top of the castle keep, Charles planted his feet firmly on the floor in preparation for the surreal distortions caused by the genie's presence. He put his hands to the vase, and he felt his eyes dilate. The room grew swimmy. "I am here," spoke the genie in his head. "Will you make a wish now?"

"Yes," said Charles. He measured his words carefully, nervous that he would misspeak or find himself confused by the genie's perturbing presence. "I do not need to wish for a castle, because I can live here in Bryen's."

"True," the genie agreed.

"What I need, then, is a court." Charles took a deep breath before committing himself to the following words: "I wish for you to summon all the half-elves in the land to this castle where they will serve me as my court."

There was a long pause before the genie spoke. "Are you sure?"

Charles was taken aback. He had not expected his wish to be questioned. "Of course," he said. "Why wouldn't I be? Are there not enough of them? There can't be too many to live comfortably in the castle. Half-elves aren't that common."

Charles heard a soft murmur of numbers pass through his ears, as if the genie were counting all the half-elves in the land. Or, perhaps, the genie was merely counting to keep his temper. When he finally spoke in his usual booming voice, he said, "You are right that the number of half-elves is in accordance with the number of courtiers needed to fill your castle. But has it occurred to you that they might not be... *pleased* by your summoning them away from their own homes and lives?"

"Are you implying that I'm bringing them here to be my slaves?" There was genuine outrage in Charles' voice. From whence he'd summoned it, he hardly knew. "There is no place for half-elves! And, this is a nice castle," Charles looked about appreciatively. It really was a nice castle. And it was *his*. "They would like it here, all of them together."

"I was only reacting to the wording of your wish, my lord. Perhaps you meant to wish for me to *invite* all the half-elves in the land to join you in your court."

The genie and Charles both knew that hardly a single half-elf would respond to such an invitation. The genie hoped it could be a learning experience for Charles; one wish was a small price to pay for an important lesson. Charles, however, thought the genie was simply trying to cheat him. The half-elves would understand his true intentions when they got here.

"I've made my wish," Charles said, his voice icy. "Now it is up to you to make it true."

The genie's voice did not speak. But as the luminescence drained from the room, and the furniture squared back to its original shapes, Charles knew it had been done.

There were a few quiet days before the half-elves began to arrive. Needless to say, some of them must have had long journeys between them and the castle. Charles used these days of respite to familiarize himself with the castle. He found an armory with which to outfit his imminent troops. He found well-stocked supply rooms. He even found a treasury with enough coin of the land to buy any supplies that were missing. When the first half-elf arrived, Charles greeted him heartily and gave him his first task: to take enough coinage and travel to the nearest town to buy chickens and livestock. The castle barns had been empty.

The half-elf, who reminded Charles a little of his brother, took the bag of gold and silver with a grim face. He bowed deeply to Charles, and he offered no resistance to Charles' new lordship over him. However, there was no joy in his demeanor. The same was true of all the half-elves as they arrived.

The only open displeasure was expressed by the few elf mothers who came bearing their half-elf babes, too young to run away and travel alone. Charles explained to the full-elf mothers that they need not stay; there were plenty of half-elf women to look after the babes. But every one of the elf mothers took exception to the idea of her babe resting in another woman's arms. The elf mothers stayed, and Charles set them up as the finest ladies in his court. He sensed that the deference did not fully appease them.

In fact, Charles was uneasy with the half-elves' easy submission. He had not told them about the genie, but he heard murmurings among the court. Were they merely biding their time?

Once all the half-elves were arrived and settled into their new home, Charles called for a grand celebration. A feast was held in one of the castle's great halls. All of the court attended, although some of the half-elves mainly served rather joining in the revelries. Well, there must be some servants, and Charles reassured himself that they were still lucky to be a part of such a grand court.

The funny thing was: many of the half-elves were happy. They liked living among their own kind, gathered into a single castle. Before, they had been spread so thinly among elves and men that many of them had never seen another half-elf before. Yet, they asked each other, why should a man rule over the kingdom of the half-elves?

The more wine was poured, the more the question rang out. *Why should a man rule over the kingdom of the half-elves?*

Of course, none of Charles' subjects put the question directly to him. They whispered it behind his back and in the corners of the hall or while leaning close to a partner on the dance floor. But Charles could see them whispering, and he had itchy ears. So, he muttered a spell and magnified their whispers to his ears.

As he sat in his throne, overlooking the revelry and

overhearing the rumors, he pulled upon his gray beard. He was startled by what he heard. His subjects not only knew about the genie, they were hatching plans to find him and claim him as their own.

Charles slipped away from the revelry and made it to his rooms at the top of the castle keep as quickly as he could. Behind the cracked open door, Charles heard noises, movement, a rustling. Was he too late? He flung open the door to find the half elf who reminded him of his brother jumbling the silk and velvet pillows on his bed.

"Are you lost?" Charles demanded in his most kingly voice.

The half-elf looked at him guiltily but did not deign to answer. Charles gruffly sent him on his way with stern orders to stay out of these rooms. Inwardly, Charles breathed a sigh of relief. He grabbed the vase. It had been sitting in plain sight.

Spinning, vertigo, and a blurring in his eyes: Charles experienced a multitude of unpleasant sensations as the genie's presence filled the room. The furniture rocked as if it floated in the ocean rather than sitting firmly on the floor.

"Have you come to make a second wish?" the genie asked.

"I have," Charles said, for he had a plan to protect the genie against thievery better than any hiding place could. "But, first, I must ask you a question. Can you work magic for yourself? Without the command of a master?"

"No," the genie answered.

Charles was relieved, but then he had a second thought. "What about burying Bryen? No one commanded that."

"True," the genie answered. "I could only do that because it was on your brother's behalf. If he had used all his wishes, or if burying him had gone against his inherent desires, I could not have done it."

"Excellent," Charles responded. He looked for more loopholes in his plan and asked, "Can you serve more than one lord at a time?"

The room fluttered as if the genie was shifting his weight. "I see that your first wish is not going well," he said. "You are worried one of your servants will try to steal me?"

Charles bristled but answered truthfully.

"If one of your servants successfully claims me, then I will be bound to him, and your remaining wishes will become forfeit."

"Then here is my second wish... that I will be your last master." There was triumph in Charles' voice.

"If I grant your wish," the genie said, wheedling, "then your third wish will be the last magic I ever perform."

"Grant it," Charles commanded.

"It will also be the last magic I ever perform *for you*."

Charles did not waver—his third wish would be his last anyway—and the genie granted his second wish.

Nonetheless, the genie's gibe did rankle Charles. The genie's magic was much more powerful than his, and now he was down to one wish. He did not know what the future would hold or when he might need the genie's magic the most. Yet, he would not be taunted into saving his third wish as Bryen had. If he could not rely on the genie's magic for the rest of his life, he would have to rely on his own.

"I will make my third wish now too," Charles said. He drew a deep breath. "I wish to be the most powerful sorcerer in the world."

There was a long pause. The furniture seemed to dance as the genie silently measured out Charles words. The mouth of the vase looked blacker and deeper than ever as the genie pondered a world under Charles' magical thumb. Phantoms of visions danced in the depth of the vase—soldiers on warhorses, elves huddling in concentration camps, a great conflagration—all horrible images.

Charles might start with good intentions, but the genie foresaw a slow hardening of Charles' heart as future good deeds went wrong. With each magical work that back-fired, Charles would grow more indignant that the world was not grateful for his magic. He would become callous, tyrannous, and dangerous. The genie could not let it happen, but he was bound by the words of Charles' wish. Thus, his deliberation eventually ended, as it had to, in acquiescence.

The genie's voice boomed a single word, "Granted," and Charles laughed out loud in elation.

He took the vase and hurried down to begin his new reign. The dancing was stopped, and there was a murmur in the great hall before Charles arrived. It seemed the half-elves had sensed the change in the balance of magical power in their world already. Charles stepped up to his throne and held the vase above his head. "Here is the genie you tried to steal from me!" he cried. "But, you will not be able to steal him now." Charles set the vase upon his throne and began chanting an explosive spell whose execution had always eluded him before. He tossed the words lightly off his lips; simple charms like these would be easy for him now.

When Charles' chanting was done, there was a slight hum in the air. The vase wobbled a little and toppled over on its side, rolling about the broad seat of the throne.

Charles' chewed his lower lip in consternation, and his cheeks colored. The embarrassment soon passed, for he realized the murmuring throng wasn't even watching him. The eyes of the half-elves were all turned toward one of the full elf mothers who had fallen into a swoon.

"Gone! All gone!" she cried. The half-elves pressed around her, offering comfort, waving smelling salts under her nose. None of it did any good. She pressed her hands to her head, then passed them over her body, as if her limbs had become foreign to her, crying, "I can feel it draining out of me!"

"What have you done?!" a handsome, young half-elf turned to Charles, accusing him with his voice and a pointed finger.

"Nothing," Charles faltered. Despite his throne beside him, and the crown on his brow, Charles had never felt less kingly. The half-elf's eyes burned into him. "I made my last two wishes. That's all."

Scorn filled the half-elf's voice: *"What did you wish?"*

Charles pulled the emerald-studded crown from his brow as he answered.

The half-elf laughed derisively in response. "And you say you've done *nothing?*"

Charles held the crown in his two hands before him. He was confused, and he felt old. "I do not understand," he said, but the half-elves were no longer interested in sparing time or attention for him. They were caught up in their own miseries and wailings. Their kind would die from the world in only a few generations—elves would become as ordinary and un-magical as men. The most talented of them already felt the loss in their powers.

Since the genie could not refuse Charles' wish, he had followed it to the word—but not the spirit. Charles was not a whit more powerful than before making his third wish, but there was no one *more* powerful than him.

It was as if the genie had reached beneath the mountains and the forests of the world and pulled out a giant plug. Swirling downward, all of the world's magic had begun draining away.

11

TOASTER DRAGON

SMOKE ROSE from Tzora's flared nostrils. Gray and pungent and entirely lacking in flame. Not a single spark. Not enough heat to rewarm a cold dinner roll, let alone toast her doughy, unbaked wings. Tzora huffed in disappointment, hoping her frustration would translate into a glowing ember inside her scaly nose. But no luck. She was still too young to breathe fire like her older sisters. And that meant she was still too young to fly. No one else would toast her wings for her.

Too young to toast, too young to fly. That's what every Breadragon always said.

"Ha!" Tlonga, one of Tzora's older sisters chuffed. "Little Tzory is trying to breathe fire again!" She aimed her crimson-scaled snout at the entrance to the family cave and snuffed out a plume of fire to make even a lava goddess jealous. Hotter than the ovens in hell. Then she flapped her well-toasted wings, crunchy and perfectly browned in the middle, and flew away into the bright blue sky.

How Tzora longed to follow her. To sail through the sky like a kite. Or a frisbee. Or a piece of toast, flung like a frisbee into the air.

If Tzora couldn't fly through the deep blue sky with her sisters, then she wanted no sight of their taunting flips and barrel rolls among the puffy clotted-cream clouds above. Tzora clambered deep into the family cave, away from the sky and away from her sisters. She crouched her way through tunnels too small for her older sisters to follow her. She spelunked her way deeper and deeper into the network of caverns, feeling sorry for herself and hating the dragging feel of her soggy, doughy wings.

Tzora passed crevasses filled with gold, cracks filled with rubies, and clefts filled with discarded magic lamps, emptied of their genies and useless. Finally she came to a chamber with a funny mound of dirt in the middle of its floor. She crept close to the mound and saw teensy-tiny six-legged creatures streaming in and out of a hole in the middle in long, orderly, single-file lines. They looked a lot like Breadragons, except no wings.

"Who are you?" Tzora whispered in a breathy, warm voice. Warm but not hot. She still didn't have the fire she needed in her belly. But as she watched the teensy-tiny creatures, she saw that their bright red bodies glowed with heat. She could feel the waves of heat rising from them.

"We are the fire ants!" thousands of tiny voices chirped in unison.

"Fire ants!" Tzora cried out, forgetting that she was speaking to creatures smaller than the tip of her sharpest claw. The fire ants had scattered in surprise and alarm at the sound of Tzora's bellowing, but when they'd reformed their lines, she whispered, "I'm sorry. I got excited. Can you... toast my wings for me?"

"We'd have to ask our queen," the fire ant chorus chimed.

"You have a queen?" Tzora asked. Though, she realized, of course they did. Every civilized society had a queen. "Would you ask her, then? Where is she?"

"Our queen lives deep beneath our hill," the ants answered. "It will take time for your question to reach her. Come back tomorrow."

And so Tzora came back tomorrow, only to find the queen of the fire ants had a task for her: bring her colony a basketful of crumbs, shed from the toasty wings of Tzora's fellow, older Breadragons. Tzora filled the basket gladly, scooping and scratching forgotten crumbs out of the nooks and crannies of her family's cave. She returned, dutifully, with the basket of crumbs, only to be disappointed with another task: two baskets of crumbs.

Day after day, Tzora gathered crumbs for the fire ants, and every day she returned to find the teensy-tiny fire ants looking bigger, rounder in the thorax, and slower in their endless queues. They had less need now to seek out their own crumbs, as they had a fully fledged Breadragon bringing crumbs to them.

Tzora was being used, and she felt fury growing in her belly like a fire.

Fire!

Tzora flared her nostrils and sneezed a tiny puff of candle-like flame. Small. But flame, nonetheless. Her scaly auburn muzzle twisted into a menacing smile, and she let her anger at the fire ants burn deeply in her belly. When she snorted again, fire streamed out of her nostrils and caught the wicker of the basket she'd been using to fetch crumbs. She aimed her nose at the fire ant hive and watched the teensy-tiny, lazy ants scurry away from her flame. She torched their hive, glorying in their tiny chorus of screams—she was a dragon after all, and her heart was full of chaos and destruction.

Then Tzora turned her new-found flame to her doughy wings, arching her long neck around and spreading her doughy wings wide. Her new-found flame kissed the dough, baking it into bread, and burned on until her wings crisped up properly into perfectly browned toast, just like the wings of all her sisters.

When Tzora emerged from the family cave that day, she flapped her toasty-wings and flew into the sky where the clouds melted against her fiery warmth like fresh-churned butter.

The moral: if you're as small as a fire ant, don't try to trick someone as large as a dragon. And if you're a dragon whose fire hasn't come in, maybe you're not angry enough yet.

12

THE PREHISTORY ZOO

I. Comfort Animal

THE WIDE TIMBER frame arch rose high above Dr. Miriam Loxley's head, presaging the size of the animals kept in the enclosure. All the movies, books, and games came rushing back to her—she'd grown up with the *Jurassic Park* franchise. She knew all of the paleontologists and geneticists involved in The Prehistory Zoo had too. Somehow, they'd taken those stories as a siren's call, instead of heeding them as a warning.

"What made you think this was a good idea again?" Loxley said.

Angie Cartwright laughed and walked right through the arch with her bucket of steaks. "Don't look so worried!" she said. "You're going to love this. Just listen to the idea, and keep an open mind."

Reluctantly, Loxley followed Cartwright up to the

curving wall of iron bars behind the timber arch. All she could see behind the bars was vegetation—ferns and palm fronds. "So what's the idea?"

Cartwright set down the bucket and pulled out a dripping red steak with a gloved hand. "You know how cheetahs are really anxious, so zoos give them their own comfort dogs to calm them down and socialize them?"

"I've heard of that, yeah." Loxley's voice got low, like she was afraid to summon whatever lurked behind the prehistoric greens. "But we're not talking about cheetahs."

"True," Cartwright said. She flung the steak, juicy and dripping, into the enclosure. It left red spatters on the concrete at their feet. A snap and rustle in the jungle of greens suggested that the steak never hit the ground. Cartwright picked up another one. "And that's why our first attempts... Let's just say, failed."

"Let's say more than that," Loxley breathed, staring into the vegetation. She could see eyes looming high above her in the dark green shadows. "Let's be very, very specific."

"Okay," Cartwright admitted. "So, as the subjects grew, the first batch, well, once they reached full size, they ate their comfort dogs." She held the dripping steak with both gloved hands and looked down at the concrete ground where red juice drip, drip, dripped. "It was heartbreaking. We knew better than to name the dogs, but you can't help getting attached anyway."

Loxley wondered what kind of dogs they'd been. Probably Labradors.

"But we found a solution," Cartwright said, flinging the second steak.

A feathery snout emerged from the jungle greens and snapped up the steak with nightmare teeth, deadly sharp and longer than Loxley's forearm. The prehistoric ancestor revived by science bobbed its head, ruffled its dusty purple neck feathers, and flapped comically tiny wings. It screeched like a murderous chicken, but motions that would have been funny on a small bird were terrifying on a creature several times Loxley's height. She stepped back from the cold iron, feeling deeply grateful for the protection of those bars. She hoped they were sturdy.

"See, the T-Rex chicks were adorable playing with the dogs, and more importantly, the chicks seemed to be picking up on the dogs' training. But as the chicks grew, they paid less and less attention to the dogs. They seemed to have trouble considering an animal as small as a normal dog to be more than, well, a snack once they hit full size. So what they needed was something that could keep up with them. You know, while they were growing. Something bigger." Cartwright threw another steak between the iron bars, but this one wasn't aimed at the feathered monstrosity. It sailed right past the T-Rex into the greenery and disappeared with another rustle. And a happy woof. "Of course, we had to mix the dog genes with a few other animals to get them big enough..."

A giant black-furred creature with floppy ears and a lolling tongue in its grinning, panting mouth emerged from the greenery. The T-Rex cawed and butted its feathered head against the gigantic dog affectionately. If the T-rex chicks had learned tricks and training from the dogs, what kind of hunting tips had the dogs picked up from the grown T-rexes?

The dog howled, baying like any goofy Labrador Retriever impatient for a treat.

"Can I throw them a steak?" Loxley asked, wondering if a steak was really enough of a treat for a creature so large.

Cartwright gestured welcomingly at the bucket and pulled an extra pair of rubber gloves out of her back pocket. Loxley pulled the gloves on and grabbed one of the cold, squishy raw steaks, trying not to think about how similar dead cow flesh was to her own living flesh.

Loxley knew she had to ask what genes Cartwright had added into the genetic code of this mixed-species dog. In order to grow a Labrador Retriever to the the size of an elephant without giving it all kinds of health issues, they must have designed an elaborate chimera with all kinds of genetic horrors and unexpected possibilities hidden inside it. Loxley's job would be to tease out the dangers, try to bandage the situation together and avoid a classic movie-style disaster. But for now, this moment, she couldn't get over the sight of that panting grin. The giant Labrador had the biggest, happiest grin she'd ever seen.

You could get lost inside that grin. Literally.

As Loxley flung the steak between the iron bars, she asked, "Who's a good dog?" and tried not to picture the inevitable—being hunted down by a pack of giant wolf-kin working together with dinosaurs. Giant teeth and claws, crunching bones and slicing flesh.

If her fate was behind those bars with teeth like swords, at least, she could try to make friends with it. Maybe when this all went to hell, that would buy her a few minutes. Maybe when they broke out from behind those bars, they'd hesitate before eating her. Maybe it would be enough. She flung another steak and shuddered. "Good dog," she said. "Good T-Rex. Have another treat!"

II. Herding the Brachiosauruses

"Look, you're overreacting," Angie Cartwright said to her wife, Dr. Miriam Loxley, as she drove the two of them across the beautiful stretch of golden savannah on the west side of Hali'corra Island. Warm air flowed through the open top of her company jeep, and she could hear the peaceful, melodic cries of the brachiosaurus herd singing to each other in the distance. She hoped that seeing the gentle, plant-eaters would calm her wife down or cheer her up. Anything other than holding her head in her hands, staring into the distance like she'd seen death itself in a cage.

Loxley hadn't taken well to seeing the T-Rex pavilion. Maybe that hadn't been the best choice for a first stop on this trip. She'd started ranting about those old *Jurassic Park* movies and messing with nature. Cartwright had expected better from a fellow scientist in a similarly unfairly maligned field, let alone her wife. Loxley worked on gene-modding humans into their fursonas, letting them live out their furry dreams, and her work had been at the center of several protests. She should know better than to judge Cartwright's work so quickly.

"I'm surprised okay?" Loxley said, voice hollow. "I knew you were working on something big..." She trailed off, thinking about how excited Cartwright always was, like she was bursting with secrets to share, but unable to talk about any of them until after she'd gotten special permission to bring her wife to the island. And even then, Loxley had been required to sign an NDA. "I just didn't realize it was *dinosaur* big."

"Or *Clifford the Big Red Dog* big," Cartwright countered, trying to cover a smile at her own joke. She parked the jeep in the middle of the field and pointed toward the tree line.

Loxley could make out the brachiosaurus herd, their legs and necks like trees, in front of the forest of prehistoric plants, each painstakingly revived and altered to grow on this particular island.

Loxley knew what Cartwright was doing. She was trying to let her wife's favorite dinosaur do the convincing. Loxley loved brachiosaurus. And giraffes. And flamingos. Anything funny-looking with a long neck. But a herd of brachiosauruses peacefully cruising across a field wouldn't erase the image in her mind of that T-Rex and its gengineered companion dog. Sure, Labrador

Retrievers were cute at any size, but they'd never been meant to be *that* big.

Even so, she was here now. It couldn't hurt to watch.

As the brachiosauruses strolled, moving away from the trees and into the savannah, Loxley made out stripes on their sides—long swaths of tree bark brown alternated with swampy green, emulating the pattern of light in the forest behind them. They came closer, and over their doleful, sonorous song, a sudden incisive *yip!* coincided with the herd changing direction. A gigantic dog came into view, circling around the slow-moving brachiosauruses. This dog had a bright orange, flowing mane and long, pointy face, split into a cheerful grin. A collie. Except as tall as a house.

"You developed herd dogs to manage the herd dinosaurs," Loxley observed drily.

Loxley had grown up with collies. Cartwright had been right that seeing one would tug at her heart strings.

"I should have shown you this before the T-Rex," Cartwright said. "I just got so carried away... The T-Rex is our crown jewel."

Loxley frowned. "This doesn't change how dangerous a T-Rex is."

"I know," Cartwright admitted. "But what we're doing here really is safe, and I didn't drag you here to help fix some horrible mistake we've made. It's not like the movies. And I guess I kinda forgot how startling it can be when... you know... you first find out about it."

Loxley shot her wife a troubled look. Now that she

knew what Cartwright had been working on, she didn't like the idea of her flying off to Hali'corra Island three days a week. And yet, Cartwright had been doing exactly that for years. Nothing had changed, except Loxley had been allowed to see behind the NDA.

"Why are you showing me?" Loxley didn't believe in hiding from knowledge. And yet, right now, she kind of wished she just didn't know that The Prehistory Zoo had gone full-on *Jurassic Park*.

In retrospect, how had she missed it? Way out on an island, with a name like that...

Loxley supposed that people had failed to see bigger things than dinosaurs when they just didn't want to see them.

Oh god, if she'd failed to see through something as big and obvious as this, what else was Loxley missing in her life? Was Cartwright keeping other secrets from her? Personal ones? Was her marriage in trouble? The hands still on the side of her head pressed harder, digging her fingernails into her scalp.

"Woah, now, Miri, don't panic, it's nothing bad." Cartwright put a hand on her wife's arm and helped Loxley to ease her hands down from her face.

The two women stared at each other, one staving off panic that felt totally irrational but seemed to be a physical response to the adrenaline of meeting dinosaurs in the flesh for the first time, and the other one... calm, smiling, almost impish.

"What then? What is it?"

"Well, we live on a really, big, isolated farm... and there's plenty of space..."

Realization dawned: "You want to adopt one of the dogs."

Cartwright's impish smile grew into a full lopsided grin. "Well, yeah, there's this one dog, Galileo. He's a scruffy mutt, and he didn't work out with the dinosaurs... but..."

Loxley could see everything she needed to know about this dog in Cartwright's face. Her wife was already in love. And it was true that their farm was big enough to safely hide a gigantic, secret, NDA-covered dog.

"Look, Galileo is the sweetest dog you'll ever meet."

And probably one of the biggest.

Loxley stared at the giant collie in the distance, running happy circles around the brachiosauruses. Dinosaurs were scary in the movies, but out there, they were just big, weird sheep for a collie to play shepherd with.

And the dog was just a dog. Domesticated. And clearly well-trained.

"Alright, Angie, let's meet this dog."

Cartwright's grin grew even wider. She knew that her wife had only agreed to *meet* the dog, but it's really hard to say 'no' to a dog when he's looking at you with big—*really big*—brown eyes.

III. Tiny Cartoon Dinosaurs

Dr. Miriam Loxley was waiting for her wife in a computer lab that looked like it could have been part of any college campus or tech startup. Rows of computers sat on desks decorated by empty pop cans and various fidget toys. If she hadn't known she was in the middle of a prehistoric jungle on a secret island, filled with genetically reconstructed dinosaurs, she would never have guessed by looking around here.

The lab was mostly empty of people. It was the weekend, but one woman in the corner looked up from her computer and tilted her head quizzically.

Loxley thought she recognized the woman from some of her wife's work parties. She raised a hand and waved tentatively. "Hi, I'm Miriam. Angie's wife. You're Cheyenne, right?"

"Oh, yeah, hi Miriam," the woman said, leaning back in her chair in a relaxed way that seemed designed to invite Loxley to come closer and chat. "So, what brings you here?"

"Angie wants to adopt one of the failed comfort dogs," Loxley said.

Cheyenne's eyebrows raised. "You must have a big estate. Anyone who can keep a dog as big as a dinosaur would have to."

"Yeah," Loxley agreed. "Huge farm in the middle of nowhere."

Cheyenne nodded.

"So, what aspect of all of this—" Loxley gestured vaguely around. "—do you work on?"

"I'm an AI expert," Cheyenne said.

Now it was Loxley's turn to tilt her head quizzically. "What does AI have to do with growing dinosaurs and giant dogs to keep them company?"

Cheyenne grinned like she'd been waiting weeks for someone to ask her that. She tilted the closest monitor around to where Loxley could see it and put her hands on the nearest keyboard. She had several each of monitors and keyboards. Her fingers flashed over the keys, sounding like a sudden downpour, and a scene filled the monitor that made Loxley think of that old game, *Zoo Tycoon*. Tiny cartoon dinosaurs and dogs lumbered and frolicked through animated forests and savannahs.

"What's this?" Loxley asked. "It looks like a game."

"It feels like a game sometimes," Cheyenne agreed, still grinning. Then her face turned suddenly serious. "Strictly speaking, the cutesy UI isn't necessary, but the program underneath it will save us from ending up with dogs who need to be adopted out like Galileo."

Loxley hadn't expected Cheyenne to know the name of the dog that Angie wanted to adopt. "I guess there's only one dog that failed dinosaur bonding, huh?"

"It's not his fault," Cheyenne said. "We started with a grab bag of dog DNA taken from all kinds of breeds and mutts, just throwing canine traits at a wall really, to see what stuck."

Loxley frowned at that image. She didn't like the idea

of throwing dogs—even microscopic parts of dogs—at a wall like overcooked spaghetti. Although, she supposed the reality was arguably worse than the metaphor—raising puppies with T-Rex chicks to figure out which ones made friends with the rapidly growing dinos and which got eaten.

"So, how does the program work?" Loxley asked.

"We take brain scans of dogs, line them up with their gene profiles, and then use those scans to create AI versions." Cheyenne went back to grinning like a cat who got to make mice run through mazes for her own entertainment and got paid for it. "We let the AI dogs play with AI dinos and see who gets along. Then we only grow giant versions of the dogs who will work well with dinos."

Loxley and Cheyenne stared at the screen in silence for a while, absorbed in watching the little cartoon dogs and dinos play. The dogs playing with the T-Rexes looked vaguely like Labrador retrievers; dogs who looked like collies circled around herds of long-necked plant-eating dinos, just like Loxley had seen in the field on the way here.

Greyhounds ran alongside Gallimimuses; scruffy mop dogs tousled with ankylosauruses. Loxley wondered what kind of implications a program like this could have if it were ever released from under the pile of NDAs that The Prehistory Zoo made everyone who knew about it sign.

Would it work on humans? Could parents someday use a computer program like this to predict whether one fertilized egg would grow into a rebellious teenager and another would be more cooperative and studious? The idea gave her pause. It was a lot of power to put in people's hands. On the other hand, didn't people already select for pleasing personalities through sexual selection, only having children with partners they liked? At least, theoretically. Would this be so much worse?

Under the weight of those thoughts, Loxley's own career—helping grown-ass adults alter their own bodies with gene therapy to develop bunny ears or cat tails to their hearts' desire—didn't seem so ethically ambiguous. Of course, she'd never found it as ethically ambiguous as all the protesters her own lab had suffered through seemed to imply.

If this place were public, those protesters wouldn't be wasting their time on her.

"It's fun, isn't it?" Cheyenne asked, completely missing the tone of Loxley's silence.

And yet, it was fun. And it was better than growing out a bunch of gigantic dogs with nowhere to go. She and Angie couldn't adopt all of them.

"Yeah," Loxley agreed. "It's fun."

"So, I guess you'll be going to the birthday party then?"

"The what?"

"Well, I mean, if Angie brought you here to meet Galileo on a Saturday, I assume it's going to be at the birthday party."

Loxley's eyes narrowed, betraying her complete confusion.

"Galileo doesn't do great with dinosaurs," Cheyenne

said, "but he's great with people. So, they've been having him do kids' birthday parties."

Now Loxley was completely lost. "But... the NDAs?" Not to mention *Jurassic Park*.

"Well, yeah, it's only for the kids of company employees so far, but he's a huge hit. When we go public, they'll probably want Galileo to keep doing them as outreach. For kids with rich parents, of course."

Loxley had been picturing Galileo in some sad pen somewhere—the gigantic dog equivalent of an animal shelter. But apparently, he was romping around with little kids in birthday hats.

"Oh, there's Angie—" Cheyenne pointed back towards the entrance to the lab. "Have fun at the party!"

Nothing about this day had gone the way Loxley had expected. She was still shaken by the unexpected terror of seeing a real, live T-Rex for the first time, accompanied by a Labrador big enough to eat her in one bite. And yet, she couldn't think of anything more fun than meeting her new dog—because really? what were the chances she'd say 'no' to this dog?—at a little kid's birthday party, surrounded by cheerful faces and plates of cake and ice cream.

IV. Birthday Party at the Prehistory Zoo

Dr. Miriam Loxley felt weird attending the birthday party of an eight-year-old child she'd never met before. She didn't have a lot of experience with children, and so their chaotic running, shouting, squabbling, cheering, tumbling and general antics whirled around her like a force of nature—beyond understanding or control.

Loxley's nerves were already rattled by discovering that her wife, Angie Cartwright, didn't just work with models of dinosaurs and their DNA. She worked with actual dinosaurs, proprietorially brought back to life by The Prehistory Zoo. Furthermore, Cartwright worked with gigantic dogs, designed to function as comfort animals for those nervous dinosaurs, removed from their own time period and turned into safari attractions.

And Cartwright wanted to adopt one of those over-sized dogs.

The dog was supposed to be here. But so far, all Loxley had seen was a gaggle of eight-year-olds on a sugar high, crashing around a playground filled with plastic climbing structures designed to look vaguely like dinosaurs. Avant-garde deconstructivist dinosaurs.

A group of adults stood by a picnic table laden with bowls of chips, popcorn, and vegetables optimistically sliced into finger food sizes, all surrounding a towering layer cake, decorated with enough little plastic dinosaurs for every one of the numerous children to get one.

Loxley recognized Cartwright's boss among the group of adults, all of them employees of The Prehistory Zoo.

Cartwright had gone over to say 'hi,' but Loxley hung back, pretending to be very busy with something on her phone. She didn't feel like being social with Cartwright's co-workers right now, let alone talking to the boss who had her wife secretly working with wildly dangerous dinosaurs, hidden behind the obscurity of an NDA.

Loxley was about ready to come to her senses and tell Cartwright that she wanted to go home. If she didn't meet this big dog, then she wouldn't fall in love with it like Cartwright had.

It didn't make sense to get a secret, NDA-covered, giant dog. They already had a perfectly good, normal-sized mutt that they'd adopted from an animal shelter like normal people.

Then Galileo came romping onto the playground. His paws were as big as beach balls. His fur was thick, curly, and sandy brown, and his brush of a tail wagged like a flag above his monster truck-sized body. His tongue flopped out of his mouth like a big pink bath mat, and his eyes were the darkest chocolate brown. Not milk chocolate. No, the high percentage stuff that Loxley ate when she really needed a good strong hit of chocolate. Dark enough to get a chocolate high just staring at them.

Damn, Loxley though, too late. As soon as you see a dog like that, you're in love.

Of course, every child on the playground felt exactly the same way, including the birthday girl. The boss's daughter.

Loxley watched with a rising sense of discomfort that she stubbornly refused to label "jealousy" as the birthday girl bonded with Galileo. The big dog did a series of tricks —turning around, then the other way, rolling over, and finally dancing on his back feet—before being fitted with a custom saddle. He gave pony rides to all the kids—two at a time; the birthday girl plus one other kid. Over and over again, the birthday girl rode Galileo around the playground, hugging his neck and giggling. He was an extremely well trained dog.

Loxley sighed. They weren't going to be taking this gigantic dog home to their farm. He was going to end up being an extra birthday present for that little girl. Loxley hoped Cartwright wouldn't be too disappointed. Maybe the two of them could go find another animal shelter mutt to adopt.

It would be easier to get excited about the idea of a new normal-sized dog if she stopped watching this boat-sized ball of joy and love prance around the playground like the most huggable, goofiest pony ever.

So, Loxley made her way over to the side of the playground where Cartwright was snacking on the array of sliced vegetables. The other adults—all parents of the party-going kids—had dispersed, mostly to follow Galileo around, desperately trying to get cute pictures of their kids riding the big dog.

What were they gonna do with those pictures anyway? It's not like they could post them to social media without breaking their NDAs.

"So, what do you think of Galileo?" Cartwright asked, nervousness tinging her voice. She clearly really wanted this dog.

"Honey, I don't..." Loxley didn't know what to say. She didn't want to be the bad guy here—especially when she was genuinely charmed by the big dog—but she also didn't want to set Cartwright up for a worse disappointment when the dog inevitably became unavailable.

"But Moo-oooo-oom!" the birthday girl cried from across the playground, interrupting their sedate adult conversation. "I looo-oooo-ooove him!"

There it was. Loxley looked over to see the eight-year-old wrapped around Galileo's front right paw like an environmental conservationist chained to a tree, staring down Cartwright's boss like the woman was a bulldozer threatening to tear down a patch of beloved forest.

The boss whispered to her daughter, took the girl by hand and managed to dislodge her arms from around the dog's leg.

Boss led birthday girl toward the table where Loxley and Cartwright stood, saying in a cheerful, announcing-to-everyone voice, "It's time for cake and presents!"

All the children came running, and the adults gathered around behind them. Loxley and Cartwright shuffled out of the way, but hung by close enough to participate in singing "Happy Birthday" and each gratefully accepted a plate of chocolate cake.

As everyone ate their cake, the birthday girl opened present after present. The presents were impressive—all kinds of plastic toys and gadgets that Loxley had never seen before—but the girl kept stealing glances at the big dog who'd curled up on the playground behind them.

Galileo snuffled quietly in his sleep, leaned against a metal structure that looked like a cross between a jungle gym and a stegosaurus. Loxley could imagine leaning against his fuzzy side, feeling his breathing rise and fall, and falling asleep just like the little girl in *My Neighbor Totoro.*

But she shouldn't think thoughts like that. Galileo was very unlikely to become hers.

Then the birthday girl was handed her last present—a box the right size for a dorm room microwave. The box wobbled as she tore at the paper, and when the top popped open, a tiny triceratops poked its pointed face out. The girl's hands flew to her face and her mouth fell open. "Sarah!" she exclaimed, as if she'd known the tiny dinosaur for years, rather than just meeting her. "Oh, thank you! Her name is Sarah, and I'm the happiest little girl who ever was!" She threw her arms around the tiny, confused dinosaur's neck.

Like that, the giant dog was forgotten.

But not by Loxley or Cartwright.

Loxley let her wife lead her by the hand up to the big, sleeping dog. His fur didn't look all that long on him, relative to his size, but when she placed her hand against his sleeping body, the shaggy curls buried her arm up to elbow.

"I hope his fur doesn't need a lot of brushing," Loxley said.

"It doesn't," Cartwright said. "So...?" Her face was tight, the smile stretched thin as she prepared for whatever answer Loxley might give.

"Yes, of course, we can adopt him," Loxley said, already

thinking about what kind of dog toys she could devise for a dog this size. Reinforced bouncy castles to serve as squeaky toys? Some of the old tree stumps they'd torn out to serve as sticks? And with that saddle, she could ride him around the farm...

As if he could hear her thoughts, Galileo sighed happily in his sleep, and his tail began to wag.

13

NO CATCH

"Waht's the catch?" I ask, watching her pet the silky soft fuzzball cupped in one palm. It's green like the inside of a kiwi fruit, and about the same size.

"What do you mean?" She lowers her head, touches her brow to the curve of the fuzzball's... back? I can't tell what kind of anatomy it has. The thing doesn't seem to have a head or face or eyes or mouth... anything recognizable. But it does purr. A soft cooing sound that soothes a troubled soul.

"There's always a catch," I say. "It reproduces too fast or turns into a monster with big teeth if you feed it after midnight."

She shakes her head at me. Amused. Dismissive.

"Or it's sucking up your blood through its fur," I continue. She just laughs. "Maybe it's going to transform into a copy of you during the night and replace you."

"Would you like to pet it?" she asks.

I reach out and touch the soft fur with my fingertips. I feel something in my chest loosen, untangle; a knot that had been choking me up ever since I came out as ace and Cal dumped me. "I've seen enough movies to know something this... cute... perfect... it has to have a catch. This is the way the world ends: not with a bang but with a purr?"

"No catch." She picks up another one, a smaller one, out of the cardboard box beside her. "They're technically plants. Just water it and make sure it gets enough sunlight." She holds it out to me. This one has fur the pale shade of a creamy key lime pie. "Would you like one?"

"Yes, please." I take the soft, warm creature in my hands, and suddenly I feel a whole lot better.

14

BIRTHDAY

"IF YOU COULD DO anything in the world for your birthday —anything at all—what would you do?"

My daughter, Layla, mirrors the question that I asked her last month about her birthday when I was looking for clues as to what I should give her, what kind of party I should throw her. She's only five, too young to be looking for clues.

If I say, "I'd spend the day in a field filled with kittens, puppies, baby tigers, and lion cubs, playing and rolling in the grass, kittens everywhere!", no one will take that as a clue that my heart's deepest desire is a kitten and then spend time researching whether the landlord will allow one, how much adopting one will cost, whether we can afford feeding it and taking it to the vet. And then feed it daily, and take it to the vet. I don't want a kitten.

If I say, "Be a dinosaur! Roar!", Layla will squeal and

shriek, adorable and worked up until I find the energy to calm her down again.

I feel too tired to be imaginative, to say, "Ride a unicorn to the moon and go roller skating on rainbows." I don't want to roller skate. Everything fantastical is either impossible or turns into something that I don't actually want to do.

All I want to do is not deal with this question, get through one more day without crying or yelling in front of Layla. Maybe grab myself a square of dark chocolate from the secret stash I keep in the top of the kitchen cupboard. But she's been following me around our apartment like a puppy all day, needy and clingy since her dad walked out on us. I can't grab a square of chocolate without giving away that secret—the one secret that's holding me together.

"I don't know what I want to do for my birthday," I say.

All wide-eyed innocence and naive selfishness, Layla asks, "What about frozen yogurt?" She loves the yogurt place—she gets to serve herself and slather the yogurt in candy toppings.

I've never liked yogurt, but it's a kid-friendly place. It's easier to take her there than a fancy restaurant with real desserts—chocolate torte, crème brûlée. It's cheaper than a vacation or even a trip to the beach. Gas is expensive. And—to Layla—it will feel like a celebration.

She expects a celebration.

"Sure, we can go to the yogurt place for my birthday."

15

THE DANCING SWORDS

FIRST, you tear the eyes out, digging your fingertips into the sockets around them, squishing the bulbs to get your fingers under them. They'll be slippy, and you'll have to squeeze hard while yanking out, or the eye won't come.

Once you have the eyeballs pulled out of their sockets, rip quickly to tear them from the gooey threads still connecting them. When they come free, throw them at the floor. Stomp on them with your boot. The heavier the boot, the better.

Now it's time to slice off the top of the head. Here's the knife. It's large and silver. It gleams. So pretty. So clean. The cleanliness won't last. Don't worry; it's sharp enough. It won't cut through the bone like butter, but if you push firmly, it will cut.

The brain is revealed. Crenelated and pinky-gray. Press your fingers into it and wiggle them, mixing the soft, mealy flesh. Blending thoughts and memories. Treasured moments, carefully collected over a lifetime become nothing more than scrambled eggs.

Now take this pair of swords. They gleam like the knife, but they're longer, thinner. Swing them through the air and hear how the air itself is cut by their sharp edges. They dance as they swing, beautiful in spite of the pain they portend.

Swing both at once, cutting long slices across the torso, first one way, then fractions of a second later, criss-crossing in the other direction. Draw Xs across the body with the hushed, breathy rhythm of the swords. They swing through the air, then cut through the flesh.

Innards fall out. Blood gushes through ribbon-like cuts.

You're almost done. Keep going.

You cannot see. You cannot think. Or remember. The pain is everything now. That and the swishing, dancing of the swords.

How are you doing it? How do you wield the knife, swing the swords, when it's your own body being cut?

You can't. You know that.

This is only a dream. And when you die, you'll wake up. You'll have to make it through another day. But when you sleep, you'll come back here.

You'll rip out the eyes. Scramble the brain. Slice your own body from every angle. It is the ultimate horror.

Yet you keep coming back. Because somehow, it's easier than the small everyday horrors, the existential uncertainties, the inescapable pressure of living.

16

BLAZE THE FIRE MONSTER

THE UNICORN STRETCHES his snowy neck, leaning his nose down to taste the dark liquid in the mug before him. He's been blowing on his hot chocolate, quietly nickering, to cool it, but it must be too hot still. He lowers his translucent horn to the surface of the drink. *Cold suffuses.* With the lightest touch, the chocolate is cool enough to drink.

"Will you tell me a story?" the Unicorn asks.

"Which one do you want?" I say, leaning my back against the front of my living room couch and stretching out my legs on the floor.

"One about me," the Unicorn says.

I nod, knowing exactly which story to tell.

* * *

"WHEN I WAS FIVE," I begin, "there was a monster that lived in the pantry. My father called him a cookie monster, and my aunt called him a cuddle monster. My mother said that when he was bigger, he'd keep us safe from the real monsters that live in our world. He'd be our guard dog. *Fight fire with fire*, she said. So, I named him Blaze the Fire Monster.

"We put an old blanket on the floor, in the corner of the pantry, and set out two bowls for Blaze's food and water. He'd curl up there, a tiny, brown ball of fluff, and I'd lean against the pantry door, idly rearranging the cans on the shelves, and tell Blaze stories about the things we'd do when we were bigger. Much like I tell you stories now.

"I couldn't make myself grow up any faster, but I thought up a way to make Blaze grow. Hotter fires burn brighter, faster, *bigger*, and, since Blaze was our little fire monster, I needed a way to make him hot. Or *spicy*.

"So, I raided the spice rack and stole every jar whose contents made my tongue sting. Poor Blaze! He ate his beef and rice pellets, liberally sprinkled with cayenne pepper almost every day."

* * *

AT THIS POINT in my story, the Unicorn wrinkles his nose, and the Dragon, the other member of my audience, snakes his slithery, slitted tongue hungrily. He snorts a puff of gun-powder smelling smoke from his nostrils, muttering, "I like a bit of cayenne."

The Unicorn shoots him a glare, and pointedly turns the attention back to me, asking, "Did it work?"

* * *

"Puppies grow. If you feed them anything, they'll grow," I say. "So, yes, Blaze grew bigger by the day. His fur grew out red and bushy, and his body filled out with strong, lean muscles. He was a wildfire of a dog, and, before I finished kindergarten, he was as big as me. Seventy-five pounds of romp-in-the-backyard, beg-under-the-table, follow-me-to-school dog. We had a blast all summer, roaming through the forests behind our house. A real estate company was planning to clear those forests out, but construction had been delayed. So the forests were as wild and untended as Blaze and me.

"By the time I started first grade, Blaze was so big I decided I would ride him to school like a pony and make a real entrance for my first day. As I braced myself against him, burying my fingers in his bushy red fur, Blaze grew grumbly inside. Before I knew it, the grumble turned into a snarl, and Blaze snapped.

"The bite wasn't deep, and my mother said I should know better than to try riding a dog like a pony. Even one as big as Blaze. But it was the first time Blaze had ever bared his teeth to me, let alone touched me with them, and I was shaken. The bandage only stayed on a few days, but every minute served as a reminder.

"I decided to stop feeding Blaze cayenne. He was big enough now. Instead, I tore open one of my mother's bags of chamomile tea, and I sprinkled the leafy bits over his food hoping to calm him. My mother always found it calming. Blaze, however, took one sniff of his tea-laced food, huffed a sigh, and blew all the little bits away.

"He wouldn't have any of the other soothing spices I tried either: rose hips, honeybush, echinacea. He liked ginger and ginseng, but the mere fact that he liked them made me wonder if they were such a good idea. So, Blaze went back to a normal doggy diet."

MY TEA IS COOLING QUICKLY, so I stop the story for a quick drink. The unsweetened lemon tea is bitter, sour, and tangy on my tongue. It's soothing, but it also makes me strong. My fantastical guests wait politely as I finish my drink and prepare to continue the story.

"LATER THAT YEAR, I decided to teach Blaze how to fetch. I got him a blue tennis ball, and took him out to our back-yard wilderness. Throw after throw, Blaze would simply watch the ball sail into the forest. He'd grumble and huff a little, like he was laughing at me for thinking he'd chase it.

"So, I gave up on the blue tennis ball. But, I didn't give up on fetch. I figured, I just needed to throw something that Blaze would be more interested in chasing.

"I offered him a variety of dog toys, but Blaze snorted derisively at each of them. A twisty pink rope. A red rubber bone. A stuffed toy squirrel with a squeaker inside. *No go.*

"That's when I got creative. First, I cut the tennis ball in half, then I stole the left-over London broil, all minced up for tomorrow's sandwiches, from the refrigerator. I duct-taped the tennis ball back together, with the minced up meat, all juicy and saucy, squashed inside.

"Blaze wasn't all that interested in chasing the doctored tennis ball, but he sure was interested in having it. That's when I got my second bite. This time, I didn't show my mom. I didn't want her to worry. I decided to keep all the worrying for myself. I thought I was tough. I thought I could handle it.

"After Kindergarten, I started first grade. I met a lot of new kids, and suddenly Blaze wasn't my only friend anymore. Or even my best one. I'd still cuddle up with him on the pantry floor sometimes, and when my head rested against his fuzzy back, the warmth of his body radiated through me as toasty as a campfire. But as the years passed, I paid less and less attention to him.

"By the age of ten, he looked like an old dog to me. Maybe he was. Big dogs don't necessarily live that long, and he was a rescue in the first place. So, we don't know how old he really was when we called him a puppy. He could have been several years old, just scrawny and undernourished..."

* * *

THE UNICORN WHICKERS SOFTLY, not wanting to interrupt my story but unable to hold back his judgement of anyone who would underfeed an animal. I agree with him, but there's not much either of us can do about the hypothetical mistreatment of a long gone dog that happened before I'd ever met him.

I run a hand through the Unicorn's mane comfortingly. The silky, ivory curls of his locks are almost as soft as his ever-melting heart.

"THIS IS where the story gets sad," I say. "This is the beginning of the end.

"I got into an argument at school. I was in fifth grade, and our classroom wasn't in the main school building. The fifth grade classes were in mobile rooms that had been added to the school by placing them at the edge of the playground. So, when our teacher came back late from lunch, my whole class—a whole troupe of twenty-some ten-year-olds—was left huddling around the locked door of our classroom, and there weren't any adults to notice.

"If our class had been inside the main building, one of the other teachers would have noticed us loitering around in the hall, making noise, and causing trouble as we waited, but not at the edge of the playground outside a mobile room. Out there, it was just us, and kids that age have a way of turning mean fast when there aren't any adults around.

"I don't remember what the argument was about, but I was articulate, imaginative, and clever. So, I probably made the class bully feel like a fool somehow, and while he couldn't outclass me with words, he knew how to pick up a rock and throw it.

"The mobile classroom was positioned on a bed of gravel, so there were plenty of rocks. Soon enough, the whole class was standing in a circle around me, jeering and throwing fistfuls of gravel.

"I ran away. It's the only time I ever ran away. I ran all the way home, but it was the middle of the school day, so there weren't any adults expecting me at home, only a sleepy old dog with fiery fur. I climbed in through his dog door and found him curled up, sleeping under the kitchen table. I crawled under the table with him and buried my face in his warm fur, drying my tears with his heat and softness. Blaze was my campfire, keeping me warm against the coldness of my classmates, the coldness of a world that ever lets children think they can get away with acting cruelly.

"My cuts and bruises weren't bad, so when I felt calmer, I dragged Blaze outside to romp through the brambly wilderness. I always felt better out there. I never had succeeded at teaching Blaze any tricks. He came when called, and he stayed close to me, even off-leash, but that was it.

"It was a cold day, cloudy overhead. I don't remember what the weather was like on most of the days of my childhood anymore, unless it matters to the story, I guess, but I could never forget the thick gray skies of that day."

THE UNICORN WHICKERS AGAIN, this time excitedly. He knows where the story is going. He's heard it before. He's heard all my stories, even before I tell them, but this one is his favorite.

His love of the story pulls me forward, even though I have mixed feelings about this memory. There is a good side to it, but in some ways, the sadness is more real. The good parts are a story I've made up. Something that helps me sleep at night. Something that gets me through the day. Like my friends.

The Dragon snarls, impatient at my hesitation. "Go on," he insists. "If we must have a story before our chess game, then go on with it and get it done."

"BLAZE and I romped through the forest, and it might have turned into a normal, forgettable day. Except Alex Golding, the class bully, chose that day to come explore the wilderness as well. It was a large patch of land, and other kids did come play there occasionally. Maybe he was looking for me. Maybe he felt bad about what he'd done, encouraging the whole class to turn against me, letting it get out of hand. Maybe he'd been chewed out by an adult and told to come looking for me to halfheartedly apologize. Maybe it was just a coincidence. I don't know. I never sought him out later to find out, because I don't really care about his side of this story.

"I do know, though, that Alex had a history of torturing animals. Yes, he was *that* kind of bully, and I think Blaze sensed it. I think Blaze could smell the cruelty rising off Alex's skin as soon as he saw him tripping his way through the forest.

"I tried to hide behind one of the dead trees, half fallen over, but Alex saw us. He called out, and he came running toward us, fast and startling, like a predator bearing down on their prey.

"To be clear, Alex really could have been coming to apologize. I don't know, because he never got the chance to say a word.

"Blaze snapped. I swear, as he lunged at my bully, Blaze swelled up in size, growing like a bonfire with a bottle of whisky poured on it. He wasn't just a dog anymore; in an instant, he became a giant, snarling, canine demi-god of vengeance.

"I have so many feelings when I look back on this moment that happened on the other side of my life from now, but at the time, I was too stunned to feel anything. I just watched as Blaze chomped down on Alex's arm. His jacket caught on fire and within moments, he was entirely engulfed in flames. A fire shaped like a fifth grade boy. A fire that used to be my dog."

* * *

My voice has gone hollow as it always does when I hit this point. Toneless, inflectionless. I don't need to express my feelings. I couldn't if I tried. They're too deep and myriad. But I know my friends understand me. I can feel the Unicorn's and Dragon's eyes on me, even though they're not real, even though they're just facets of myself, projected outward onto imaginary friends: a tape recorder to capture the words of my story and automatically transcribe them, and a digital chessboard that will play against me when I'm ready. That's what I see when I look with my eyes, but when I look with my heart, the Dragon's eyes are green and piercing. The Unicorn's eyes are gold and loving.

* * *

"They didn't stay that way. The flames licked upward, climbing toward the sky, crawling away from Alex, leaving him clutching his arm to his chest and looking almost comically horrified but free of fire.

"As soon as he gathered his wits—at least, what wits a bully like that has—Alex ran away from the comet tail of fire, rising past him, but I ran toward it, reaching the empty place in the forest where the conflict had happened just in time to burn my hand on the last wisps of fire before they flitted out of reach like the whimsical flip of a sleeping dog's tail.

"My dog, who had been my best friend for half of my life, my bonfire, my companion, my guiding light—my Blaze—had became a ball of fire rising into the sky, already out of my reach, but the sharp bite of that burn on my fingers felt like his last kiss. One last time his tongue licked me.

"I stood there in shock, staring up through the naked winter branches of the trees all around.

"On that dark, gray, cloudy day, I watched orange flames rise into the sky, and the thick layer of clouds cleared for them. For one moment, the sun shone down so brightly through a gap in the clouds that it hurt my eyes. The fire that had been my dog joined the rays of the winter sun, and when the clouds closed back up again, I knew Blaze had run away for good. We wouldn't find him, no matter how long my parents looked, we never would.

"It felt like the sadness would well up inside me, and I'd have no way to put it out. No fire to warm me anymore. But then I saw movement in the trees. A beautiful white creature like the shadow of a deer on the snow..."

* * *

"It's me!" the Unicorn whickers delightedly, as bright and clear, as profoundly real as he can ever be.

"Yes," I agree, "it's you."

* * *

"THE SHADOWY WHITE creature approached me so shyly. I knew I couldn't move or he would run away, so I held as still as stone."

* * *

"I WOULD HAVE COME to you anyway, even if you had moved," the Unicorn demurs, turning his head to the side so he's looking at me coyly out of the corner of one of his golden eyes.

"You wouldn't have," the Dragon chides. "You know it. Yet you insist otherwise."

"Shh," I hush them both. "We're almost finished. Let me finish?"

My friends grow quiet, and I tell them the final words, finishing my story.

"I held so still that this fawnlike creature with snowy, downy fur approached me, and when he got close enough, I held out my burned hand. I don't know why. But he knew.

"The willowy white deer lowered its head, bowing toward my burned hand, and as I watched, glistening tears filled his golden eyes. He cried, and the perfect tears spilled out over his lowered forehead, meeting right at the point of his forelock. The tears glittered in the cold winter light like crystals as they froze, fresh tears spiraling past the frozen ones before freezing themselves, growing together into a shining, translucent, icicle of a horn.

"The horn grew until the frozen tip touched the burn

on my hand, suffusing the bright pink flesh with soothing coldness. It instantly stopped hurting."

* * *

THE UNICORN'S golden eyes glow like they did the very first time I saw him. He loves this story.

"You healed my wounded hand," I say. "And then you stayed, and over time, you helped to heal my wounded heart."

Unicorns can smile. Did you know that? I know it. He smiles every time we get to the end. I say the final words like a ritual. I know I have them right this time, finally, after so many practices, I know exactly how the story ends:

"When I was ten, my dog ran away, and I invented an imaginary friend. If I hadn't lost my dog on that day, he would have died by now anyway. But my Unicorn? He's still here, decades later, listening to my stories."

* * *

I TURN off the tape recorder, take a sip of my lemon tea, and power up the digital chess board.

The Unicorn has gone to sleep, lulled into dreams by his favorite story, but the Dragon is more than ready now to play.

17

IN THE ROOTS OF THE WORLD TREE

Alia heard water dripping all through the city. Every surface was damp, cold and slick. She smelled mold in the air. It came in great huffs as the wind moved. The summoning circle would open around her, and suddenly, mold would be all she smelled. She hated it. She loved water, but not like this. She longed for the open ocean of her home realm, but she'd been called here. To Dornsair, the city beneath the hanging roots of the world tree. The rotten bottom of the world.

Her home in the open ocean was an entire world away in a dimension where the sky stretched out like a sandy beach, glittering with stars. Here the closest thing to stars were the roving colonies of lightning bugs who lived high in the world tree's branches. Exhibitionists. Showing off their civilization as if it were something to envy. Though they had never seen the phosphorescence of the fire dancing eels in the depths of the sea.

And yet... it wouldn't be as moldy up there.

Down here, among the hanging tendrils of roots, burrowing creatures had made their homes. Moles and worms and whole competing monarchies of ants. Someday, when the queen of the Red Empire called Alia here through her summoning circle, surrounded by drones standing at every point of the pentagram and worker sisters standing in a circle around them, the felotter would turn tail, run from her calling, and climb up to meet the butterflies and squirrels in the branches high above. She'd waste weeks among them, infuriating the demanding queen.

But today was not that day. Alia wanted to return home and see the felotter pups in her enclave graduate from their first swimming classes. She wanted to eat the feast of rock shrimp and mollusks in celebration while her younger sister shook her thick tail and twisted her long spine in the goofy dance of triumph she always did when she was proud. And the fastest way home was to do what Queen Seltyne wanted. Then she would be sent home through the summoning circle, instead of slowly collecting enough life-leaves to summon her own portal, high in the world tree's branches.

Alia bowed down before Queen Seltyne. The red queen, who stood only as tall as Alia's knees, folded several pairs of her arms across the burnished maroon of her exoskeletal breast.

"Why have you summoned me?" Alia asked.

"A monster is terrorizing my people."

"Again?" Alia tried not to let her weariness show in her voice, but she feared the word came out dry and disinterested.

"This is a new one, and it keeps eating my people."

Alia could sympathize with wanting to eat Queen Seltyne's people. They looked a little like lobsters, and Alia imagined they might be quite tasty. Yet, Queen Seltyne and her retinue of wizards-in-training had her on a short leash. They could summon the felotter from her own realm any time they wished, and if they were unhappy with her, they could most likely bind her in the space between realms, unable to step out of the summoning circle into the realm of the world tree and also unable to return to the oceans of her own world.

Alia sighed and said, "Tell me what you know."

In sequence, Queen Seltyne's royal advisors told Alia the stories of their workers and drones being stolen from shadowy corners, disappearing without a trace, except for the crumpled, empty exoskeletons they left behind. Queen Seltyne feared for the safety of her youngling chrysalids, hanging in the central pupal chambers. "You must find the culprit."

Alia nodded solemnly. She might dislike the way that the Red Empire summoned her without warning, but she had grown fond of them anyway. She had spent many seasons protecting them from fears, both real and imagined. They were an annoying infestation in the roots of this world tree. But they were hers to protect, and it made her feel powerful and important to protect them.

"I will find it."

The felotter left the royal summoning party behind and took to the cavernous passageways of their hive. She sniffed the mildewed air and squinched her nose. She ruffled her whiskers, scenting for the traces of magic. The Red Empire's battle drones were powerful enough warriors that they could usually fight their own physical battles. When the queen summoned Alia, it usually meant their foe was of a magical disposition.

So, she followed the tingle in her whiskers, down one corridor and into another, until she found herself at a crumpled pile of red armor. An empty exoskeleton. She was too late to save this warrior. Something had sucked the poor creature out through the joints of its own armored body, slurping up the organs inside.

Alia pressed her nose close to the armor, letting her whiskers feel its hollowness. Except, it wasn't totally hollow. She nosed at the armor, and the dried, desiccated pile shifted. Inside, she found a newly pupated youngling, quivering, frightened. Alia had never seen one of the members of the Red Empire so young before—it had wooly tufts of chrysalis silk clumped around all of its joints. Its eye stalks were as large as those of an adult, even though the rest of it was tiny. The eye stalks waggled in their tufts of silk, and its relatively huge eyes blinked. It looked like a sheep crossed with some army ant.

"Are you lost?" Alia asked.

"Are you going to eat me?"

Alia was tempted, but the tiny creature's voice was

such an adorable squeak that she didn't think she could live with herself if she harmed it. "No, but I think someone did eat the warrior whose armor you're hiding in. I'm looking for them. Do you know where they went?"

The youngling waggled its eyestalks again and also the pair of antennae behind them, in a gesture that Alia understood to mean yes. "Climb up behind my ear," the felotter said, "and whisper to me the right way." The youngling would be safe enough, hidden behind her round ear.

The youngling's many feet tickled as it climbed over Alia's fur. Once settled behind her ear, it guided her down the corridors, deeper and deeper into the shadowy corners of the hive, until finally she was staring at a shadow too dark to be a mere shadow.

Alia glared at the shadow. Her whiskers felt aflame with the magic roiling, boiling, and pouring out of the darkness. "I know you're in there," the felotter said.

A burst of darkness shot out at her, but it bounced off of her fur. Felotters' hearts were too full of the sunlight in their ocean world to be susceptible to attacks of dark magic. Another burst of darkness bounced off of her, and another. Alia sighed. She reached into the puddle of gloom and groped with her paws until she felt something bumpy, slick, and porous. Some kind of skin. She squeezed down, and once she had a good grip, she pulled hard, yanking the bumpy-skinned creature out of its nest of gloom.

A flippered foot pulled out of the shadows first,

followed by a squishy tank of a body—no neck, no separate head; just a big bumpy lump, split by a frowning pair of bulbous lips, and with four limbs sticking out, each ending in flippered feet or hands.

The frowning mouth opened, and a long tongue shot out at Alia, but it bounced off of her fur, just like it had when cloaked in shadows. She held the shadow toad up by its hind foot and watched it dangle.

Tiny feet behind Alia's round ear tickled her, and the youngling squeaked.

"Does it look as scary when it's pulled out of the shadows?" Alia asked.

"Yes!"

Alia laughed at the youngling's answer, but the shadow toad's eyes bulged. "What's that?" it galumphed.

"One of the babies of the people you've been eating," Alia answered, squeezing the toad's ankle brutally. "And it's under my protection."

The shadow toad smacked its wide lips. "Young. Tender. A delicacy..."

Alia could feel the youngling shivering behind her ear. It had looked tasty. Tiny and delectable. She could just imagine the fresh carapace snapping between her teeth. Would the tufts of chrysalis silk be sweet? Like the flesh of fruit? Or savory like strands of kelp. Alia could feel her mouth watering.

"We can share," the toad said. "More than enough for both!"

Alia was tempted.

But there were rock shrimp and mollusks waiting for her at home. Sometimes the line between food and friend could be so thin. She swung the toad by its stretched out leg, and its thick body thwacked against the wall. She thwacked it again and again, until the moaning stopped. Then she dragged its body back to the summoning hall, stood in the center of the summoning circle, and held the shadow toad up high.

"I've defeated your monster," she said. "Now send me home."

Queen Seltyne and her royal advisors clacked their mandibles in admiration and waved their eyestalks and antennae gratefully. Alia took the youngling from behind her ear, and placed the adorable little bundle of silk tufts and stick-like red limbs at the queen's many feet.

Alia enjoyed her moment of being worshipped as a hero.

But as she felt the magic of the summoning circle course through her, replacing the vision of dark tree roots with wide, open, sun-sparkling oceans, she knew that she'd had her fill of protecting the Red Empire. The next time they dared summon her, she'd get her fill a different way, and she would finally feel their delectable-looking limbs between her teeth.

18

PANDA-MENSIONAL

I POINT at the star map again, angrily saying, "Come on, Meijing! We only have a few hours of air left!" But the black-masked eyes blink at me impassively, profoundly uninterested in the yellow spot on the view screen under my fingertip.

We're only five jumps from home. Three if we didn't have any cargo. Or one jump back down to the planet of Gloaming, but Meijing won't jump our spaceship either way. I knew it was a risk to keep doing cargo runs this month, but I never imagined Meijing would leave us stranded like this. I guess that'll teach me to trust a dumb animal. Even one with quantum spaceflight capabilities.

"I told my girlfriend I'd be home an hour ago," Jace says irritably. He's my cargo boy, and every word out of his mouth makes me feel old. I can't imagine taking the ability to travel from Gloaming to Earth in less than an hour for granted. I remember when the scientists first discovered Gloaming, and anyone audacious enough to dream about going there was a laughable fool. Not a visionary.

Now I can look out the window of my spaceship and see the gleaming cities of Gloaming glitter along its twilight meridian. And it's all possible because of this big, useless lump of a cuddly panda bear.

Jace offers Meijing another handful of bamboo to munch, but the panda only raises a hind paw to itch at her control collar. It's a device that creates an electro-magnetic field that ensures all her jumps are constrained to the right vector.

I'm tempted to snatch the handful of twigs from Jace and beat Meijing about the head with it, but I don't think that will bring my spaceship any closer to landing on a planet with breathable atmosphere. Besides, Meijing looks too much like a children's plushie. I can't hate her any more than I would a marshmallow.

"God," I say, "Why didn't they put engines on these ships?"

"Engines?" Jace asks.

He's such a youngling.

"Yes, engines," I say. "Engines to fly the ship back down to Gloaming."

He blinks, confused, and I explain.

"Before pandas, spaceships had rocket fuel and engines. They were blasted through the atmosphere by giant explosions, and they flew. Like birds, but straight up."

Jace laughs and shakes his head. He's part of a generation that thinks quantum jumping is a perfectly normal biological adaptation. Scientists are even working on incorporating it into human DNA now. Then we won't be so dependent on pandas and their strange moodiness every twenty months.

For the moment, however, I'm trapped in orbit of Gloaming inside a spaceship that amounts to a giant, airtight box. The only engines it has run the limited atmosphere scrubbers, the force field that forces Meijing to carry the ship with her when she jumps, the lights, and the computer where I keep records of my cargo log and Jace plays video games. It's more of a camper than a real spaceship.

The only piece of actual space-faring technology I have is Meijing, my panda.

Pandas would have died out if the scientists hadn't gengineered new strains of high protein bamboo for them. It's the craziest combination of quantum mechanics and wildlife preservation ever. We'd have never even discovered that pandas have a gene allowing for quantum mechanical space jumping if we hadn't improved their diet enough that they had the energy left over to use it. Having a carnivore's digestive tract and a vegetarian's diet is a real bummer, I guess.

"I'm taking her control collar off," I say. "She keeps itching at it, so maybe it's bothering her." Jace stares at me like I'm crazy, but I can't think of anything else to try. I've already tried pleading and bribing Meijing with every delicacy of gengineered bamboo I have onboard. She won't eat any of it. I know from experience that this twenty-month itch that pandas get can last for days. Sometimes the whole month, and our air won't last that long.

Besides, what's the worst that can happen? Meijing may be stubborn and stupid, but I can't believe she's actually suicidal. I know her better than that. So, maybe she'll drag the ship on a few jumps along a non-optimized vector, but that won't hurt us. And at least it might get her jumping again.

Meijing perks up the moment the collar comes off her neck. The difference in her demeanor is subtle but instant. Before my hands are fully away, I feel the wavering gravity-like pull of a quantum jump. My stomach lurches sideways, then up, then sideways again. My feet stumble as the ship jumps once, twice... three times... I count twelve jumps in total before we stop.

Jace curses and says, *"Where are we?"* He's looking out the window, and I can see green trees out there. But the sky above them is not Earth's sky. We are not home.

Meijing scrabbles at the ship's door, running her blunt claws noisily along the metal. I'm too busy being thankful that Meijing has finally been jostled out of her slump to realize what Jace is doing until too late. Like a well-trained human with a domineering pet, Jace opens the door and lets Meijing out.

Now I'm too busy being thankful that the air here has

turned out to be breathable and—hopefully—non-toxic to give Jace the telling off he deserves.

Speechless, we follow Meijing as she lumbers excitedly into this alien forest. We dare not lose sight of her; she is our only ticket home. I hear other large figures crashing through the bamboo-like trees around us, and my heart races. But I can soon see that the other figures are pandas too. All of them.

"Is this what happens every twenty months?" Jace asks as we step into a clearing filled with pandas. "All the unconstrained pandas come here?"

"And all the constrained ones are miserable," I say, feeling bad for all the times I kept Meijing from coming here.

For the rest of my life, I know I will never forget this sight. The clearing is filled with flowers. They're built like hibiscus, but their petals radiate through every color from ultraviolet through infrared in a pulsating cycle. And, apparently, to pandas, they taste delicious. It's a frenzied panda smorgasbord out there. All the pandas are running about, throwing pawfuls of bamboo leaves like confetti, and eating the rainbow flowers by the fistful. Some of them even look like they're dancing.

"That flower must only bloom once a year here," I say. "And this planet must have a longer year than ours..."

Jace nods. "We should bring a sample back."

"Yeah," I say. "Maybe it can be reverse gengineered and forced to bloom more often. Maybe we could grow it ourselves. Then Earth and Gloaming won't have to shut down all transportation every twenty months for this interplanetary panda holiday."

It hits me then, *interplanetary. This planet.* I look up at the crimson sky, filled with pale-faced moons and wonder exactly which vector Meijing followed to bring us here.

"We've discovered a whole new habitable world," I say. And, unlike Gloaming, this one won't require atmo-domes or terra-forming. While every planet we've discovered using telescopes has been a hostile ball of rock or ice, covered in swirling noxious gases, this one is beautiful. I could even imagine living here one day.

"How many more worlds do you think pandas know about?" Jace asks.

"Who knows?" I say. I look around at all the bundles of black-and-white fuzz, happily munching flowers around me, and I realize that the pandas are the true explorers here. Human scientists may have unleashed the panda's potential, but human scientists didn't discover this world. The pandas did. After all our years running cargo together, I knew it couldn't be wrong to trust my panda. Pandas may have replaced spaceship engines, but they are more than mere machines.

"So... " Jace says, "How are we going to drag Meijing back to the ship? How will we get her control collar back on?"

"We won't," I say. "I think it's time we all started controlling pandas a little less and trusting them a little more. I'm sure Meijing will meet us at the ship when she's ready to take us home... Until then, I'm going to explore."

19

THE EMPTY EMPIRE

IT TOOK a hundred years to design and build the first planet. Multi-dimensional bulldozers and hyper-spatial cranes arranged the mountains, the icy spires, the cozy sea-green valleys in-between. Everything was perfect; ready for a feathered avian species to take roost in the frozen castle-like heights or maybe a variety of vine-swinging primates to set up their homes in the valleys. But no one came.

So I built another world—a moon to circle the planet. To follow the theme, the moon's face was formed from glassy mirror-like ice, great stretches and planes of ice. Hoofed equines could pound their way around the moon, reveling in those wide, broad planes. But the equines didn't come.

The planet and the moon shone at each other, reflecting each other's empty beauty, waiting.

No one wants ice worlds anymore, I thought. My next

planet was red and dusty, and it only took a few years to build, smashing asteroids together, gluing them in place. But no reptiles came to bask in the red world's sun-burnt warmth.

I was good at building worlds now— I could churn them out, one every several years. So, I kept building: a green planet, wishing for a civilization of tiny rodents; another covered in oceans, hoping to become inhabited by sentient fish; an entire world carved out of a giant purple gem—I don't even know who would live there. But it's beautiful.

Each of them waited.

Each of them is waiting.

I keep building worlds, hoping that some day the creatures will come, but there are too many other worlds out there for them. Too many places to live. Yet, I keep building. Some day they will come.

Until then, my empty empire is perfect and serene.

20

NOT SPIDER-MAN AND THE SEVEN
ANGEL DONORS

THIS IS NOT a story about Spider-Man, because Spider-Man is owned by a company. This is a story about a young boy, on his first day of high school, who was bitten by a spider and fell asleep like a princess in a fairytale. He fell asleep for the life of the author—which in this case would be his parents—plus seventy years.

Understandably, his parents were very upset. They placed their son in a glass coffin like Snow White or Sleeping Beauty—but not Princess Aurora, because she's owned by a corporation too, so really, just the generic, public domain version—and dressed him in his favorite clothes, which happened to be his Spider-Man Halloween costume, which he had purchased lawfully from a department store, let's call it Mal-Wart, who discouraged their workers from forming a union.

The boy's parents couldn't take time off of work to grieve for their sleeping princess boy, because they worked at Mal-Wart, and without the protections of a union, they couldn't afford any time off. However, the Mal-Wart they worked at agreed to let them set up their son's glass coffin in the gardening department as a publicity stunt. At least, they could look through the panes of glass and see his sleeping face every day during their fifteen minute breaks.

The other workers at the store came together to start a GoKickMe campaign in support of the grieving parents and their sleeping son. Many of them donated a few dollars here or there, but nothing that could change the fundamental situation.

Of course, the campaign would only be fully funded if an angel donor came forward to buy into the highest tier of support—cure Not Spider-Man of his torporific afflic-tion and in return, be rewarded with seven years of his labor as an unpaid intern, and also, seven additional years of labor from his firstborn child as an unpaid intern, and so on, and so on, ad infinitum. His parents weren't too concerned about promising away years of the lives of their hypothetical grandchildren and great-grandchildren. Given that Mal-Wart didn't provide any of them with health insurance, their son probably couldn't afford to have children, and if he did, they'd likely all die from global warming before they were old enough for intern-ships anyway.

The first potential angel donor to present himself to the bereaved parents during one of their breaks in the garden center beside their son's glass coffin was another teenager from his high school. The boy had been one of Not Spider-Man's friends since middle school, and he insisted that he could awake the sleeping boy—who he'd apparently had a crush on since elementary school—with True Love's Kiss.

Not Spider-Man's parents were unimpressed with the science (entirely non-existent) behind the boy's pitch and sent him away unkissed, as they didn't feel they could offer consent on their sleeping son's behalf. Especially not for such a half-baked notion.

One by one, other potential angel donors came to the parents with similarly half-baked ideas. One mad scientist proposed transplanting a spider's heart—which would be more compatible with the venom flowing through the boy's body—in place of his human heart. The parent's objected that a spider's heart would be much too small, and the scientist countered that he could clone a human-sized spider if they would give him some seed money.

Unsurprisingly, the parents declined, and their son went on sleeping.

Eventually, another worker at the Mal-Wart came to the parents with a beautiful, shimmering cloak in her hands. She had aspirations of becoming a famous fashion designer, and she proposed to cure Not Spider-Man's torpor with this cloak woven entirely from the silk of spiders who had been fed upon only free trade coffee beans and the most highly caffeinated sparkling water on the market. Surely, their silk could wake him up.

The aspiring fashion designer had been up all night,

every night for months, feeding the spiders and weaving their silk. Also, chomping on coffee beans and drinking caffeinated sparkling water.

With bated breath and high hopes, the grieving parents opened the coffin, draped the shimmery cloak awkwardly over their son's shoulders, and then watched in awe as he leapt up for the first time in months, did a perfect pirouette even though he'd never taken a gymnastics or dance class in his life, and then laid back down to sleep. His eyes never opened. Their eyes filled with tears.

The aspiring fashion designer, however, had planned ahead and had the foresight to stream the occurrence on her insta-fame account. Within a matter of minutes, the post of the Not Spider-Man boy doing a pirouette in his sleep had gone viral. By the end of the hour, she received an order request from the Metropolitan Gothopolis Opera to weave a dozen similar cloaks for their upcoming performance of Swan Lake. Similar orders began pouring in from dance studios all over the world. Her career was made!

Although, she would have to get by without seven years of help from an unpaid intern.

The international fame of the fashion designer's video inadvertently helped Not Spider-Man's parents: suddenly, they began receiving angel donor pitches from much farther afield, instead of simply from interested parties in their hometown. A notable billionaire even sponsored a pharmaceutical research team to find a cure, using actual reputable science and none of the fairy tale nonsense that

Not Spider-Man's parents had been dealing with up until that point.

However, once the cure was synthesized—using a simple process and cheap ingredients—the pharmaceutical company refused to give it to the parents for less than 3.4 million dollars, and they patented the recipe, promising to savagely sue anyone who threatened the proprietary nature of their invention.

Not Spider-Man and his parents found themselves no better off than they'd been before. Although, Not Spider-Man didn't seem to care very much. He was still sleeping.

At her wit's end, Not Spider-Man's mother—an amateur astronomer who had been running the SETI@home screensaver on her computer since she'd been a high school student herself—set up her radio equipment and sent a desperate, last-ditch cry for help out to the stars. She included her heartfelt plea, accompanied by complete copies of the DNA sequencing for both her son and the spider who had bit him.

Maybe, in all the reaches of the galaxy, there was a more advanced race of beings who could come to her aid. All she could do was hope.

Amazingly, she was right. There were more highly advanced beings in the galaxy, and they heard her plea.

The silver spaceships came to Earth on the anniversary of Not Spider-Man's fateful spider bite. They surrounded the planet, hovering over every major city, exactly as the movies had always predicted they would, and then they filled the airwaves with their answer.

On every television, phone, and computer screen in the Mal-Wart—and presumably across the world—a spider of unearthly beauty appeared. Its clusters of black eyes gleamed with deep emotion; its long legs shuffled with a quietly suppressed grace and elegance; and its wiggling mouth parts somehow conveyed a smile that made every human who saw it both sad and strangely peaceful.

"Thank you for alerting our species to the unauthorized use of our personal DNA here on this unregistered planet. Be assured, we will seek out and punish those responsible for illegally seeding this planet with unregulated lifeforms nearly four billion years ago. For now, as per galactic guidelines, we have begun releasing a powerful anesthetic agent into your atmosphere before beginning the extraction of every unlawful instance of our proprietary proteins and amino acids, which should return this world to its previously barren, pristine state..."

Very few humans stayed awake long enough to hear the rest of the alien spider's announcement.

21

THE SPIDER IN HER LUNGS

MOIRA FELT a tickle in her throat. She pulled the handkerchief from her pocket and covered her mouth before coughing. It was a hacking cough that wracked her body, deep into her lungs. She felt the slime of silk on her tongue and spit the silky strands surreptitiously into her handkerchief before tucking it back in her pocket.

"Your cough seems worse today." The only customer in Moira's shop was a bride-to-be, a rich socialite marrying a famous poet. Their wedding would be broadcast across the entire solar system. She was running her hands reverently over the shimmering, gleaming wedding dress that Moira had almost finished for her. It wasn't simply white —it was pearlescent like a cumulonimbus cloud that had accidentally wandered into a sunny day and glowed with hidden sunlight.

All that was left to make was the veil.

"I hope working on my dress hasn't been wearing you

out." The bride hugged the silky bodice to her own bosom. "It's perfect. I don't know where you get this silk. No one else can get Numi Silk at any price—not for three solar systems in any direction. I checked. The spiders are too hard to keep alive."

Moira smiled primly, holding back the tickle that had already returned to her throat. "This dress is my masterpiece," she said. "And how I get the silk is my secret. I'll have the veil for you tomorrow."

The bride paid Moira enough credits to fund another trip to Numinous VI—a journey involving three space cruisers and a hyper sleep. A journey that Moira no longer had the energy for. She couldn't sleep that long. If she didn't cough out the silk in her lungs often enough, the Numi Spider would fill them.

As soon as the bride was gone, Moira closed her shop for the day and doubled over coughing. She spread the handkerchief over her face and caught every silvery strand of silk that she hacked out of her lungs. The silk glistened in the handkerchief. Moira would add it to the veil.

In the back room of the shop, behind the counter with the cash register, Moira did her sewing. She took the wet silk, freshly coughed from her lungs, and spread it out over a screen to dry it into sheets of useable fabric. For the wedding dress, she'd spread the silk thickly, drying several layers to make a fabric strong and opaque enough. For the veil, she only needed a single thin layer to create a fabric as light and diaphanous as mist. It would be beautiful.

For other projects over the years, Moira had dyed the silk bright colors, but for a traditional white wedding gown, its natural shimmery shade was perfect.

Moira hemmed the sheets of silk, carefully sewing pearls along the edges. As she worked on stitching one layer of the veil, the spider in her lungs spun the silk for the next. She coughed and stitched late into the night.

"You're spinning awfully fast tonight," Moira said to the spider in her lungs. She'd never seen it—except on an x-ray, long ago. The newly hatched spider had been nothing more than an eight-legged splotch of light on that x-ray, but Moira liked to imagine that her spider glittered like gemstones, ruby red, a living piece of jewelry hidden inside her chest.

The doctors had said she would die. She had inhaled a minuscule egg, and by the time her cough developed, her body was already addicted to the spider's toxins. It couldn't be removed without killing her, and its webs would eventually suffocate her. One wrong breath, months earlier and star systems away, had sealed her fate. But Moira and the spider had shown the doctors. They'd found a way to work together, and she'd lived with her death inside of her for years, assisting her daily to become one of the most successful seamstresses in the whole system.

Moira simply could never sleep for too long; she had to wake up and cough, clearing away the cobwebs.

Lately, it felt like the spider was growing stronger and spinning webs faster. Or maybe, Moira's body was simply breaking down on her after years of fighting. Either way, Moira drifted off several times during the night.

As dawn glowed dimly through the window, Moira held up the finished veil. The dawn sunlight twinkled in the layers of fabric, catching tiny rainbows in the folds. It was so beautiful, Moira caught her breath at her own work. Then she coughed again.

"It only needs a few more pearls," she said to herself, laying the veil down. She knew that she could call it done, and the bride would never know the difference. But Moira was a master of her craft, and for herself, she knew a dozen more pearls would make it perfect. "But maybe... I'll lie down a while first." She tapped her hand on her chest and said, "Hear that in there? We're taking a break. No more spinning." The words were punctuated, short of breath as she said them.

Moira drifted in and out sleep, feeling her breath grow more and more shallow, but she was too tired, too tired to get up.

Finally, Moira awoke to the full brightness of afternoon sunlight. Her lungs creaked when she tried to breathe, and she saw something on the tip of her nose.

The spider was small and green, not at all how she'd imagined it. Moira tried to speak, but her lungs were too full. "You've laid your eggs," she wanted to say. "Our eggs." Instead, she stared at the spider as it drew forth its strands of silk and began to wrap her in a cocoon—a layer of fresh silk that was at once a wedding dress of her own, binding her to the spider dancing over her body, and her burial shroud.

Moira closed her eyes and thought about the baby spiders growing inside her now. They'd eat her when they hatched. But she drifted off into a dream-filled sleep long before that.

In her final dreams, Moira sewed the last pearls on the veil.

22

BIRTHING CLASS

Standing in the hospital lobby, Daniel spread his hands over the shirt covering his flat belly. He tried to imagine the alien life growing inside him, but it didn't seem real. He didn't feel any different than he had a week ago.

A couple women walked by Daniel, chatting with each other. The base's hospital was otherwise quiet at this time of evening. Daniel turned back toward the row of glass doors that led out to the dry, desert air of Eridani Mu, wanting to leave the hospital. The buildings of the human base were under the shadow of twilight now, but the majestic spires of the alien city in the distance were still lit by the pink-and-orange tinged sunset. In only five years since the humans had crashed here, those spires had grown and stretched until they dwarfed the human base. The aliens' work was awe-inspiring. Unlike humans, they were naturally suited to this environment. Their technology and progress far outpaced what humans could do on their own, stuck on this backwater world.

Daniel put his hand to his belly again. He tried to remind himself of why he was here. He wanted to be a part of the progress on this world in any way he could be. No matter how strange.

Another man walked through the glass doors into the hospital lobby. "Are you here for the birthing class?" he asked Daniel.

"Yeah," Daniel said.

"Do you know where it is? This is my first time." The man laughed nervously. "I guess that's obvious. If it weren't my first time, I wouldn't need the class, would I?"

"I guess not," Daniel said. "Want to look for it together?"

The man talked with Daniel as they walked through the halls of the hospital looking for the class. His name was Mike, and like Daniel he was the last one in his company to be impregnated. "Most of the guys are on their second or third time," Mike said. "One woman, I think she's up to five. Talk about dedication!"

"No kidding," Daniel said.

"I could see they were starting to wonder why I wasn't doing my part. We've got to earn our meal packs somehow, right?"

When they found the room, it was crowded with people. Their ages ranged from graying hair with a few wrinkles down to one girl whose angelic face looked so young that Daniel would've sworn she was fourteen.

Except she was here. There were children on base, but the rules were very strict. The doctors couldn't properly repair bodies that were too young or too old. The girl must have been eighteen, at least.

Chairs were set out in a big circle around the room. Daniel took a chair beside Mike. Daniel didn't feel like talking, but Mike started chatting right away with a couple women who introduced themselves as Lorelei and Andrea. They looked like sisters.

"I've never felt anything else so relaxing," Lorelei said.

"It was like a really great, week-long nap!" Andrea said with a deep belly chuckle.

Lorelei swatted Andrea on the arm and said, "Oh, you keep saying that! But, you know it was so much more."

Mike leaned forward and said, "It was sensual, wasn't it?"

Andrea blushed, but Lorelei nodded, touching her fingers to her neck.

As Daniel watched, he realized that he'd unconsciously put his fingers to his own neck as well. He remembered the pinching sensation as the larval body had grabbed him, reaching behind his head with an amorphous pseudopod and latching on. It grabbed his neck first, but then it drew itself against him, enveloping his body and wrapping around him. He could taste its flesh against his lips, briny like oysters or mussels. It pressed against his eyes, holding them shut. All of it felt in the darkness behind closed eyes.

The visceral nature of the memory struck Daniel so suddenly, he gasped.

Mike laughed; Lorelei smiled; but Andrea caught Daniel's eye. Daniel realized that she'd been joking about her experience of being impregnated, because she felt the same way he did: it had been too personal to talk about openly.

A nurse wearing green scrubs called for quiet and started the class with an outline of what they'd be doing—a short presentation, breathing exercises, a video of an actual birth, a break with snacks, and then a visit from a special guest. The nurse handed out half a dozen or more pamphlets and information sheets on different colors of paper.

Daniel flipped through the papers and pamphlets as the nurse, along with several assistants, gave their presentation. The papers mostly had medical information—how to take care of yourself during the recovery, postpartum groups to join, etc. The presentation was about the warning signs that your birth was about to begin and making sure that you made it to the hospital early enough. Apparently, it could be really dangerous if you didn't.

They weren't talking about what everyone wanted to hear: the lifecycle of the aliens. But whispers passed through the audience, telling hushed rumors of one of the aliens visiting the hospital. Maybe they'd all get to meet one and finally see the adult phase. Only the initiated and the few who worked directly with the aliens got to see them.

During the breathing exercises, everyone stretched out on the floor in the middle of the circle of chairs. Over all the funny breathing patterns, Daniel heard Mike and Lorelei talking quietly about how exciting it was to finally feel like they were part of the amazing changes happening on their planet.

Daniel pictured those spires in the distance—at once mechanical and organic—twisting their way into the sky. He tried to imagine the aliens that must live there—not the larval stage that had impregnated him but the mature phase of their lifecycle. The child growing inside him would live in those spires someday, build them taller, make this world strong and powerful. They would regain space travel. Probably faster travel than had stranded them here in the first place. Other planets would envy the nation that humans and aliens were building together here.

"All right, everyone," one of the nurses called out. "It's time for the video now. Back to your chairs." Once everyone was settled, the nurse said, "Now, I know this video can be kind of shocking. Graphic, even. But, I want you to remember that this is completely natural. This is the way that our two species were always meant to coexist. And, besides, we have cutting edge doctors here to take care of you. There's nothing to fear." The nurse started the video.

On screen, a woman lay on a hospital table, naked except for white sheets draped over her upper and lower body. Blue-gowned, face-masked doctors tended her. Her breathing was heavy but not erratic.

"Notice the breathing pattern?" the nurse said, standing beside the video. "Just like we practiced."

The woman's breathing sped up, faster and faster. Her eyes were wide. If Daniel hadn't known better, he'd have thought there was terror in them. Horror. The skin on the woman's chest, just below her ribcage, began to bulge and crawl. The flesh rippled, darkened, and then—the students in the birthing class all gasped—melted away, leaving a gaping hole in her abdomen. An infant nestled between the glistening pink of the woman's shockingly revealed organs. Its face was all eyes—faceted and silvery—and its body was all tentacle-like arms and hands and tiny, tiny fingers. Its multitude of fingers wiggled and stretched. Then the creature skittered out of its hold in an explosion of cracking sounds and disappeared off-screen.

Ragged, shrill screams emerged from the woman in the video, but the doctors weren't fazed. Instantly, they went to work, mending the hole in the woman's abdomen with a prepared stretch of lab-grown skin, gleaming metal tools, white gauze, and a pale purple foam.

"Look at that professionalism!" the nurse running the video said.

One of the assistants, without looking away from the video, added, "A few broken ribs is completely normal, but they heal fast."

The video cut to a new scene: the woman who had been lying naked on the hospital table was sitting up, dressed in a hospital gown, and smiling. Someone from off camera asked, "How do you feel?"

The woman spoke slowly, easily but slightly slurred, like she was drugged. Or maybe just really tired. "Great," she said. "Never better."

"Your offspring has already made it to the alien city," the voice off-camera said.

The woman's smile widened. "God," she said. "I've never seen anything so beautiful. I wish I could be there with it."

The voice off-camera said, "In all the ways that matter, you are. That city is a monument to their love for us. The food they export to us daily is a tribute to what you—and every other host—has done for them."

There were tears in the woman's eyes. She tried to speak but was overcome with emotion and could only look away, brushing at the gleams in her eyes.

The video ended.

"Does anyone have any questions before our break?" the nurse asked.

Lorelei raised her hand. "How long does she have to wait before it's safe to do it again?"

"Eager!" the nurse said. "I like it. Our doctors ask that people wait several months to let their bodies heal. Since people heal at different rates, it's best that you check in with your doctor and get a green light before signing up for another ovum."

Daniel remembered his ovum: large enough to hold an adult human curled into the fetal position; translucent, milky white; and, warm and sticky to the touch. He'd heard that they'd found clusters of the ovum numbering in the thousands when they first started mining this planet after the crash. Back before the spires. The ovum were desiccated and lifeless when they were found underground, but exposure to the surface atmosphere revitalized them.

The first impregnations were accidents. Now, you had to undergo a health exam and sign medical waivers to be assigned an ovum. All that paperwork and, then, as soon as he was in the room alone with it... The pseudopod had burst the ovum's milky white skin, tearing its way out so fast. He barely saw the larva before its amorphous body pressed against him, blocking out everything except the sensation of its soft flesh and the subtle taste of shellfish.

Daniel's heart began racing. His chest felt funny.

All through the break, Daniel watched the others, talking excitedly, planning parties with each other after their births, exclaiming over the brief glimpse of the alien they'd seen in the video, speculating about how many years it would be before the aliens had space travel, and they could all take to the stars again. He knew he should join them, but he couldn't muster the enthusiasm. He couldn't help feeling frightened and shaken by what he'd seen.

"Okay, everybody, break over!" one of the nurses sang out. "Time for our very, very special guest!"

Another nurse went to a door in the back of the room and said before opening it, "I know that you've all been dying to meet the aliens we share this planet with... well, let me introduce you to one of their queens."

Everyone fell silent.

"Of course, there are many queens over in the alien city, but this one has come here today especially to meet you!" The nurse opened the door, and the darkness behind it writhed. A creature stepped forward that was almost too tall for the room. Its body stooped, curving like a question mark. Multitudinous appendages—arms and tentacles of all lengths and sizes—lined its sides asymmetrically, and its face was the same cluster of faceted, silvery eyes.

"Oh my god," Lorelei said. Other voices around the room echoed hers. At first, Daniel thought they were horrified. He was. But, then, he realized they were expressing awe. Why didn't they see a monster? Was this what was growing inside him? Inside all of them?

Andrea held her hands to her belly like she was clutching a precious treasure. Lorelei was saying *beautiful* over and over again. Mike, at least, looked worried, but he said, "I guess it's normal to feel nervous." He tried to share a laugh with Daniel, but Daniel didn't feel like laughing.

A woman on the other side of the room stood up from her chair and shouted the words that Daniel was thinking, "What's wrong with you people! Can't you see this is a monster?"

The nurses rushed toward the woman, trying to quiet her down. "Please, ma'am," one of the nurses entreated. "You're upsetting the queen!"

The woman struggled against their restraining arms. She kept shouting. "We've been tricked! We've all been tricked!"

Daniel wanted to help the woman, but he noticed the queen moving. Terror froze him in his seat.

The woman pointed at the alien queen and screamed, "Parasite! What have you done to us?"

The queen's arms and tentacles spread wide, looming over them. She stepped toward the screaming woman, reaching out to her with those mismatched rows of limbs.

The woman shrieked and grabbed a chair. She threw it at the queen, but a long tentacle, surprisingly strong, whipped it out of the way. The queen's massive body hunched up and then sprang forward. The queen pounced on the woman, immobilizing her with winding tentacles and more restraining arms than the nurses had. Faceted eyes large enough to reflect the woman's entire face stared her down, mere inches away from her own scared eyes.

Daniel smelled perfume in the air like sea foam, tangy and fresh. The woman's screaming stopped, and she relaxed into the queen's embrace.

The nurses took the woman and helped her, limp and calm, out of the room. The queen settled back into her curved posture; her many limbs folded across her body. Daniel wanted to demand an explanation. He wanted to grab a weapon and point it at the queen. But he felt the presence in his belly—the alien presence—holding him down like an anchor. No matter what he did, he would still have one of *that* growing inside him.

Daniel wanted to rip it from his belly and strangle the infant with its own tentacles, rip off its arms, and leave it tattered into shreds. He seethed inside. What was wrong with everyone? All the people who'd done this before? All the workers who transported goods from the alien city? Had everyone succumbed to these monsters?

They'd either succumbed or been made to like that woman. Nothing was worth this. He'd rather starve on this rock than barter his body for the food these monsters could grow and the technology they could build.

"We're sorry for the disturbance," one of the nurses said. "That was clearly a very unstable individual, and we have people helping her. Now, if we can move on, I'd like you all to breathe deeply, put your hands on your bellies, and I'm going to guide you through a meditation."

Daniel breathed deeply, and the sea foam scent in the air filled his lungs. Had the smell grown thicker? He needed a plan, but the droning voice of the nurse and the soothing ocean smell dulled him. He couldn't think clearly. He couldn't plan. He felt his worries floating away.

"Now picture the life growing inside you," the nurse said.

Daniel pictured it—unmatched arms, tentacles, faceted eyes and all—deep in his belly. He felt it writhing.

And it was beautiful.

23

THE BLOOD PORTAL

HANNA STEERED the spaceship with one arm, punching buttons, turning knobs, and flipping switches. Her other arm was wrapped tightly around her young son. His face was buried against her shoulder. He wasn't crying any more. His breathing had stilled. He was sleeping, but he still clung to her with his arms and legs that seemed so long and gangly compared to when he was a baby.

Hanna didn't have energy to cast another portal large enough for the spaceship to pass through, so she would have to find a place to hide in this dimension. A habitable planet. A mineral rich asteroid field. A nebula, thick with space dust, at the very least. Her magic wouldn't recharge without matter and gravity fields to draw on. Yet, so far, all she'd seen were stars, barren stars, and their gravity was too strong. It would overload her in her weakened state.

Hanna shut down her spaceship's sensors and flew

blind through the velvety darkness. She closed her eyes and felt Owen, her little boy, breathing against her. She let an entire universe fold down to the quiet space inside of herself, and then she reached out with her mind, listening for voices in the darkness.

She heard a murmur. She tilted her head, and she made out a cacophony of quiet voices, almost too distant to hear. A space station, filled with people. A pocket of atmosphere and gravity where sound waves folded space, vibrating, tingling against her spatial magic sensitivity.

Hers was not the right magic for this job. Owen's father's magic, blood magic, would lead him to any space station filled with people—filled with blood—like an arrow to a bull's eye. Like a bloodhound to blood.

But Hanna had no choice. She could sense nothing else out here in the darkness. She had nowhere else to go.

She turned the spaceship consoles back on, set a course towards the gentle, barely perceptible tug of gravity in the distance, and fell asleep as soon as the autopilot took over.

"Mommy, wake up," Owen said, poking her cheeks and lightly touching her eyelids. "There's a fairy man on the viewscreen. He says, 'Welcome to the Darkness Bazaar.'"

Hanna opened her eyes to see Owen's cherubic face much too close to her own. His beautiful eyes were filled with love and questions. He trusted her, but he sought answers. She squeezed him, looked over his shoulder, and saw the fairy man, frowning on the viewscreen. He had pointed ears, silver hair, and gossamer wings behind the flowing cloak he wore, but the scene behind him was clearly a top-of-the-line, bleeding-edge-of-technology control room. And when Hanna looked through the portholes beside the viewscreen, she could see the space station—wheels spinning, tori turning, hanging in the darkness like a gyroscope lost in space. A space station without a star.

Yet, even without a stellar—or even planetary—mass nearby, the gravity fields here felt rich and velvety. They soothed Hanna's spatial senses, worn raw by ripping portal after portal to escape her husband Brison.

"What kind of realm is this?" Hanna asked. "No planets, only a wandering space station?"

The fairy man's frown turned to a smirk. "You're lost." He seemed pleased. Apparently, the Darkness Bazaar was more comfortable with aimless wanderers than unexpected purposeful visitors. Perhaps, this place was hiding from something too. "You should dock."

THE FAIRY MAN met Hanna and Owen at their airlock. He explained that they were welcome to keep their ship docked at the Darkness Bazaar for as long as they liked. There were docking berths to spare. However, when she wanted to leave, Hanna would need to consult with the ruling council and log an appropriate debarkation route. She couldn't tell if this was for her own safety—the gravity wells around the station were clearly unusual; she could feel it—or if it was to help keep the station hidden. She guessed the latter.

Inside the space station's docking ring, Hanna and her son found a twilight realm lit by flitting lightning bugs and glowing flowers hanging from twisting vines clinging to the bulkheads. More of the fairy people—delicately boned and very tall with colorful butterfly wings sprouting from their backs—manned stalls with magical and technological wares. A vendor selling replacement robot arms—upgrades with extra attachments—stood alongside a shop selling potions and power crystals. Hanna wondered briefly if a transformation potion could hide her and Owen from Brison, but unless it altered their bodies all the way down to the blood, he would still find them.

The Darkness Bazaar might prize its obscure location, but it wouldn't obscure the pull that Owen's blood had on Brison. She didn't have much time, a day at most, before Brison found them.

Owen tugged on her sleeve and pointed towards a vendor selling robot snakes. "Can I have one? Daddy still has Jaame..."

Hanna shuddered at the memory of the scaly, brown, sightless leech that Brison had told Owen was a pet. Jaame was not a pet. At least, it hadn't been Owen's. It was a blood bank that Brison used to strengthen his magic, and Owen had been a source of blood other than his own that was genetically bound to him.

Before Hanna could answer her son, a commotion ran

through the bazaar. Fairies gasped and pointed at the arching ceiling that looked out on the star-studded night. Swirls of red spiraled in the blackness, looping and knotting, tangling and untangling. An explosion of blood in the vacuum opened the ragged mouth of a passage that cut through the layers of dimension.

And Brison's ship flew through. He'd found her already. He'd found Owen. Hanna wished she could cut the ties of blood that bound her son to that man.

"Please, don't make us run again," Owen said, hugging Hanna's leg and looking up at her with pleading eyes.

"We have nowhere left to run to..." Hanna said, feeling defeated. But she pulled herself together. She had to. For Owen. "Come on, I'll buy you a robo-snake after I get us... a snack." She led Owen by the hand through the crowd of fairies, over to the potions stall.

She couldn't help glancing up at the sky, watching Brison's ship dock, as she picked through the glass bulbs and vials. Finally, she found two labelled Cthonion. She didn't want to transform herself and her cherubic child into monstrous creatures with tentacles on their faces, but it was the only sentient alien species that she knew for sure used blood based on hemocyanin instead of hemoglobin. So, if the potions were truly transformative, not merely illusions (which they almost certainly were), then maybe, just maybe, Brison wouldn't recognize Owen in Cthonion form.

It was a terrible plan, but it was all she had. Hanna tried to buy the potions, but the fairy selling them didn't recognize her credit chips as legal tender. She tried to barter, offering anything she had on her spaceship, and eventually the spaceship itself, but the fairy wasn't interested. He offered her a job; she could work for the potions. But Hanna didn't have time for that.

Time ticked down, and Hanna considered stealing the potions. Before she could decide, time ran out.

"Daddy has Jaame with him!" Owen cried. The boy twisted his hand, escaping Hanna's grip, and ran off through the crowd of fairies.

Hanna cried out too, an inarticulate sound between an admonition for Owen to stop and a plea for him to come back. The boy didn't listen. He only had eyes for that blasted leech he thought was his pet.

Standing in the berth where his ship had docked, in front of the re-sealed airlock, Brison had the damnable leech draped over his shoulders. It was longer than his arms, covered in crinkly brown scales like dried leaves, and instead of eyes, it had a triad of sticky red mouths, smacking and slurping, reaching toward the little boy who was jumping up and down, eagerly, in front of his father.

Brison lifted the leech off of his shoulders and placed it on Owen's, beneficently as if it were a gift rather than a curse. The little boy wobbled under the weight of his pet, giggled, and clapped his hands.

Hanna remembered how pale his face had been when she'd finally gathered the courage to run away. But here he was again, the leech's mouth latching onto his tiny neck. Owen smiled and squirmed as if the leech's bite was nothing more than a pleasant tickle.

Hanna walked through the crowd in a daze, drawn inexorably toward her son. If she ran, alone, Brison wouldn't care. She could start her life over, but it would be without Owen. If she fought to save her little boy... She'd felt her blood boil and sting with Brison's magic before. It would be a horrible way to die.

Horror, then.

"Get that leech off of my son!" she shouted. The crowd of fairies cleared out of her way, avoiding the family drama playing out amongst them.

"Jaame's not hurting me, Momma."

Brison laughed cruelly and ruffled Owen's hair. He thought he had won, but the boy cringed away from his father and said, "Don't touch me."

"I brought your pet to you," Brison said.

Owen's voice got very small; Hanna could hardly hear him. "You yelled at Momma. I think you hurt her."

Brison's face turned bright red. He'd never been good at hiding his anger. "Your mother—"

Owen cowered, hiding his face behind one of Jaame's scaly coils. The leech's body pulsed with the blood it was sucking.

Brison modulated his voice and tried again. "Your mother stole you from me."

Owen peeked out between Jaame's coils, his little face contorted in confusion. He didn't understand the idea of being stolen. He wasn't a possession. That's not how his mother treated him, at least. Hanna could see these thoughts reflected in the bewilderment filling his eyes.

"I have you back now," Brison said, holding a hand out to their son. "Let's go home."

"Back to our own dimension?" Owen asked. He didn't take his father's hand.

"That's right."

"Not without Mom."

Brison gave his son a withering stare, filled with scorn. He held up his hand and clenched it into a fist.

Hanna who had been helplessly watching their exchange fell to her knees, doubled over in pain. The sound of her own blood buzzed in her ears. It was rushing and singing, fighting to free itself from the veins that held it in. Brison's intent was clear—if the mother was in the way, get rid of the mother.

"Stop!" Owen cried.

And the pain stopped. Hanna gasped in relief. She'd never expected to experience another moment without pain again. She looked up to see Brison doubled over now, screaming and clutching at himself, as if trying to hold his blood inside. It was already leaking out of his nose and the corners of his eyes.

Her son was doing this to him. Protecting her. Destroying himself. Owen's fists were raised above his head, clenched tight. Hanna could see the phantom of the man her cherubic son would become—another cruel, cold-hearted blood mage, wielding the warm beating liquid of life itself as a weapon. She couldn't let that happen. He couldn't murder his own father. So Hanna summoned every bit of her own magic, pulling on the gravity fields and folds around her, feeling out the architecture of space. She gasped. The dimensions here were pressed together tightly like the pages in a book, instead of scattered like leaves on the wind. No wonder the Darkness Bazaar prized its privacy—it was sitting in a hub between realities. She could tear a portal to any other universe from here with a fraction of the energy it usually took.

Magic flowed into Hanna like a gushing stream. She crafted the gravity, sculpting it with her spatial sense, and ripped a man-sized portal through the layers of dimension into the space beneath her husband's feet. A special portal. A portal for only him.

The portal looked like nothing more than a black shadow; a double of his own shadow, but darker, deeper. It was a Brison-shaped window into a black hole, and the dimensional-rip sealed itself back up the moment that Brison was sucked through like an opened book slamming shut.

"Where'd Daddy go?" Owen asked, his hands falling slack at his sides. He looked small, scared, and harmless, but the vision of him like his father still haunted Hanna.

"I sent him home," she said, trying to believe that in some spiritual sense it might be true.

Owen nodded solemnly.

The leech let go of Owen's neck and nuzzled his perfect cheek with its glistening mouths. The boy stroked its scaly head. "Can we... not go home?" he asked, uncertain. "I don't want to see Daddy again. At least... not right now."

Hanna tried to take a step towards her son, but instead she stumbled and fell to her knees, exhausted from the power of the gravity magic that had flowed through her.

A fairy woman with swallowtail wings rushed over and helped her up. "Are you all right?" she asked, wings flapping slowly behind her.

"I will be," Hanna said, and the fairy woman nodded.

Hanna looked around the fairy land inside this wandering space station. It troubled her that none of the fairies had come to her aid against Bryson, but then that had also been true in her own realm.

The intersectionality of the dimensions here in the darkness spoke to Hanna's spatial senses, amplifying her magic. She shouldn't have been able to cast a portal that quickly, even such a small one. She could get used to that kind of power.

Besides, she had a job offer, assuming it was still good.

Working for the potion vendor would give Hanna time to recover; time to decide what to do with her beautiful and terrifyingly powerful young boy.

"How about we stay here?" she said.

"Okay," Owen answered. He scritched the leech draped over his shoulders and said, "Will you still buy me a robo-snake? I think Jaame would like a friend."

Hanna shuddered. Her son had been right; somewhere along the line, the leech had become his.

24

———

DARK FATHER

I DIDN'T CRY. I didn't flinch. I barely reacted at all.

Even the soldiers on the bridge—trained clones, grown in vats, raised to be soldiers—exclaimed in horror and shock. How could anyone order the destruction of an entire planet?

But Erith Danaya is more than a warlord to me. He is my father. Not the absent kind. He didn't abandon me and my mother, though every day I wish he had.

Erith raised me. Not in a benevolent way. Not in a way you're grateful for. Not in the way that leads you to want to care for your parent when you've both aged, and they need you more than you need them.

No, Erith dragged my mother and me with him, on his space cruiser. Dragged from planet to planet, unable to escape because anywhere we stopped, we had none of the local currency. No friend. No contacts. Not even enough knowledge of the local geography to know where we could find a hospitable city, anywhere with an embassy that would take us. Protect us.

But then who could protect us from Erith Danaya? He has the Supreme Commandant behind him. No planet in the galaxy is safe from him.

Not even the planet itself; I don't just mean the people.

You see, I know him. So I was not surprised.

After the ensign at the weapons station yelps, she pulls herself together. She is a soldier. And she obeys his order.

Green.

Blue.

The sparkling cities on the crescent of the night side.

They all burn.

Green and blue are lost in a horrifying inferno of orange, yellow, red, and finally brown and gray. Dead rock.

It almost breaks me that the fiery inferno that just engulfed an entire planet—the planet I'd almost escaped to; the planet where I'd hidden my twin toddlers with my mother, hoping like breathing that Erith would never find us—was beautiful.

Oh my god, I'm a monster. I'm just like him. I watched my mother and babies die, and I found the fire they died in—even if for only a split second—beautiful.

I don't deserve to live. I'm just like my father.

And he doesn't deserve to live either.

Erith turns to me in his long, regal, navy blue robes. They swish around his heavily booted feet, and his mouth, visible under the silver visor of the helmet he wears, twists into a grim, self-satisfied smirk.

He's proud of himself for killing a whole planet. For killing my babies. My mother. They're just pawns in a game to him, and he thinks he's won.

"Now tell me," he says, "where are the headquarters of the justice crusaders?"

a while It never can be now...—I had my arm cut off.

I would cut my whole body to pieces if it would bring my home back. I can hardly even understand that the charred rock I'm looking at, only moments ago, was a verdant world, where my mother and daughters hid in a forest by a pond. They can't be gone. It makes no sense. How can someone exist one moment and not exist the next?

How can this be real?

As if in a dream, I activate my robotic arm. The false skin boils away, and with a musical hum that I had hoped to never hear, the laser coils power up.

A beam of light flashes along my arm from shoulder to fingertips. The restraints around my wrist melt away, and the light—blue and cool, like the oceans that no longer cover half of the rock that was moments ago my home— burns through my other hand where the restraints held it too close.

Now I yelp, as I didn't before. I feel my body make the sound before I've even managed to process the pain caus- ing it.

I think my other hand is gone. Oh well. I won't need it

much longer. The soldiers around the room rush to stop me. But they're already too late.

As pain and shock overwhelm my body, I swing my arm.

Before I die, I see him.

Erith Danaya crumples, folds in half, burning and sizzling. Cut down by the blue laser coursing across my robotic arm.

He's dead before I am.

The rest of you will have to sort out the galaxy without me, try to stop anyone else from taking his place and anyone else from using that weapon ever again.

But I did what I could to make it better.

I took him down with me.

25

GRIZZELKA'S BRIDEGROOM

RED LIGHT from the five suns streamed down through the church's stained glass windows. The colored glass of the windows tried vainly to tint the light, to paint pictures with it on the packed pews below, but the redness was too powerful. The intricate, rainbow-filled depictions of many-winged angels and many-mouthed chimera bled together into indiscernible pools of red, orange, auburn, and sickly magenta. The distorted light colored the crowded interior of the church like a crime scene, covered in splattered, congealed blood.

On the dais at the front of the great hall, Rhun's bride stood, resplendent in lace, pearls, ruffles, and diamonds—all of the sugary sweetness of silk and satin that her attendant minions had been able to gather, all of it draped over her bulging tentacles. She looked like an octopus who had choked to death on a rack of wedding dresses. She had never looked more lovely.

Rhun had never felt more scared.

He stood at the end of the aisle, willing himself as powerfully as he could to let himself be seen, but he could not overpower his instinctive vanishing spell. So he stood. Quaking. In his best gray suit, with his long pink hair reaching lankly to his shoulder blades and his gazelle-like horns polished to a black shine. He looked exactly the way the Goddess Grizzelka had asked him to, exactly the way his parents had insisted. All he had to do was drop his vanishing spell and walk down the aisle.

He would be her fourth husband, and his parents assured him that if he were well-behaved—a good, obedient husband—his bride would most likely not eat him. At least, not right away. He could live for years, enjoying the nightly embrace of those tentacles (he thrilled at the thought, unsure if he was terrified or excited) and all of the honor that came with being the Goddess's only living consort.

He should be happy.

But he couldn't make himself seen. No matter how hard he willed himself visible, his quivering body stayed stubbornly invisible. He could not marry the goddess if she could not see him. And even with an eye at the tip of every tentacle (beautiful purple eyes) and a cluster of ten on her belly (glowing yellow eyes that showed through a cut-out in her dress), the goddess could not see through his vanishing spell. No one could.

The red light from the five suns above fell impassively through him.

Rhun sighed and slumped, ready to give up and go, when he suddenly saw one of the guests, sitting in the back pew, sit up straighter. Had she heard his sigh? Over the tinkling harp music?

Harpists played so beautifully when they knew only one of them—the best—would survive the ceremony. The rest would become Grizzelka's wedding feast. Truly, Rhun could not be betrothed to a more terrifying and wonderful (she was wonderful, right? right?) goddess or god in all of the seven underkingdoms.

Yet Grizzelka stood at the front of the church, impatiently checking the gold and platinum timepieces strapped to each of her tentacles, wondering where her bridegroom was... and this woman in the back pew was now staring Rhun directly in his eyes. He pushed the fringe of pink hair back from his face, nervously, and he felt tears spring to the corner of his eyes. Perhaps he was imagining it, but he felt like the woman was looking at him. And he'd never felt so thoroughly seen before.

"Are you okay?" the woman mouthed. Her face was round and plain, her hair brown and dappled like a fawn's. She looked like a dryad more than a demon. A creature of golden sunlight, filtered gently through green leaves, instead of red light blaring down harshly on craggy rocks and lava streams. Was she in the wrong realm?

The woman tilted her head and flared her nostrils. Her brown eyes were unfocused—staring at him but maybe not seeing him. Rhun realized she could smell him. She could probably smell the fear on him. He most likely reeked of it. The woman stood up, gestured surreptitiously toward the entrance to the church, right behind Rhun, and then she slipped out, without any of the other guests noticing her.

Rhun followed. The guests didn't notice him either. Impatient as they were, they did not expect and could not see a groom so frightened by his bride that he'd been overcome by his own instinctive vanishing spell.

Outside the church, Rhun shed his gray linen suit jacket and pulled off the pink silk tie that perfectly matched his hair. He dropped both offending articles of fancy clothing on the stone steps and felt freer with every step he took away from the life that had been prescribed for him.

Twisting spires of purple and blue crystal surrounded the church, a veritable forest of them. The church had clearly been built at the base of the valley beside the crystal spires for the location's natural beauty. The valley was much cooler than most of the surrounding mountains, protected as it was from the blistering breezes that wafted from the three nearest volcanoes.

Rhun frowned. The woman he'd been following was gone. She'd given him the courage, the prompting he'd needed to walk out on his own wedding. But she had left him alone. Between two spires at the edge of the crystal forest stood a raptor, half Rhun's height and covered in brown feathers—soft and speckled like a fawn's. The raptor tilted its head, and Rhun recognized the movement. The raptor was the woman. She was a shifter. Or a were-raptor. Either way, her presence in this demonic realm made much more sense now. A dryad would burn up, burst into flame in a realm such as this one, filled with so much fire and evil. Glorious evil. Except, Rhun wasn't so sure anymore. Evil had sounded more glorious to him when he wasn't standing before it, promised to be married to it, and expecting to be eaten by it if he ever stepped out of line. Evil is so much more exciting in the abstract.

Rhun wished he were a little boy again with only nubs of horns on his forehead and harmless dreams of tentacled goddesses filling his head, instead of beautiful spiraling horns that could not protect him and a tentacled goddess actually awaiting him. Grizzelka would not be forgiving of a bridegroom who ran away. If she planned to eat him eventually as her husband, nothing would stop her from eating him as a coward who couldn't even go through with marrying her.

Rhun's resolve almost failed him. His knees grew weak, and he nearly turned around to run up the aisle to the loving death that awaited him. A death that would wait longer if he faced her straight on. Courageously. As she would want him to. As his parents—the Nor-Eastern Zephyra and her favorite satyr—wanted him to.

Courage failed him. Rhun followed the raptor-shifter, leaving the church and his prescribed fate behind. He followed her into the crystal forest, and she led him on a path that descended into a hole, most likely burrowed by a giant grub, and through a twisting warren of passageways. They came to a hub room with portals to seven of the seventy realms. The portals swirled on the walls of the cave-like room; gold and silver pools that pulled the eye toward them, begging the viewer to reach out and touch.

Rhun knew there were hub rooms hidden all over the realm, but he'd only seen one of them once before—when his parents brought him from his birth realm to this one as a child before his horns came in. He remembered feeling compelled to touch the portal and then being shocked, frightened, and confused when the silver-gold surface had sucked him in. He'd assumed the compulsion to touch had been a child's whimsy, but now he felt the same compulsion and recognized the spell-power behind it. The dark magic.

The raptor shifted back to her humanoid form, like a reflection disturbed and distorted on the surface of a rippling brook. "You looked like you needed an escape—a chance to think and talk," she said. "I know somewhere we can go." She stepped up to one of the portals with a coppery cast to its swirls. Strangely, it was the portal that Rhun felt least compelled to reach out and touch.

"Who are you?" Rhun asked. He hadn't known half of the demons and angels at his own wedding, but most of them made sense with their arching bat wings and cow horns and visages of cut glass, so beautiful and horrible that merely looking upon them could make you fall to your knees. This woman-raptor was so... natural. She didn't fit. Yet she felt familiar. Safe somehow. And even though she shook her head, refusing to answer his question, he followed her into the coppery swirls of the portal.

On the other side, Rhun expected to find green trees and dappled yellow sunlight. A wooded glade with rivulets of blue water and doe-eyed forest animals, songbirds filling the air with music that didn't carry the underpinnings of fear, the strain of musicians expecting their host to gobble them up using her grasping, choking, strangling tentacles.

Rhun felt the thrill of fear (or excitement?) again as he remembered Grizzelka's ash-gray tentacles, bursting out of the lacy white wedding dress that could not constrain them. She was voluptuous.

Instead of a pleasant meadow or forest glade, Rhun found himself in a dingy, dark beer pub, crammed full of rowdy revelers and reeking of yeast, sassafras, and cheese. Not at all what he had expected, but it answered a calling in his soul he'd never listened to before. He'd never been allowed to.

The woman slipped through the crowd, up to the bar, and shouted something to the bartender. Rhun couldn't hear her over the noise of the crowd. But the bartender gave her two tankards of mead, and she brought them—one in each fist—over to a small, round table in the corner. Rhun joined her, took the second tankard, and sipped the pungent liquid. He'd never drunk alcohol before. He'd had to stay pure for Grizzelka. The fizzy, warm liquid tickled his tongue, glowed in his belly, and buzzed right up to his brain. He felt light headed. Almost dizzy. But free.

Across from him, the woman smiled and said, "My

name is Iuscae. We knew each other as children."

"In my birth realm," Rhun said. He'd been so young when he left, he barely remembered it. He certainly didn't remember her.

"In Cloriander," Iuscae corrected, and Rhun felt a flash of shame that he didn't even know the name of the realm where he'd been born. He'd lived all of his life awaiting today, training for today, learning the ways to be a pleasing husband to the great Goddess Grizzelka.

Iuscae drank deeply from her tankard, and Rhun marveled at her ability to hold her alcohol. She was shorter than him but not as skeletally thin. She was probably used to drinking; she probably hadn't been sheltered the way Rhun had been.

Rhun couldn't imagine drinking so deeply from his tankard; it would rise straight to his brain and knock him right off his feet. He was sure of it. Yet, Rhun took another sip and let the pleasant warmth lift his spirits. Grizzelka was going to eat him, and he would be nothing more than a snack, not an honorable meal. He'd be eaten without ceremony. Without candles and a fine silver platter. No tablecloth. No table even, probably. Just swallowed whole, as if he were nothing more than a harpist who hadn't played beautifully enough.

Maybe he needed another sip of the warm mead. Or maybe not. Maybe its warmth wasn't lifting his spirits after all...

Why had he run away? Why had he ruined his life? He'd never know the sublime pain and pleasure of being eaten in tiny bites, pulled apart by tentacles stronger than he could imagine gripping him with sucker disks like a million tiny kisses.

"I'm ruined," Rhun said.

"You're free," Iuscae countered. "Did you really want to be the consort to the Goddess Grizzelka?"

Rhun didn't know what else he could be, but instead of saying so, he drank deeply from the tankard of mead. His head grew foggy, and he felt himself growing translucent, vanishing again. This beer pub with its endless possibilities frightened him as badly as Grizzelka with her one, clear path.

"Free," Rhun repeated sadly. "I don't know what that means."

Iuscae shrugged, leaned back, and put her feet up on the seat of an empty chair. A waiter brought a platter of fried and greasy foods to their table. Apparently, Iuscae had ordered them when she was at the bar. "I bet you've never eaten calamari," she said, lifting a breaded circle from a paper-lined basket. The red-and-white checked paper was stained with grease.

Iuscae was right. Rhun had never eaten such base, plebeian food. He'd been fed water-rush salads and boiled greens, fetched from other realms for him. He'd been kept trim and fit. Healthy as can be. He reached into the basket and took one of the greasy loops of calamari. It crunched and squished between his teeth, and the greasy flavor exploded on his tongue. So rich. So salty. "It's delicious."

"Squid tentacles," Iuscae said with a devilish grin. She'd

never looked more like she belonged among the demons still waiting for him at his wedding.

Rhun hoped they still waited. Maybe... If he left now, he could slip back into the church and down the aisle. His indiscretion would go unnoticed. And he could continue his life as it had been meant to be.

"So you like them," Iuscae said. "The taste of freedom." She popped several more of the tiny, breaded tentacles into her mouth. A perversion of the natural order. She was a temptress.

And Rhun was tempted.

He tried the snacks from each of the other baskets—fried cheese, fried jalapeños, fried shrimp. Everything fried. Everything delicious. But the calamari was the best, and with every bite, the squish between his teeth reminded him of his betrothed.

He was meant to squish between her teeth—the red-lipped mouth on her face and the maw on her belly, under the cluster of ten yellow eyes, and also the beaked mouth hidden between her tentacles. She was a glorious hybrid of creatures, and the more he imagined staying here, the more he longed for her.

"You're thinking about going back," Iuscae said. She shook her head. "Do you know how long a demi-mortal like you can live for? If he isn't eaten?"

Rhun did not know. His education hadn't included information like that. Information that would be useless to him.

"Thousands of years." She mouthed the words, barely whispering them.

Rhun couldn't even imagine what to do with all of that time. And he wasn't sure why Iuscae cared. "How did you come to be at my wedding?" he asked.

Iuscae's face rippled, fading from woman to raptor again. In her feathered therapod form, all of her softness was revealed as nothing but a cloak over sharp teeth and curved claws. She was a predator, and Rhun was prey. An antelope; a gazelle; a herd-animal separated from his herd.

The beer pub was filled with demi-mortals—satyrs, dryads, taurs, and less recognizable creatures. In many ways, they were more like Rhun than the demons and angels at his wedding—full immortals. But he'd had a place among them. Here he was alone in a crowd.

The waiter came to the table again, this time bearing a single plate of chipped, off-white china: a tentacled delicacy glistened upon it. Ash-gray tentacles, speckled with black, as much like Grizzelka's own tentacles as any simple squid's could be. Garnished with lemon and cilantro.

"I will not eat that," Rhun said.

"You don't have to," Iuscae said. She unwrapped a fork from a dingy, sky-blue, cloth napkin. She speared one of the tentacles, lifted it to her angular muzzle and slurped it into her toothy mouth with the aid of a long, serpentine tongue. "You don't have to do anything that you don't want." She gobbled up several more tentacles. "But you should know—they are delicious. Better than the fried ones. More succulent."

Rhun turned his face away. He had run from his fate out of fear, but he would not pervert the natural order of the universe. He watched the patrons of the bar, and he tried to picture living among them. Could he be a bartender? A dryad and satyr in the corner were playing darts. Would he play darts?

Rhun rose from his seat without thinking and let his feet carry him to the beer pub's front door. He opened it and looked outside—the pub was in a forest, but not the picturesque glade he'd imagined, nor the stark crystal forest they'd come from. The forest here was dark and dank, dripping with spider webs, and he saw eyes—tiny, pale eyes—peeking out at him from the thick crowns of all the trees.

Iuscae came up behind Rhun and whispered in his ear, "There are other realms. You could spend lifetimes exploring them." She flapped her downy raptor wings, showing their speckled under-feathers. She was glorious. Different from the Goddess Grizzelka, but glorious too. Rhun had always loved birds, all sorts of birds, especially prehistoric ones. "You could explore them with me." She could be his home. She began telling him about all the realms she could take him to—mushroom forests, asteroid fields stretched across the velvety blackness of space, ice castles, oceans with iridescent blue-green waves. There were so many.

But Rhun had a home, among the purple and blue

crystal spires in Grizzelka's realm. Inside the pearl and marble palace she'd built for him, and him alone, filled with silk pillows in his favorite colors and oil paintings of him on the walls, attendants trained to play his favorite music and prepare his favorite meals, all under the lava red sky. It was time to go home.

Rhun turned back toward the tavern, and he saw Iuscae's toothy grin, too close to his delicate neck for comfort. Would she rip out his throat and eat him if he refused her offer? The Goddess Grizzelka would. Rhun couldn't risk crossing her. "I'll go with you," he said, telling her what she clearly wanted to hear. "But..." He needed a ploy that would get him back home. "...take me back to the church to get my nuptial bag. It has my clothes and toiletries in it."

"I can buy you new ones." Her teeth were so sharp, and they had none of the voluptuous softness of Grizzelka's tentacles.

"I want my own," Rhun said. He stared Iuscae down, unflinching and unwavering. He had something to fight for. Eventually, the raptor woman relented.

Iuscae took Rhun by the hand. In her raptor form, her hand was a scaly talon at the end of her feathered wing-arm. Nonetheless, she curled her scaly talon gently around Rhun's hand, and she led him back through the crowd of the bar to the coppery disc of the portal. Together they stepped through. This time, Rhun felt the magnetic pull—Grizzelka's realm called to him through the portal, calling him back home.

Without Iuscae leading the way, Rhun would have been lost in the underground tunnels beneath the crystal spire forest for hours before he found the church of his wedding again. Following her feathered tail, with the downy feathers splayed out like a fan, Rhun found his way to the church before the wedding guests—and his bride— had given up hope.

As he peeked through the doors, Rhun could see that the scene in the church was much the same as when he had left. Demons and angels shifted impatiently in their seats, forked tails twitching and folded wings straining against the constrained space in the pews.

In the cracked open doorway, Iuscae leaned in close to Rhun and whispered, "Do you want to slip inside invisibly again?" She looked him up and down. He was not invisible. "Or if you tell me where your things are, I can get them. While you stay out here."

"I'll get them," Rhun said. His vanishing spell flushed over him, sending him into transparency long enough for Iuscae to step back. The warmth of her breath, implying the sharpness of her teeth, withdrew from Rhun's neck, and he stepped confidently into the church's main sanctuary. This time, his vanishing spell dissipated as soon as the red light from the stained glass windows above touched the tips of his gazelle-like horns. Their polished, burnished twists gleamed in the light. He walked down the aisle, too quickly, out of beat with the harp music— thinner than it had been before, as some of the harps stood on the dais un-played, abandoned by their musicians who had likely already been eaten—that sprang into a lilting rhythm to invite the bridegroom to approach his bride.

Each twinkling note of music twanged against Rhun's heart like the promise of a kiss from one of Grizzelka's tentacles. He hoped he was not too late. He hoped, when he reached the dais, she would marry him and make him her celebrated husband, rather than a meaningless snack. She couldn't know his indiscretion? His attempt to run away? Could she?

Yet as Rhun stepped up on the dais beside Grizzelka, he saw a gleam in the cluster of yellow eyes on her belly, a knowing gleam. Three of her ash-gray tentacles reached toward him, and Rhun flinched, shying away. He was ready to marry her; he was not ready to be eaten. But the tentacles stretched cautiously, gently, until just the narrow tips with their purple eyes touched his hand, lifted his hand, and pulled him, so lightly that it was more of a request than a demand, toward her.

A request from a goddess. Rhun stepped close, and Grizzelka whispered to him. "You've come to me willingly."

Rhun whispered back, "Of course."

"No," Grizzelka said. "Not of course." She turned her head toward the crowd of angels and demons watching them. In the back of the church, Iuscae still leaned against the wide wooden doors to the church. The raptor winked at him, and then she nodded at Grizzelka. "You always had a choice, and I made sure you considered it."

"You knew—" Rhun began.

The maw on Grizzelka's belly twisted into a mysterious smile, and the lips on her face mirrored the expression. "You had doubts, and you needed to explore them. Now you come to me of your own free will, as it should be."

Iuscae had been working for Grizzelka the whole time. She was a temptress sent to test Rhun's devotion.

He had passed the test.

"You always know," Rhun breathed. He squeezed the three tentacle tips still wrapped tenderly around his hand. The ash-gray flesh squished and then squeezed back. He lowered his head, feeling unworthy to look upon Grizzelka's greatness. "You know everything worth knowing, and you know me better than I know myself. You are my goddess. I worship you."

"Say that again," Grizzelka said. "The last part. And louder."

"I worship you," Rhun repeated, his voice raised to where the words echoed through the sanctuary of the church.

"And I," Grizzelka said in a voice like a thousand snakes hissing as they crawled out of the depths of hell, "accept your worship." Her slithery voice filled the church with deafening power. "You are my husband."

Tears sprang to Rhun's eyes as relief and gratitude flushed through his body like a fever breaking. He had fulfilled his destiny. He was home.

The goddess Grizzelka reached five more tentacles

toward her bridegroom and enfolded his body in an embrace. She drew him against her, and then she dipped him backward into a passionate kiss. As her mouth engulfed his, each tentacle wrapped around his body and kissed against him with their multitudinous sucker disks in a gentle softness, promising years of love to come before he finally became a ceremonial meal to be deeply, slowly, and luxuriously enjoyed as he filled her belly. He would be a part of her greatness forever.

26

DIAMOND DUST HEART

DOWN AT THE PRECINCT, we'd been calling the big crime lord in town Diamond Dust, because that was our only lead. Whenever the big busts went down, the only clues left behind were microscopic traces of the expensive substance. Most of my fellow detectives thought Diamond Dust was an addict, hooked on smoking the stuff. But none of us had any luck tracking Diamond Dust down through the trafficking patterns of the illicit drug. I had a different theory.

Most of my colleagues are organics. Sure, there's another android down in accounting. But I'm the only synthetic sentient on the detective floor. So, I had to be careful. Especially with a theory like the one I'd been developing... See, I know that there are several different methods for constructing the mechanical battery that powers an android—our hearts, if you will. One of them involves a reservoir of galvanized diamond dust.

I don't have a diamond dust heart. Too expensive. I was built in a basement by a lonely old roboticist who'd never had a daughter. She built me to be her Pinocchio. Joke's on her—I was so real that I ran away from home, got mixed up with a gang, and then swept into the police force as part of a Last Chances program. I never looked back. But I expect I caused Dear Old Mom as much heartbreak as any organic daughter ever could have. Dreams do come true!

Anyway, diamond dust batteries shouldn't leave behind traces of diamond dust. But one could, if it were leaking.

My theory was that the whole police department was being led in circles by an android with a leaking heart. A very expensive android. You can see why I wouldn't want to share that theory, being an android myself.

Best case scenario, my colleagues all laugh at me. Worst case, they decide I can't be trusted, because apparently, androids have a propensity for becoming mob bosses. This is the problem with being the only one of your kind around. You're always the example. Win or lose, you don't do it for yourself; you do it for everyone of your kind. And they can all lose and drag you down too.

That's why I hatched a plan. I can sense microscopic traces of diamond dust with chemical spectralyzers in my nostrils. Yes, I can literally sniff out tracks of diamond dust. Most of my colleagues need to check a bulky spectralyzer wand out from the supplies division. But I was able to throw a trench coat on over my spiky back (the way that my mechanical plating comes together gives the back of my body a hunched, irregular quality; I don't like to talk about it) and sniff my way through town like a dog.

I didn't want any of my colleagues to know I had this power, because they already give me enough trouble about my slightly elongated face, almost muzzle-like, without knowing I can sniff footprints out like a bloodhound.

Sometimes, I simply don't know what my mother was thinking when she designed me. Wouldn't life be hard enough as an android without a weirdly hunched back, muzzle-like snout, and super-human senses?

I shake my head. But I keep pounding the pavement, waiting for the bright and tingly scent of diamond dust. I don't hit pay dirt until I make it out to the docks. Where else, right? So, I skulk around the various piers, waiting until after dark when I can slip into the warehouse with the strongest diamond dust smell without having to flash my badge.

The sunset is glorious. I don't know what it looks like to human eyes, but to my own mechanical eyes, the spectrum of hues along the horizon, reflected in the wine-dark ocean, is pure poetry. Times like this, I wonder why I became a cop instead of staying in school, keeping out of that gang, and learning what I would have needed in order to become a poet or a painter... Someone who creates beauty instead of someone who hunts down ugliness. Seeks the darkness out.

The sun finishes setting, and I slip into the warehouse.

The tingly, bright scent of diamond dust tickles my nose so strongly in here that I know I've either tracked down a major drug deal... Or Diamond Dust is here.

I draw my zapper from the holster at my side and hold it in front of me, wary. Ready. I follow the scent to a back room, behind a row of mechanical monsters—the kind of sub-sentient mechas that were all decommissioned after the last war. The mechas loom over me, ancient metal constructs who bear about as much resemblance to me as dinosaur skeletons do to humans. Except humans love their dinosaur skeletons. These mechanical monsters creep me out. I know humans would stow me away in an abandoned warehouse like this in a heartbeat if they decided androids had a predilection towards crime.

I hope to whatever gods out there who would listen to an android like me that behind the door to this backroom, I'll find a motherlode of drugs and not an android with a dark and leaky heart.

I kick the door open, aim my zapper into the room and shout, "Hands up!"

Behind a desk, leaning back with his feet up, cool and relaxed, sits a bulky metalloid man. An android. But he's not humanoid—his face is long and narrow; his hind legs are thick, and his arms are short; he has three horns—two on his brow and one extending from his nose. He looks a little like a metal dinosaur wearing a pinstripe suit.

"What the hell are you?" I ask, angry and worried. This is my worst fear realized. If I take him down and take him in, the force will congratulate me at first. But then they'll grow cold. Distant. Calculating. They'll wonder how long it will take me to turn into a mobster like this man. Unless, maybe… he's not like me? I don't have horns. I am not a dinosaur.

"You finally caught up with me," the man says. He hasn't put his hands up. His arms aren't long enough to hold his hands above his head even if he did.

His arms aren't long enough for me to cuff his hands together with normal handcuffs. I'll have to rig together two pairs. Who the hell would design an android like him?

Then he answers the question in my heart by saying, "It's nice to meet you, little sis."

I lower my zapper, realizing what I've known all along: I may have been mother's first daughter, but I was not her first child. I was the child she could afford to make after my more expensive older brother ran off. Finally I understand the shape of my muzzle, the spikes on my back.

Mother always did love dinosaurs.

"Are you ready to join the family business?" he asks. "We can run this town together."

Who am I to fight fate?

Besides, he's family.

27

STING ONCE AND DIE

Selina knelt in the middle of the empty Hamilton Middle School room. She'd pushed the desks and chairs up against the walls, leaving the floor clear for the bull's eye pattern she'd drawn with salt. The only light came from the soft cold glow of the moon behind the shuttered windows and a flickering warm radiance from the ring of candles around the outer edge of the bull's eye. In the middle, the very middle, she carefully placed the brittle body of a dead bumblebee on the circle of salt. She had considered using a wasp, but she was looking for justice, not vengeance. A solution, not escalation.

Selina traced her finger tips through the carefully drawn concentric circles of salt, drawing the simple pattern into complex spirals. All the while, she chanted. Nonsense syllables in a sing-song voice, tripped over her tongue, spilling out the anguish and pain she'd felt. The terror. She was tired of living in terror. What had been lost could not be brought back, but she could end the cycle.

The silver moonlight flickered, as if the entire moon were a candle and someone had breathed too closely to it. And the candlelight steadied. A fairy appeared, the size of a small child, maybe five or six, with translucent wings and bobbed hair, like one of the Beatles. The students who had died in this room were so young, they might not have even known who the Beatles were... Selina choked back the tears that always lived on the edge of her eyes now.

The fairy looked almost painfully precious, wearing a black and yellow striped leotard with a lemon colored tutu. "This is an interesting form you've chosen." The fairy's voice was high and clear. There was no way to tell its gender.

"Bees sting once," Selina said. "Then they die."

"True," the fairy observed, flapping zir wings very slowly. "It's a very powerful spell. It will need a blood sacrifice."

Selina laughed—one bitter barking sound that lacerated her throat with its suddenness.

The room was drenched in blood.

Sure, the floor, the walls, the desks—they'd all been cleaned. Thoroughly. But the blood would always be there. The fairy looked around, nodded once, and said, "Oh, I see. Well, then, the price is paid." The words were spoken by a face that looked too young to make such a serious proclamation.

Before Selina could thank the fairy or change her mind and plead to take the spell back, the moonlight steadied; the candlelight flickered; and the fairy and the dead bumblebee were gone. Selina swept up the salt and returned the desks and chairs to their usual, orderly rows.

* * *

ALL OVER THE COUNTRY, scrabbling, scraping sounds appeared inside gun safes.

Those gun owners, the cautious, conscientious, careful ones, who had kept their guns in metal boxes, locked up tight, were the lucky ones; they had time to find out about the effects of Selina's spell, and time to dispose of their guns safely.

But in many households, there was no metal box protecting the legal owner of a toy meant for murder from the consequences of their foolish choice.

The country dripped with blood. But this time, it wasn't the blood of innocents. That's what Selina told herself as she watched the news roll in, sitting on her bed, staring at her phone, unable or unwilling to look away from the horror, shaking and sobbing, and listening to the scraaaatching, scrrr-rrr-raabbling, scraaaaping sounds inside her own gun safe.

These were the birth pains of a better nation. One without guns.

But Selina didn't know if she could handle the blood, on her hands this time, long enough to see the results. That's why she'd bought the gun and safe.

Selina clicked on story after story about right-wing extremists shot hundreds of times by their hoarder-like stockpiles turning on them. But there were also stories about women who'd bought a single gun, ostensibly for safety in spite of what all the studies show: guns don't make you safer. And Selina's heart ached for them.

She reached for the biometric safe, unlocked it with her fingerprint, and then watched the creature inside—spiky with gunmetal gray fur and fast with its six stubby legs—emerge from the darkness within, seeking its legal owner like a heat-seeking missile. That was her.

The gun's mouth was round like an O. For a beat, Selina stared at it, and the creature stared back. Then with a bang, it was over.

One sting and dead. Both of them. Owner and gun.

28

THE WERE-RAPTOR AND THE SEAMSTRESS ROBOT

ANGIE AND TYLER'S hands touched the green-gold brass of the magic lamp at the same time. The metal was slick with creek water, and they had to dig away the mud and wet moss that had half buried the lamp using their bare hands. Their fingers smeared the mud, leaving their hands and the lamp dirty. Someone must have thrown it into this creek, deep in the woods, years ago.

Angie and Tyler had strayed from the trail hours ago, and Angie kept oscillating between feeling thrilled to be alone with him in the forest... and terrified that she was making a dangerous mistake. She and Tyler had only been dating a few months. He seemed perfect and kind, but she knew that abusive men used a honeymoon period to lure their girlfriends in and then isolate them. Right now, they were pretty isolated.

Still, how many men would dig up old junk in the forest with her and pretend it was a magical treasure?

Most adults didn't seem to remember how to play and have fun. Tyler did. She loved that about him.

Both Tyler and Angie washed their hands off in the cold creek water, and when the brass lamp looked as good as it was going to—still rusty and mis-colored—Tyler said, "Shall we make a wish?"

Angie smiled. "Yeah, we should. What would you wish for?"

"You first," Tyler said, sitting down on a big sun-baked boulder beside the creek. Angie perched on a smaller rock beside it.

"Okay..." she said. "You won't laugh?"

"I won't laugh." He held one hand up, palm out, as if he were solemnly swearing.

Angie tugged at the edge of her hiking shorts, slightly shorter and tighter than she'd like, and she straightened the t-shirt that had always been too boxy for her but now was also a little too tight. She didn't want to get a larger one, because that would involve admitting that she needed a bigger size. And there were far fewer fun t-shirts in the next size up. "I want a seamstress robot."

"A what?"

"You know, like, a robot that can measure me and sew clothes that fit absolutely perfectly. Sort of like a cross between a 3D fabric printer and... well, a really, really good tailor."

Tyler didn't laugh, but his mouth quirked kind of like he was tasting a lemon. "Can't you just go buy clothes? Or order them online?"

It was easy for him to think that, sitting there in his jeans and shirt, made from fabric several times thicker than the flimsy stuff used for women's clothes, that came in sizes measured in inches instead of a numbering system come up with by Cthulhu. Shopping for clothes in stores took hours, and the selection was so limited... And when Angie ordered stuff online, it was like playing roulette. Half of the time, the object that arrived looked nothing like she'd ordered, and sure, she could send it back, but that takes time too. And it was demoralizing. Trying on clothes that were too tight in all kinds of random places and too baggy in others? Ugh. It was Angie's least favorite activity.

"Besides, you already have a lot of clothes that you look good in." Tyler grinned in the way that Angie always felt like she was supposed to feel was a loving compliment... but somehow felt more like a leer.

"They're too tight," Angie mumbled.

Tyler laughed. "Yeah, that's why they look so good. But I mean, if you really want a seamstress... couldn't you just do it yourself?"

"Sewing takes a lot of time," Angie said. She tugged at her shirt again, wishing it didn't show the exact curve of her breasts and belly underneath it so well.

Tyler shrugged. He didn't care about Angie's time.

"Yeah, whatever, what would you wish for?"

Tyler's grin shifted into the one he got whenever he knew he was about to be really, really clever: "I'd wish we were both were-velociraptors who could shift back and forth at will!"

"That would be pretty cool..." Angie admitted. Although, she couldn't help thinking that it would be even harder to find clothes that fit her then.

Suddenly, the light shifted as if the sun had come out from behind a cloud, but the angles were all wrong. Angie realized that the new light was coming from the lamp, and it glowed brighter and brighter, until it left a sunspot shape in her vision. When her eyes cleared, a lumpy, curvy green-skinned woman with bulbous eyes and a wide, wide mouth like a frog stood... well, hovered... since her extremities kind of disappeared into a green mist... before them.

"You only get one wish," the genie said. "You touched my lamp at the exact same time, so you have to share it. Figure out what you're wishing for, and *agree* on it."

"Uh..." Tyler looked stunned. But he recovered quickly. "The velociraptor one, right?" He glanced cursorily at Angie, not really long enough to see her reaction. "You said that was cool. We both like that one."

Angie was having trouble believing what she was looking at. And shouldn't they be wishing for world peace or something? But somehow, she found herself saying, "Okay..." She did that, when she knew Tyler wanted her to say "okay;" she often started to say it before really thinking through what she wanted for herself. It wasn't her favorite thing about herself, but it was a habit she didn't know how to break.

"Granted," the genie said. She turned her wide, bulbous face toward Angie and said, "Now get rid of him."

Angie felt her body shifting, rearranging, changing shape: her legs grew thicker and more curved. Her butt extruded out into a long, balancing tail. Her face lengthened, and her toes grew giant claws. And her instincts sharpened inside her belly. She felt the slow boil of anger that she was always pushing down bubble over, and her right leg shot out, extending a claw that sliced across Tyler's neck before he had finished changing.

Tyler fell into the creek, blood spilling around him, looking like a science experiment gone wrong. Something from a bad b-movie. Half-lizard, half human with a giant pocket knife clutched in his talon-hand. Where had that come from? In his rush to pull it out of his pocket, he seemed to have spilled a pile of white plastic sticks on the ground... zip ties.

Angie shuddered. She looked at her reflection in the creek. Tilted her head. She was a gorgeous velociraptor. She felt so strong. And then—completely under her own control—she shifted back into human form. Her clothes were shredded, ripped and distended.

"Now," the genie said, "tell me more about this seamstress robot."

"I thought we'd used up our wishes..." Angie kept herself from looking back at the creek. She didn't want to see Tyler, dead and half-transformed, with her human eyes. She wasn't as fierce in human form. Even if she was pretty sure that the genie had just saved her life. She couldn't believe that she'd been so stupid as to come out here with Tyler. Somehow, all the clues she'd been ignoring for months—stories about his previous girlfriends who were all crazy bitches who'd mysteriously ghosted on him after he'd brought them out here—had been impossible to push aside in velociraptor form.

"Look, you may not have any more wishes, but I can still do magic for myself. And I'm sick of living alone in a lamp at the edge of a creek, abandoned deep in the forest. So, bring me home with you, and well, I'll see what I can do."

Angie already had some ideas for flowy tops and stretchy waistbands that wouldn't be ripped apart by her tail when she shifted into raptor form. "Sure," she said. She picked up the lamp and tied it onto the shreds of her clothes that had survived her transformation, and then she transformed back.

Angie ran through the forest, talking to the froggy genie woman floating beside her, and they cooked up plans for a wonderful life together, full of practical robots and comfortable, well-fitting clothes.

29

SAFE HERE IN CREST CITY

@UnicornGirl231: O MUH GOD i jus saw a zombie eating sumone's arm and the ARM FELL OFF #zombiesarereal #zombiesarehere #evenincrestcity

@KarenCane: You're in Crest City? How do you know it was a zombie?

@LiteralGhost1: Is the zombie virus airborn? Will a mask protect me? Do I need to hold my breath around zombies? Maybe I'll just stay inside...

@UnicornGirl231: If you smell them it's too late for you. Ruuuuuuuun.

. . .

@LiteralGhost1: If it's already too late, shouldn't you just kill yourself instead of risking infecting more people by running around like a chicken with its head cut off?

@UnicornGirl231: Ruuuuuuuuuuuuuuuun

@DudgerDailyGazette: 13 STUDENTS IN DUDGER CITY COLLEGE DORMS HOLD A ZOMB-KISS PARTY, 3 EATEN, 2 TURNED... SO FAR

@KarenCane: Who the hell even wants to kiss a zombie?????

@GiveMeFr33dom: You will not stop me from kissing who I want! Goddamn libs wanted it this way, and now they gotta live with it! Im kissin first zomb I see that's halfway attractive

@AltRightIsAlright: Rather kiss a zombie than a libtard snoflake!

@LiteralGhost1: Yeah, well, I don't think a lot of liberals want to kiss you either, AltRight. Besides shouldn't you be out there shooting zombies with your precious guns? Not kissing them?

@AltRightIsAlright: I can shoot an kiss zombies both ifn I want! You cant stop me!

@MickTheRick: They don't tell you that you can smell the zombies. Ugh. Why don't they ever tell you that? Crest City reeks, and that's just from the wind blowing their scent in from Dudger, 20 miles away.

@MickTheRick: How fast can zombies travel?

@MickTheRick: Is it safe to go to sleep tonight?

@MickTheRick: Where do we get evac info for the Crest City/Dudger area?

@KarenCane: Just lock your doors and windows. Leave your lights off. Zombies aren't smart enough to break in.

. . .

@MICKTHERICK: Excuse you, but I watched my mom die, slowly, rotting to pieces, behind a glass window in the local hospital. I couldn't give her a last hug. She didn't even understand me as I said goodbye. So don't spread dangerous misinformation like that zombies won't break into your house if you keep the lights off. They broke into my mom's house, and she was as quiet and careful as can be. Now I don't have a mom. Just horrible memories.

@LITERALGHOST1: Yeah... you're mom did SOMETHING to attract the zombies. They don't bother breaking into empty looking houses for no reason. They're not smart enough to imagine someone might be hiding. They're like trexes in Jurassic Park—drawn to noise and light.

@MICKTHERICK: You calling my mom stupid or me a liar? Cause I'm telling you THEY BROKE IN. SHE WAS QUIET AS A MOUSE. NO LIGHTS. NOTHIN.

@LITERALGHOST1: Like she didn't turn on her phone and check Tweeter? Riiiiiiight. They prob saw her phone screen glowing. Sorry. Your mom was probably nice and didn't deserve it. But she was not smart and not careful. Zombies eat sloppy people. That's that.

. . .

@KarenCane: Oh god I can't sleep. Just keep checking Tweeter to see how close the horde of zombies are...

@DudgerDailyGazette: PACK A ZOMBIE ESCAPE PLAN BACKPACK! BE READY!

@DudgerDailyGazette: WHICH FRIENDS WOULD YOU LET SHELTER INSIDE WITH YOU? AND WHICH WOULD YOU LOCK OUTSIDE WITH THE ZOMBIES???

@DudgerDailyGazette: THE TOP TEN ITEMS TO KEEP AT HAND WHEN THE ZOMBIES GET TO YOUR TOWN—AND NO, THEY'RE NOT ALL AXES AND FLAMETHROWERS!

@JoannaFreeFall: Feelin real lucky to live in Crest city today—most bigger towns got wiped out by the alien saucers back at Christmas and any town smaller doesn't have the resources to keep the zombies at bay. #Blessed #CrestCityBestCity #CrestCity4Evah

@GiveMeFr33dom: CREST CITY IS GON!!! ALL

RESIDENTS ARE ZOMBIESSSS!!!! DO NOT GO THERE!!!!!

@JoannaFreeFall: Um... I don't know where you get your news, but I live in Crest City, and in case you haven't noticed, I have better grammar and punctuation that you do. So, uh, yeah. Not a zombie. I call fake news.

@AltRightIsAlright: OH NO ZOMBIES CAN USE TWEETER NOW

@JoannaFreeFall: *Hangs head and le sigh* Some people. (Would almost be better off as zombies...)

@KarenCane: I think he's a bot. Don't feed the bots.

@MickTheRick: Great. Zombies in the physical world and bots in the digital one. Those alien saucer ships should have wiped us all out.

@AltRightIsAlright: Not a bot. And not gonna let the zombies get me like they got YOUR MOM, MICK. Gotz my AR15 in one hand and a flamethrower in the other. Zombies can kiss my ass. And so can you.

@UnicornGirl231: DO NOT USE FLAME THROWERS ON ZOMBIES. GOD the whole west coast is in high fire alert, do you want forest fires AND zombies??!! Just use guns like god intended.

@UnicornGirl231: Goddamnit I'm serious. If you kill one zombie with a flamethrower and it burns your house down, WHERE RE UOU GONNA HID FROM THE OTHER ZOMBIES!!!!???

@DudgerDailyGazette: 5 SIMPLE STEPS TO BUILD YOUR OWN ANTI-ZOMBIE FLAMETHROWER FROM SIMPLE HOUSEHOLD OBJECTS

@DudgerDailyGazette: Breaking news: Crest City burned down by wave of flaming zombies

30

EIGHT WAYS

BLAKE HAD HEARD octopuses were smart, but it was hard to believe, looking at the blurring mass of muscle. He scooped the hand net into the cold water of the storage cell, like a plastic tub set into the deck of his small fishing boat. Tentacles writhed in a squirming reddish brown mass below. He couldn't even make out a single individual creature in there. Just limbs. Squishy, slippery limbs.

A tentacle wrapped around his wrist, kissing his skin in the funny way of a vacuum sucking against your palm. He tried to shake it off, but another tentacle reached up and looped around his wrist, a little higher than the other. Suddenly, he noticed a pair of eyes looking up at him— Halloween orange with black bars for irises, much like a goat's. There was a mark between the eyes; a jagged scar. He'd seen that scar before.

"Look at all the good it did you to escape." Blake

laughed. "Ornery little morsel. Right back into the frying pan for you."

The scarred octopus was the only one that had ever escaped from the kitchen at Eight Ways, by squirting water at Dave, the head chef, and then slipping its way across the tile floor, over the counter, and out an open window.

This time, the scarred octopus was prepared and had friends. Tentacles kept wrapping around Blake's arm, sucking and releasing, using their sucker discs to climb higher and higher. Up his arm, to his shoulder. Blake shook his arm and scoffed at the stupid creatures, more amused than scared. Then their beaks, tiny sharp mouths hidden between their arms, started nipping him. The pain was like needles—thick needles stabbing and grinding.

Blake opened his mouth to scream, but tentacles stuffed their way inside, slurping down the back of his throat and wrenching his jaw wider and wider until it cracked.

* * *

As the boat docked, Dave watched through the panoramic windows of the Eight Ways kitchen. He and Katarina were almost done closing the place up for the night. All they needed was the delivery of fresh octopi for tomorrow.

Blake lurched his way out of the boat, a silhouette

against the coastal town's lights reflecting on the water in Van Gogh-like smears.

"What the hell?" Dave said, wondering why Blake wasn't carrying a tub full of delectable fresh octopi with him after deboarding. "He's coming back empty handed?"

"That's not Blake..." Katarina whispered. She'd only been working at Eight Ways a few months. But she could see that the silhouette wasn't moving right. Not like Blake. Not like a person at all.

"What do you mean?"

It was a clear night, and they'd been able to see the fishing boat's lights for the whole hour Blake had been out at sea, pulling up the clay pot traps. No other boats had come near.

The silhouette lurched toward them, making its way down the pier.

Katarina put down the knives she'd been sharpening and backed away from the windows.

"You're being weird, get back to work," Dave said. He went to open the dockside kitchen door. "Hey, Blake," he called out. "Where are my blue plate special darlings?"

The only sound, beyond the lapping of the waves, was a squelching and rattling as Blake approached. When the light from the windows hit him, he was reddish brown and squirming all over, like something had torn off his skin, leaving only the muscles beneath. But the muscles writhed too much, and in places, the bones shone through. White and clean.

A few more steps forward, and Dave recognized the

lumpy shapes of octopus bodies, stretched over Blake's skeleton, nestling inside his ribs where his heart and lungs should be. Their tentacles worked together, wrapping around the bones and moving them like a marionette's sticks, replacing the flesh and muscle they'd already eaten. Strange eyes peered out from his pelvis, from his shoulder, his legs. Everywhere tentacles writhed and alien eyes stared.

The octopus with the scar between its orange eyes had wrapped itself around Blake's skull and operated his broken jawbone, as if pantomiming silent laughter. Inside the skeletal mouth rested a smaller octopus—daffodil yellow with brilliant blue rings. Deadly poisonous.

Dave started to back away, but too late, too slow. He couldn't believe what he was seeing, so he didn't run or struggle, even as the writhing mass of tentacles reached out to him with both of the skeleton's arms, grabbed him by the shoulders, pulled him close, and kissed his face with a poisoned bite.

Dave fell to the floor, spasming and shaking. He'd be dead in minutes. Another skeleton, dressed in useless flesh, waiting to be cleaned.

Katarina choked back a sob, hiding behind the farthest counter. She watched as the skeleton filled with octopuses rambled through the room, rattling and squelching, bending in ways a human skeleton shouldn't. It ran sucker disc covered tentacles over every surface, touching everything it could. She held her breath when the lurching figure came near her, waiting until her head pounded and her lungs burned, before gasping for air.

The octopuses didn't see her with their strange eyes. They dragged Dave, still quaking from the poison, with them when they went. Back to the sea.

Katarina cried, shaking as if she'd been poisoned by the blue ring octopus's bite herself. She fell asleep—too scared to move, too scared to stay conscious—curled up against the hard wood of the counter, and dreamed about the octopuses coming back, filling Dave's skeleton as well as Blake's. Gathering more and more skeletons until they built an army. She woke to the bright glare of morning light, bouncing off the sea.

All around her, like tiny pearls, tiny seeds, everywhere the octopus creature had touched... Eggs clung to all of the surfaces, and as the sunlight shone through their milky membranes, she saw the tiny orbs filled with minuscule fetal tentacles waving inside.

31

TAKE THEM TO THE HAPPINESS ZOO

EXHAUSTED, Junie watched her five-year-old daughter and two toddler sons play with Gorvall. They stacked up colored blocks and knocked them down. Gorvall's long gray fingers helped pry apart the building blocks that stuck together. The colorful towers reflected in his large, teardrop-shaped black eyes.

Another one of Gorvall's bodies, identical to the first, sat at the dining table with Junie. "Your children will be perfectly happy."

A third of Gorvall's bodies picked up the stuffed toys—bunnies and dolls—that had been strewn and trampled during an earlier game. Junie knew that Gorvall was only trying to ingratiate himself to her. It was working.

"Why do you need my consent?" What she really wondered was why a multi-dimensional being would be running happiness studies on human children. But she didn't ask. It would be rude. Or, maybe, she just didn't want to know the truth.

Gorvall's body sitting at the table with her shrugged. "Rules. You know how it is."

"Oh, sure," Junie agreed, as if it was a given that bureaucratic tape extended to every government, even interstellar, multi-dimensional ones.

The kids did look happy playing with Gorvall. Emily balanced one of the blocks on her head. The twins, Nick and Eric, laughed.

What was she thinking? Junie couldn't send her children away to live their lives in some sort of space zoo or science experiment. Or whatever Gorvall really wanted them for.

Then Nick shoved Emily. Eric grabbed the blocks and threw them at her face. Emily shrieked, "Moooooom! The babies are BUGGING ME!"

Junie's head throbbed. Nothing gave her a headache like Emily's voice. Instead of shouting, she said to Gorvall, "Take them." It was for their own good. They'd be happier in a life-long experiment on how to optimize human happiness than with a mom yelling at them, never getting them to bed on time, and basically failing constantly.

"You've made a wise choice." Gorvall—all of his bodies —and the three children vanished in a blur of sparkles.

Junie knew her husband would be furious when he got back from his month long conference, but, for now, she was going to get a full night's sleep.

32

WHEN HE STOPPED CRYING

KARYANNE KNEW RIGHT AWAY when the fae replaced her son. The baby had been crying days straight, since he was born. Karyanne didn't even know how long that was. She woke to darkness. She woke to brittle morning light. She woke to darkness. She woke to full, ripe, afternoon light slanting through the venetian blinds. It was all the same. It was all baby screams, and her eyes glued shut from tears and exhaustion, and the back of her head hurting, and her body aching all over.

Sometimes, she kept Ewan in the bed with her when he finished nursing and curled her body around him while he wailed. When he nursed, he bit her breast between sobs. It was the closest he came to not crying.

Sometimes she tried to sleep through his hysterical sobbing as it emanated from the crib across the hall. That was almost worse. At least, when she wrapped her warm body around Ewan, she felt like she was doing something —trying to ward the sadness away with the comfort of her flesh.

The baby didn't care.

Ewan's red face wrinkled with screams. And sobs. Tiny tears traveled down the creases of his face. He wasn't even a pretty baby—with his red face and red fuzz of hair, he looked like demon spawn. But he still felt like a part of her own body, and his screams tore at her heart from the inside out.

That's how she knew immediately when he stopped screaming—

Ewan was gone.

Karyanne pushed herself painfully out of her bed and padded across the hall. She looked over the wooden crib railing to see a peaceful, serene baby's face. Sound asleep. More beautiful than any baby she'd ever seen before. Her stomach twisted inside her, and it felt like emotion was trying to wring her out like a wet cloth. But the tears wouldn't come. Just dry sobs, shocked and heaving. She sank down beside the crib, leaned against its decoratively carved wooden leg. The wooden carvings dug into her shoulder, and Karyanne tried to anchor herself to that feeling.

If she felt discomfort—sharp, painful discomfort— maybe she didn't have to feel anything else. Discomfort was trivial and could be brushed aside as easily as shifting the way her shoulder hit the wooden crib leg. But if it was sharp enough— If it dug into her shoulder deeply enough—

The sound of the front door opening. The sound of heavy footsteps. Then a whisper—loud but breathy—from above: "Karyanne? What did you do? He's quiet!"

Aaron leaned over the crib. Karyanne put her hands around the rough fabric of his pant-leg, bunched up around the top of his boot. She looked up to see a wide grin break across her husband's face.

"He's so beautiful when he's sleeping!" Aaron reached out to touch the changeling child. Then he sank down beside his wife. "I thought he'd never sleep. I thought..."

Aaron didn't say it. He'd never say it. But Karyanne knew. He'd been gone from the house longer and longer each time. At first, he whispered excuses and kissed her behind her ear before leaving. Last time, he just tore at his hair, cursed under his breath, grabbed a change of clothes from their shared dresser, and disappeared.

Karyanne couldn't measure the days, but he looked like he'd had a full night's sleep. Somewhere. She hadn't. Not since Ewan had torn his way out of her and begun filling her ears with screams.

She had prayed for him to stop. She'd prayed for the screams to stop. She'd taken down the special mobile her crazy old grandmother had made to protect the baby from fae—the one with bright red dragons and silver knights wielding swords. It was too scary for a baby, and maybe its bright colors had been upsetting Ewan. That's what she lied to herself, anyway. But she knew what she was doing. She just didn't believe it.

She didn't believe her grandmother's stories. She didn't believe that her red hair and gold-flecked blue eyes meant the fae would want her baby. She didn't believe in fae at all.

Aaron leaned his head against Karyanne's. He grabbed one of her hands and stroked the back of it with his roughly callused fingers. "You're a good mother. Whatever you did, it finally worked. That wee boy knows you love him. Knows his mother never left his side this whole week."

Aaron stood up and pulled Karyanne after him. He looked down on the sleeping changeling child. Karyanne couldn't look at the fae baby who'd replaced her own flesh and blood. So she looked at Aaron.

"You know?" Aaron whispered. "I think his hair is darkening up already. Gonna be a brunette like daddy! I guess we won't have another redhead in the family." Aaron turned to look at her, his brown eyes soft with love. He ran his fingers through her long hair, maneuvering his thick fingers deftly whenever they ran into the tangles gathered from days without a shower. Then he cupped his palm against her cheek. She loved the skillful feel of his hand on her again. She'd been terrified he'd never come back.

Had she traded her son for her husband?

In her grandmother's stories, the fae raised stolen

human children as princes and queens. They lived a hundred years, eating honeyed food and drinking nectar, all in the beat of a heart. Her son could meet her tomorrow, a grown man, older than she was, having lived an entire life and crossed back to this side of the veil. She could be a grandmother herself by now, to half-fairy children living in the land of fae.

Her red-haired son was gone, on the other side of a veil she could never see. All Karyanne could do was hope he was okay—that he hadn't been raised by a cruel fairy, trapped in a cage constructed of human bones, and whipped with entrails until he obeyed. Enslaved by fairies. Fairies could be cruel, couldn't they?

Of course, they could. They'd taken her son.

Karyanne looked down at the changeling finally. The babe's face was smooth and pale, cherubic. The soft fuzz on his head was a shade of brown reminiscent of young tree bark, and there was a slight point to his ears, almost too subtle to see. He breathed evenly. The sound was soothing. Even if it wasn't the breathing of her own baby.

"Can we..." Karyanne hesitated over the words. It was a strange request. "Can we call him something else? I don't think Ewan is the right name. He doesn't..." She couldn't stop herself from crying, but Aaron didn't find it strange. She hadn't slept for more than a few minutes at a time for days. "He doesn't look like an Ewan."

"I don't think he's had time to get used to his name," Aaron said, lightly. As if they were talking about nicknames, nothing more. "And you know I wanted to call him Greg for my dad."

"The middle name, yes." Karyanne reached toward the changeling, but she let her fingers float just above the curve of his smooth forehead. When she touched him it would be real. "Greg," she said.

She placed her fingers on the baby's head, and Greg sighed contentedly. Her fairy child.

Karyanne's body doubled over with violent sobbing. She sounded like Ewan had.

Aaron guided her out of the nursery room. "Come on," he said. "You don't want to wake him up. And you could use a shower. Maybe a foot rub first?"

Karyanne nodded, tears still streaming down her face and falling to the carpeted floor. She wanted to tell Aaron, unburden herself of her awful failure and the bottomless chasm of loss she felt. But he'd never believe her. No one would. The mad ravings of a sleep deprived new mother? She'd sound like her crazy old grandmother.

Instead, she cried quietly and fell asleep while Aaron rubbed her feet. She awoke hours later, still lying on the couch, with a plate of Chinese take-out on the coffee table beside her. She could hear Aaron cooing to the changeling babe in the next room.

She hoped her red-faced, red-haired Ewan was happier in the fae realm. She hadn't known how to make him happy.

Aaron brought Greg to her, wrapped in a blanket covered in Winnie-the-Pooh characters. From all the baby books, Karyanne knew he was still too young to smile, but she could have sworn those cheeks dimpled when his unfocused moss-green eyes saw her. She took the baby in her arms. The strange but beautiful imposter.

Maybe she could make Greg happy.

And maybe someday she'd tell her grandmother.

33

FEMCLOUD INC.

CHLOE LAY on the table in the doctor's office, wearing a paper sheet over her legs and one of those weird gowns that opened in the back. She didn't want to be pregnant, but she didn't want to need an abortion. She couldn't help thinking about David—it had to be David—and what amazing genes he must have. He'd talked like a character out of a fast-paced TV show, everything clever, insightful, and... much too articulate. They'd argued corporate law for hours, until she'd shouted at him in a flurry of frustration that she was done arguing, and he should leave her alone. Instead, he'd kissed her. God, he was handsome, too.

But, no, she didn't want a baby, even a brilliant and handsome one. She wouldn't let a few squishy, hormone-inspired feelings derail the rest of her life.

Dr. Orton wheeled an ultrasound machine into the room and set it up. She slicked Chloe's flat belly down with goo, and then slid the wand around in it. "Let's see if we can find a heartbeat, shall we?"

Chloe's own heart clenched at the word "heartbeat." Maybe she should try to look David up after all...

The blue images on the screen of the ultrasound looked like nothing to Chloe. Then, the machine clicked. An atonal mechanical voice said, "*...will repeat every minute of the first trimester.*"

Dr. Orton looked troubled.

"What's the machine talking about?" Chloe asked.

"That... uh... wasn't the machine talking," Dr. Orton said. "That sound came from your uterus."

"What?" Chloe didn't understand. She argued with Dr. Orton—surely the machine was broken—until the atonal voice began speaking again.

"*Greetings, new FemCloud employee. You have been recruited by David Livell, founder and CEO of FemCloud, to join FemCloud as an Incubational Assistant. If you do well, you will be promoted to Administrative Caretaker at the end of your preliminary nine-month term. Your sexual actions with David Livell constitute a legally binding agreement. Any action that you—or anyone else—take to damage the corporate property that has been entrusted to you as an Incubational Assistant is in violation of this agreement and will be prosecuted to the full extent of the law. We hope that you enjoy working with FemCloud and will continue serving us for the next eighteen years. This message will repeat...*"

34

BRAIN-DEAD BABY JESUSES

THE SNOW CAME DOWN in flurries. It swarmed outside the window of Miley's dorm room, brushing softly against the third story window in gusts of wind. Tiny flakes. White crystals, pinging against the glass.   Miley had been checking the weather app on her phone, watching the forecast fluctuate back and forth all week—snow on Friday, no wait, now on Saturday, back to Friday, and then only freezing rain. She'd been praying for snow.

The snow was finally here, but online classes don't get cancelled due to weather. So, while her eyes kept straying from her laptop screen to the window behind it, Miley had to finish her essay before she could bundle up, go outside, and catch those tantalizing flakes on her tongue. Her fingers itched, impatiently, as she typed, and she kept switching tabs from her essay to Facepage, telling herself that frequent breaks actually helped her concentrate.

"So unfair! Snow outside, and I'm stuck inside writing about economic theory!" Miley posted.

Two sentences of economic theory later, her Facepage tab lured her back with two notifications.

"Ha ha loser," from Brendan. She couldn't believe she'd ever had a crush on him.

And "Snow? What snow? You live two buildings down from me?" posted by Carol.

Miley snapped a picture with her phone of the flurry outside her window. The white flakes glowed in the light of the camera's flash. She posted the picture, saying, "See —SNOW. Told you prayers get answered, Carol. God is good."

Miley had been trying to convince Carol to come to church with her for more than a year. Carol was a good person. Miley would reach her eventually. No, God would reach her.

After a couple more sentences of essay writing, Miley checked Facepage again. This time, Brendan had posted an article link. He was always posting junky liberal fake news to her timeline. This one was especially weird: "Nano-drone Bio-Engineer Uses Facial Recognition Software and Social Network Hacks to Identify Pro-Life Women and Artificially Inseminate Them."

Miley's cheeks burned. She wished she'd never told Brendan that she was pro-life. It had been one of those nights where a group of friends stays up until dawn, sitting in a circle, telling each other everything. Quintessential college. She'd thought that she and Brendan were getting really close; she'd been thinking about admitting her crush to him. But then abortion came up, and he'd said he'd never sleep with a girl who was pro-life—too dangerous. Miley had told him that if he really loved a girl, he wouldn't sleep with her until they were married anyway. It got worse from there. The more Miley explained her beliefs, the more awkward and quiet everyone became.

It was hard being Christian at a liberal college.

Miley went back to work on her essay, but a few minutes later, her phone buzzed—a call from Carol. Miley answered, and Carol said in a rush, "Did you look at that article about the nano-drones?"

"What, Brendan teasing me again? No, I didn't."

"You should read it."

Miley skimmed the article, but it was clearly ridiculous—it claimed that swarms of nano-drones were flying around the country, finding women who had said pro-life things on the internet, and then entering their bodies. Once inside, the nano-drones re-engineered the women's own eggs into sperm and altered the sperm's DNA so that the ensuing immaculately conceived babies would develop with an unusual, non-fatal form of anencephaly. Normally, anencephalic babies live no longer than a few hours after birth; these specially engineered babies would be able to live long, brainless lives.

The money quote from the mad scientist behind it all read, "I intend to create an army of brain-dead baby Jesuses to waste the energy of pro-lifers. Or else cause a whole lot of hypocrites to get abortions." He was already in jail, but his nano-drones were supposedly still at large.

"This article is extreme crazy-sauce. Why am I supposed to read it?"

"I checked it on SnoopTruth," Carol said. "This one checks out."

A tingle of fear passed down Miley's spine. Even if it was a hoax, the idea was still appalling. Miley had never even had sex. She couldn't get pregnant with a brainless baby. That wouldn't just stop her from finishing college... It would take up the rest of her life. "Why would anyone do this?"

Carol didn't answer, but her silence spoke volumes. They'd had some pretty ugly fights about what Carol called "abortion rights" versus a baby's right to life. Carol didn't understand that God gave babies their souls the moment they were conceived.

Except... what if God didn't make the baby... a nano-drone designed by a Godless scientist did?

No, that was wrong. Only God made babies, and even atheist scientists could be God's tools. Miley looked out the window and saw God's majesty right there—beautiful and pure, nature at its finest. She needed a break from all of this—college life, liberal "friends," her essay on economic theory. Maybe it was time for that walk in the snow.

Before Miley could hang up the phone, Carol said, "Look, I found another article... It... It describes what the nano-drone swarms look like. I'll... send you the link."

"I'm not interested," Miley said, but the article popped up on her Facepage anyway. The picture looked very familiar. It looked exactly like the picture she'd posted earlier of the snow.

"I don't think you should go outside tonight," Carol said.

Miley hung up on her.

She stood up, leaned over her desk, and looked out the window more closely. The white crystalline flakes beat at the window pane. But one story up and one story down, the air was clear. All around the dorm, except for Miley's window, the air was clear. The snow had come for her.

Miley sat back down and began scrolling through Facepage, deleting every post where she'd mentioned God or the sanctity of life, hoping it wasn't too late. But she knew the drones had already identified her. The snow was watching her. It lusted for her.

A stone crashed through the window, and a voice from outside screamed, "Pro-life bitch!"

The flurries swirled through the broken glass, and Miley spread her arms wide to accept them. To accept God's future for her and the love He was bringing her, no matter what form it came in. The first flake tingled as it touched the tip of her tongue.

35

THE CHRISTMAS TREE BARN

THE CONCRETE FLOOR of the basement was freezing cold right through Becca's socks, and the air smelled moldy. She hadn't properly aired the basement out since it had flooded most of a year ago, last spring. Becca yanked on the corner of the old, beat-up cardboard box with the robotic Christmas tree in it, and the box scraped across the floor as it pulled out from under the tool shelves.

The cardboard was darker on the bottom, lighter on top. Water damage. Becca hoped the tree's wiring wouldn't be shorted out. She didn't think she could face trying to fix it herself; her mother had always kept the tree running. She was a wizard with electronics. Had been a wizard. A wave of sadness washed over Becca, and she shoved the ratty, heavy box right back where it had been.

Becca rushed upstairs and closed the basement door behind her, like she could shut her grief away with a slab of wood.

"What about the tree!?" Jenny whined. "You said we could put it up! Kennedy's family got their tree out weeks ago!"

Becca grabbed her coat from the hook beside the front door, and one for her daughter as well. She tried not to cringe at being compared to Kennedy's perfect family, yet again. They were the kind of family that ate meals at a dining table with homemade pot roasts and fresh steamed green beans. Instead of neon orange packets of macaroni and cheese with canned tuna and frozen peas dumped in.

"Come on," Becca said. "You've been bugging me all week about those new, live Christmas trees. Let's go take a look."

The Christmas Tree Barn was actually a party store that had gone out of business earlier in the year. It was one of those temporary stores that pops up for a few weeks right around the holidays and disappears afterward, like all the Halloween costume stores. The smell of pine needles was overpowering, as soon as the store's front doors slid open, and "Jingle Bells" roared cheerfully at them over low quality speakers.

When they stepped inside, the whole place had been set up like a pet store on adoption day, when the local shelters bring all the foster dogs in. Except behind the waist-high puppy gates, instead of dogs were rows and rows of trees—some decorated, some not. But all of them... dancing. Their branches waved. Some of them twirled. Others seemed to be playing chase, crawling over the warehouse floor with their exposed roots. A couple of them leaned over the puppy gates, playing some kind of self-decorating game with bright-eyed toddlers whose parents were definitely going to be buying pet trees for Christmas.

Becca wanted to turn around and leave. But her own daughter, usually a surly teenager with a snarky comeback for everything, had bright eyes, and her mouth had fallen open, speechless. Becca risked reaching over and grabbing her daughter's hand. Squeezing it.

Jenny squeezed back and turned to look at her mother with a glowing smile. "There are so many!" she said. "And Kennedy told me they dance! But... but..."

Jenny didn't have to finish her sentence. Becca knew that she was picturing their old, robotic tree with its rotating branches. Becca had spent many happy days, lying beneath that tree as a child, listening to it tell her Christmas stories and making up riddles about what was in her presents. It had been a top of the line robotic tree back then. Now... Well, apparently, the world had come full circle—live trees to fake trees to robotic trees with limited AI, and now live trees again, gengineered to be... this.

"Can I help you?" asked a woman in a cheap green blazer with a nametag that read, "Hi, I'm Angelica, Your Christmas Elf-Helper!"

"I'm surprised they don't make you wear Santa hats or blinking light necklaces," Becca said, though she immediately felt bad for being snarky at a retail worker... especially in front of her daughter, who didn't need any encouragement in that direction.

Angelica laughed and said, "Here at *The Christmas Tree Barn*, we like to let the trees do the shining. Besides—" She held a hand up beside her mouth, pretending to be conspiratorial. "—the Doug Firs are such hounds for decorations, I'm sure they'd steal any holiday bling I tried to wear!"

Now Jenny laughed, and it was the kind of whole-hearted, wholesome laugh that Becca remembered from when she was younger, not a teenager's snide snicker. "Kennedy told me that they decorate themselves."

"That's true," Angelica agreed. "Just put out your box of ornaments, and they'll have a ball playing dress-up. If you don't have ornaments, give them a pile of crafting supplies, and they'll make some!"

"I have to admit," Becca said. "These trees are charming."

"If you listen closely—" Angelica placed a hand theatrically beside her ear. "—you'll hear that they can even sing along with the carols."

Jenny walked toward the closest enclosure of frolicking Christmas trees as if pulled forward by their magic. Totally enthralled. "They sound... like cellos... or violas."

"Yes, they vibrate their needles to make the sound," Angelica explained.

"They're so active," Becca said. "What's to stop one from flailing around and knocking over all my furniture?"

"Oh, they can see." Angelica pointed at the nearest tree. "See those clusters of red berries on their branches? They look festive, but they're actually photosensitive. Primitive eyes. Our trees can recognize faces and everything. They're approximately as smart as Labrador Retrievers."

A horrible thought occurred to Becca. "What... happens to them after Christmas?" She didn't want to ask, but she needed to know. One of these trees couldn't get disassembled and boxed up in the basement for eleven months a year. "And how long do they live?"

Angelica's cheerful voice turned serious: "We do take them back, if you don't want to keep them. But they're very easy pets—set your tree free in your backyard, and it'll get all the sun and water it needs, given the weather in this region. Also, they can be trained to be excellent gardeners. If you don't have a yard, they can be trained to water themselves in the shower and care for potted plants."

"Really?" Becca asked with surprise.

"Oh, yes, teach one of these trees to take care of your garden, and you'll have a perfectly pruned, expertly tended garden for years to come. Because they do live for years. And..." Angelica's voice got even more serious. "They get attached to families they spend Christmas with. So, we really *don't* recommend returning them."

Becca nodded solemnly. She wondered if one of these trees could be trained to hold down the ribbon with the tip of one of its branches while she wrapped presents after Jenny was in bed. It would be nice to have a companion for that. And... it would be nice to have a pet that didn't require more attention than she could give. With only her and Jenny in the house, they couldn't properly take care of a dog.

For the first time this season, Becca was feeling hopeful. "I guess it's time," she said, "to pick out a new friend."

36

PEN PALS WITH THE TOOTH FAIRY

ELLA DIDN'T LIKE APPLES, but she'd been trying to wiggle her loose tooth out for an hour. Now it was almost bedtime, and if she didn't eat something with a big CRUNCH, then she wouldn't get to introduce the tooth fairy to Santa Claus. So, she took the crunchiest looking apple from the kitchen counter—one of the horrible green ones that her mother liked—and sank her teeth into its sour flesh.

Bingo. She spat out the mouthful of apple into her palm... and her tooth too!

Ella slipped her tooth into the envelope that she'd already prepared with a letter inside and the words TOOTH FAIRY in scripty letters on the front.

"What's that?" her mom asked.

"I lost a tooth!" Ella proclaimed proudly, waving the freshly sealed envelope. "I've got to go put this under my pillow!"

"Okay," Mom said. "But hurry back. It's time to set out the cookies." She got out the special plate that they always used on Christmas Eve for Santa.

Ella ran to her room and placed the envelope carefully under her pillow; then she ran back and eagerly helped pick out an array of cookies for Santa—two Oreos, a snickerdoodle from Grandma, and the gingerbread man that she'd decorated herself. She wanted to put out even more—Santa needed to be kept busy, so he didn't leave before the tooth fairy got her letter—but Mom insisted four was enough. So, with a stroke of inspiration, Ella added a stick of gum from her personal stash. Santa would have to stick around longer to chew the gum.

Once the plate of cookies was placed on the mantel, and Ella's head was on her pillow, everything was in place. Tonight would be the most magical night of her life—she was going to introduce Santa Claus and the tooth fairy! If only she could stay awake for it...

IF ONLY HER little girl would fall asleep, Charlene could work the magic for her and finally go to bed herself. Instead, she heard Ella tossing and turning, occasionally giggling to herself in her dark room. So, Charlene watched another episode of CSI and tried not to think about how tired she'd be tomorrow. Maybe she could sneak in a nap when they got to her sister's house.

When it finally seemed safe, Charlene slipped into

Ella's dark room, slid her hand gingerly under the little girl's pillow, and pulled out the tooth fairy envelope. Usually, Charlene would simply hide the envelope with the other envelopes of Ella's teeth in the back of her sock drawer, unopened, but she'd seen Ella secretively writing something after decorating the envelope that evening. So, this time, she tore the envelope open, and inside she found a letter:

* * *

DEAR TOOTH FAIRY,

I read a book about you, and I think you have a lot in common with Santa Claus. 1) You both travel fast. 2) You both like children and work hard. 3) You are very generous. So, I lost my tooth tonight, so you could meet Santa Claus. I know you will fall in love. Please invite me to the wedding, because I introduced you. OK?

Love,

Ella

* * *

CHARLENE BLINKED at the letter a few times, trying to figure out what to make of it. While she thought about the situation, she worked on her evening's Santa Claus duties —she slipped all the prepared goodies into Ella's stocking, returned the Oreos and snickerdoodle back to the cookie jar with the other identical Oreos and snickerdoodles. She ate the gingerbread man. It tasted like love. Her daughter had made it for her—even if her daughter didn't know it.

Finally, it was time to prepare a return envelope from the tooth fairy. As was usual, Charlene put a couple quarters, nickels, and dimes into the envelope. Also a sheet of stickers.

Should she write a letter back? What would it even say?

Charlene got out a piece of paper and sat down to write.

* * *

Dear Ella,

Thank you for thinking of me! Santa Claus and I had a nice time tonight, but I'm not looking for anyone to marry. Besides, he's already married. He and Mrs. Claus are very happy together.

However, as you mentioned, I do work hard, and it can get a little lonely. Would you like to be pen pals with me?

Love,

TTF

* * *

Charlene stared at the letter for a long time before folding it into thirds and tucking it into the envelope. It could be hard to talk to her daughter. The girl was always lost in the clouds. Charlene wanted to be a part of those clouds. She wondered what surprise her little girl would come up with next.

For now, Charlene slipped the envelope, heavy with coins, under Ella's pillow. Ella made magic for her every day. It was nice to be able to give a little magic back.

Tonight, Charlene would fall asleep and join her daughter in dreaming about a rotund man in red crushed velvet dancing with a spritely woman sporting translucent, fluttering wings.

37

ST. KALWAIN AND THE LADY UTA

SNOW BENT the boughs of the karillow trees, and ice silvered the soft buds at their tips. Spring had come too early this year, and all the eager young plants would pay a price for their enthusiasm. Flowers killed by frost.

St. Kalwain didn't mind the snow. His black fur was thick and warm. He found it insufferably so whenever he kept the company of humans. Their houses were always warmed by raging hearth fires. Their walls held in the heat. And they insulated themselves with layers of cloaks and clothes. They expected him to layer himself with clothes too. He remembered a time when he chose to wear clothes out of modesty. Now, he preferred to sleep in the wild. In the snow. Alone and far from humans.

Deep in the forest, St. Kalwain didn't hear hoof beats often. When he did, they were far off and the sound began to recede long before the smell of the steed reached his nose. There were no roads near his dell, so there was no reason for travelers to come by. Unless they were lost. Or looking for him. The only paths were those made by his own misshapen feet, too like a wolf's to comfortably wear shoes. Yet, the skin of his footpads was still too human and too tender to entirely go without. St. Kalwain made do with scraps of cloth, tied tight around the bare-skinned parts of his otherwise furry feet.

Today, though, the sound of the hoof beats kept growing closer, and St. Kalwain scented oats, mint, and the salt of sweat in the air. He perked his ears to listen closely for any more telling sounds, but he was not in the mood to help lost travelers today. He'd done enough good deeds to last a lifetime. He stretched and yawned, then settled back even more comfortably in his hollowed out dent at the base of a tree.

The hoof beats grew closer for a while, then slowed and meandered aimlessly through the woods. "Kalwain?" a sweet voice sang. "Saint Kalwain?" It was the voice of a young woman, and the sound made St. Kalwain flatten his ears and draw back his lips in a snarl that he knew from memory was more wolf than man. The accursed mirror that could show him his snarl hung in a locket about his neck. It was only the size of a farthing, but he dreaded the sight of himself in it. Nonetheless, if a sweet-voiced young woman had come to call on him in his reclusion, it could only mean one thing. And he would not give up his retirement easily.

St. Kalwain opened the locket and steeled himself

against the glaring reflection of his hideously yellow eyes. He stared himself down and whispered the couplet that would summon the faerie queen's attention. The words felt like a collar around his neck, but within seconds his hateful reflection frosted over. The image of his captor queen appeared in its place: alabaster skin, raven hair, sharply arched eyebrows, and eyes that sparkled like the edge of a knife. She was beauty. She was death. She was the hand at the end of the chain that held him here in the wilderness away from the life he'd once lived.

"My queen," he said to the image in the glass. "There is a woman seeking me in my forest. Did you send her?"

The faerie queen frowned, an expression as frightening as ice cracking beneath your feet yet as delicate as a single petal floating on the wind. "Of course I sent her," the faerie queen said. "You are my champion, and she needs a champion."

"I have done good deeds in the name of Faerie for half my life," St. Kalwain said, bitterly. "I am known in every village across this land. My own people have made me a saint—in spite of your curse. Yet, never are my deeds enough for you. You will not release me from my curse. So, I will champion for you no more."

The faerie queen laughed, and icicles broke, shattering on the trees all around. "You think I can't make you?" she said. "I can bring you back to Faerie. If you won't work off your curse."

St. Kalwain didn't flinch. He'd been to Faerie, and he'd rather die than live in that terrifying land again. But he knew where he stood. "You can bring me back to Faerie anyway," he said. "I won't dance for you anymore."

There was laughter in the faerie queen's eyes, but it died away as St. Kalwain looked at her. "Very well," she said. "This will be your last service to me. Assist the lady who seeks you in your forest now, and afterward I will set you free."

St. Kalwain's heart leapt at the sound of those words, but they were hard to believe.

"I warn you, though," the faerie queen added as her image began to fade in the locket, "Fail me here, and you will sit by my side, a royal hunting hound in the land of Faerie forever."

St. Kalwain remembered the faerie queen's throne room. It was lit with a sickly green glow, and sounds echoed like water droplets in a musty cellar. The walls were living flesh, embedded with chattering teeth and watchful eyes. Dried bracken and branches of thorns were set in vases as if they were exquisite flowers. At the center of the room, raised on a dais, was the faerie queen's throne, built from human bones. St. Kalwain shuddered, picturing himself forced to curl at the foot of that throne like a loyal dog.

"And, so," he said to the emptied mirror as he closed it back in the locket, "I will dance for you again. As always." He sighed, a long drawn-out breath between his muzzle's sharp teeth.

The sweet-voiced maiden continued to call St. Kalwain's name in the distance. He could hear that she'd dismounted her horse and walked by its side. She would be expecting a clothed man with the face of a wolf, not the naked beast-man he had become. St. Kalwain reached into the branches of his tree and found the bundle of clothes and other human affectations he'd stored away. He pulled out a broad cloak and slung it around his shoulders. It draped nearly to the ground. It would do. The rest he swung over his shoulder to bring. He'd need the brush and combs, and the full outfit of shirt and trousers if he was going to follow this girl back to civilization.

"Saint Kalwain?" she called. "I know you're here. The faerie queen sent me. Please come out!"

St. Kalwain approached her, setting his paw-like feet carefully in the snow. She would not hear him. He stayed behind the trees where she could not see him either. But he could see her. Her cloak and her horse were green like springtime. Her hood was edged in white fur, and her hands were buried in a white fur muff. But her cheeks were pink with the cold anyway, and her breaths hovered in the air, telling clouds of fog.

"Please come out," she repeated. "My village needs you."

"What is it this time?" St. Kalwain bellowed, still hidden behind the trees. "The tyranny of a bad man? A dragon?" He stepped quickly through the thick of the forest, watching her turn about, trying to spot him. "Or maybe a gryphon that steals away babies to eat in the night?"

"A dragon," she said, giving up her quest to see St.

Kalwain and speaking instead to the faceless forest. "You've slain dragons before."

"Five of them. Yes," St. Kalwain said. "I chopped off their heads."

"Then you'll come with me?" she asked, lowering her hood. Her hair was light brown and simple, her features plain but pleasing. "I know of your curse," she said. "You don't have to be afraid to show yourself to me."

St. Kalwain laughed, a booming bark that he expected would frighten her as it echoed through the forest. Yet, the girl stood as steadily as ever. "*Me* afraid?" he said, mockingly.

It should be the girl, alone in the forest with a wolf-faced monster, who was afraid. Nonetheless, St. Kalwain's foot faltered as he stepped from his shield of trees and into the young woman's sight.

"What could scare a demon like me?" He asked the question rhetorically, voice dripping with sarcasm, but she had been right. He was afraid. St. Kalwain expected the beautiful young woman would flinch at the sight of him, like so many women before, but the lady Uta did not flinch.

"You're not a demon," she said. "You've slain five drag-ons, saved countless lives, and you're going to rescue my village."

St. Kalwain stood more than a foot taller than her, but she stared up at him, holding his gaze better than he could hold hers. "I'm the lady Uta," she said. "And you are a saint."

Abashed, the unhappy saint said, "I'll get my sword." It was hidden high in the branches of another tree. He never fought with a shield or armor. They only slowed down his lupine reflexes. "Will your horse let me ride? We can travel faster if we ride together."

Not all horses would let a wolf-demon take to their backs, but the lady Uta assured St. Kalwain that her steed would. Even more surprising to St. Kalwain, the lady Uta did not lie and claim shyness on the part of her horse to cover shyness of her own. He'd faced fair maidens before who claimed their horses were afraid of him, when he could smell no fear on them. It was the maids themselves who wished to avoid sitting close to him in the saddle, his toothy snout behind their heads, his dangerously clawed paw-hands settled at their waists. Yes, fair maids would cost their villages hours and days of time under the tyranny of a dragon to avoid the beastly touch of their savior.

The ride to Uta's village was three days through the forest and another five across open countryside. The lady Uta had cheese and dried fruits in her saddle bags, but St. Kalwain had no taste for such a meal since the faerie queen's curse had changed his form. Whenever they set camp for the night, he left the small fire to hunt up live game. Uta cooked the rabbits and pheasants he brought her. Though, if he hadn't been sharing with her, St. Kalwain would have happily eaten them raw. That was his way in the forest. Sitting at a fire and eating cooked meat had grown foreign to him. Not that he denied its appeal.

The firelight cast dreamy shadows, and its orange glow glinted off of Uta's hair like copper. The wood smoke smell was a comforting reminder of his youth. It took him back to the days of his childhood when he would sit on the hearth, idly poking the family cooking fire with sticks and straws until his mother noticed. She'd chide him and tell him to stop. No one chided him now. The lady Uta merely watched with dark eyes, singing her lullabies to Jescha, the green steed that carried them all day. Jescha whickered. And the night wore on into the dark.

On the final morning of their journey, St. Kalwain and Uta awoke to a cold fog curling over the snowy ground. It swirled around Jescha's tail as she swished the verdigris hair.

"We're half a day's ride from my village," Uta said. "Is there anything I can tell you... anything I can do... to help you prepare?"

St. Kalwain mounted Jescha behind the lady Uta and thought about all the questions he could ask her. All the questions she expected him to ask. He could ask about the dragon—*how many knights have fought it? how did it kill them? what does it look like? what color are its scales?* But, in the end, fighting dragons was fighting dragons, and St. Kalwain had never found that preparing for it helped him very much. In the moment of decision, it would be steel against scales, and there would be no tricks. For if there was a trick that made it easy to slay this dragon, then the village would not have called on him, eight days' travel away and hidden deep in the forest, findable only by those that the faerie queen fancied to help.

So, instead, St. Kalwain asked as Jescha cantered with them across the snowy hills, "Why is your horse green?"

The lady Uta laughed, and it was an altogether different animal than the last laugh St. Kalwain had heard. Unlike the faerie queen's ethereal, demonic laughter, Uta's laugh was hearty and human. St. Kalwain could feel her body rock with it; he wished he could see her face.

"All right," she said, loudly enough for him to hear her through the muffling of her fur-lined hood. Though, without his canine ears, he might not have been able. "I'll tell you that story," she said. "If you like."

As they cantered on, the lady Uta told St. Kalwain about the forest beside her father's cottage. As a small girl, she would wander freely through that forest, unchecked by her loving but distant father. Most often, her rambles took her to a small glade filled with wildflowers where she would knit herself flower chains to wear. One day, she found a plant with five-pointed leaves, dark green on the underside and a soft silver on top, growing out of the broken snag of a fallen tree. She worked one of those star shaped leaves into the chain of flowers she was wearing as a crown on her head. Then, as she was on her way home, the young lady Uta happened upon another person in the forest.

This person was taller than her father, but the individual's long hair, delicate cheekbones, and style of dress convinced the young Uta that it was a woman. To this day, though, she could not be sure. "I am sure, however," the lady Uta explained to Kalwain, "that it was a faerie from the faerie queen's court, and this courtier had been sent to our realm to find Starlight's Wort. The courtier recognized the leaf in my crown as what she was looking for, and she promised me a reward if I showed her where I'd found it.

"So, I took her to the broken stump, and she told me that Starlight's Wort only grows in the decaying remains of trees that once housed wood nymphs. I was enchanted. Wouldn't any little girl be?"

St. Kalwain grumbled, "I haven't known many little girls, but it sounds grisly to me. Dead wood nymphs."

The lady Uta laughed. "Yes, I suppose that's one way to look at it, but all I was thinking was that a wood nymph once lived in my forest. Anyway, the faerie asked me what I'd like for my reward, and I said I'd like to see her faerie wings."

Now St. Kalwain laughed. He'd known faeries too well for too long to remember a time when he pictured them as good forest sprites with dazzling butterfly wings.

"As you clearly know," the lady Uta said, "the faerie courtier told me that real faeries don't have wings. I was dreadfully disappointed, but I came up with a different request."

"You asked for a horse," St. Kalwain said. "That's a good request."

"Yes," the lady Uta agreed. "I asked for a horse of my own. I wanted a companion. So, the faerie courtier took a strange looking pea pod out of the satchel of herbs at her waist. She opened the pod and gave me a single pea. She told me to feed it to my father's old mare, which of course I did, and that old, old mare soon grew pregnant. Although, there were no stud horses around. Her foal was Jescha." The lady Uta patted her green steed affectionately on the neck.

"So, Jescha has been touched by the faerie queen like me," St. Kalwain said.

"Yes, she's been blessed," the lady Uta said.

"Ah, then, not like me."

"What do you mean?" the lady Uta said. "The faerie queen has made you a saint."

"No," St. Kalwain said, the fur on his shoulders bristling under his cloak. "My own deeds have made me a saint. The faerie queen made me a beast."

"You think you're cursed?" the lady Uta asked. "You think you would have done all those great deeds and saved all those lives without the faerie queen's touch on you?"

Maybe not, St. Kalwain thought. But no one had asked him if he wanted to be a saint.

The lady, the saint, and the miracle steed rode on in silence. By the time they crested the final hill and could see Uta's village in the distance, the fog had melted away and the snow glittered with sunlight. It was a cold March.

Villagers spotted the travelers long before they reached the first cottage. St. Kalwain and Uta watched as the village streets filled with people. Everyone was excited to meet the saint who'd come to save them.

"There will be a feast tonight," the lady Uta said. "In your honor. Then, tomorrow, you can face the dragon."

St. Kalwain smiled bitterly as the lady Uta brought their steed to a halt. He was familiar with the feasts that villages held in his honor, the night before he was meant to do battle. They were farewell feasts. A hero's goodbye. In case he did not succeed. No village wanted to be responsible for the death of a saint without even giving him a proper sending-off to Heaven's gate. Of course, there would be no gate to Heaven awaiting St. Kalwain if he failed here. Only walls of flesh and a throne of bone.

"Very well," St. Kalwain said to Uta, helping her down from Jescha's back. Then, he turned to the gathering crowd, raised his voice and said, "I hear you have a dragon here."

The crowd, as an entity, murmured. A few young children shrieked, as if the very word 'dragon' had summoned the visage of the dreadful beast before them. Then, an older gentleman, still able-bodied but gray around the edges, stepped forward from the crowd. He carried a pennant—a narrow, tapering flag that had been inscribed with a wolf's paw and the letter 'K.'

St. Kalwain shuddered at the sight of that hated symbol. He wanted to hide his hands—those offending paw-like monstrosities—that had inspired the symbol. But the man holding the pennant reached forward, found St.

Kalwain's right hand, and drew it forth into a hearty handshake.

How brave you must feel for touching me, St. Kalwain thought. The man hid his discomfort well. At least, from anyone only looking at him with their eyes. His scent, however, gave him away. St. Kalwain hated his nose for always telling him how fake the pleasantries and compliments were from the people in the villages he helped. Perhaps, he could have settled down and made some sort of life for himself somewhere, instead of skulking in the woods like a wild animal, if it weren't for his nose. But the faerie queen hadn't just given him the face and gnarled paws of a wolf. She'd given him a wolf's keen senses as well.

After shaking St. Kalwain's hand, the man introduced himself as the mayor of the town. He gave a speech, thanking St. Kalwain for honoring their village with his presence; praising St. Kalwain for all the great deeds he'd done in the past; and prognosticating St. Kalwain's certain success on the morrow. It would have all been quite inspiring if the stench of nervous uncertainty, flavored with a hint of revulsion, hadn't been wafting off the man's body.

The crowd applauded. Then, people parted to let the mayor and his charges pass. The people began disappearing back into their houses, returning to their normal business. Some of them scurried off to set up the evening feast. The lady Uta went with them. In the meantime, the mayor led St. Kalwain on a tour of the small town. It wasn't an impressive metropolis, but, then, St. Kalwain had found that most dragons were mean-spirited, lazy creatures. And small, helpless towns were easier to victimize.

St. Kalwain saw little damage to the town. A few buildings had suffered scorch marks, but there were no charred ruins. Likely, the town had chosen to pay the dragon off with sacrifices of livestock and treasure. Most dragons settled for such sacrifices, though St. Kalwain had once faced a six-legged silvery drake who actually insisted his offerings be human and virginal. That had been an ambitious dragon, and almost strong enough to back his ambition. The battle between him and Kalwain had lasted nearly a fortnight, and afterward the church convened and christened the tired, battered, beleaguered wolf-boy a saint.

St. Kalwain had been happy for a while then. He tried settling down in the town he'd saved. He'd built himself a homestead cottage and courted a maiden who had bathed his furry brow during his recovery. He brought her flowers, picked fresh from the forest. And fresh slain venison. But his keen ears let St. Kalwain hear her one day inside her house when he came to call. Her words reached him before he reached the door to knock, and they struck him like blows to the face. *Hideous. Disfigured. Beast.*

He abandoned his cottage and took to roaming. For a while, he sought out villages in distress, trying to earn release from the faerie queen's curse as soon as possible. Over the years, though, he took to staying longer and longer in the depths of the forest. Eventually, he gave up on ever coming back.

Then the lady Uta had come for him.

The feast that night was held in the great hall that served as both church and town hall. It had high ceilings and tall windows of stained glass. St. Kalwain imagined the stained glass would be brilliant in morning light, but, come morning, he would have more on his mind than colorful depictions of holy figures and sacred scenes. Tonight, they glittered darkly in the lamplight. The long tables were laid with fresh baked breads, pots of jam and preserves, boiled eggs, and meat that had been cooked in savory spices to cover the smell of age. St. Kalwain could remember enjoying spiced lamb as a young man. Now, it smelled rotten to him, and he shuddered to see people eat it. He kept to the eggs himself, wistfully wishing that he could duck away in the night to hunt down a rabbit or bird.

That possibility seemed unlikely. There was a desperate, frantic quality to the feasting and celebrating of the villagers. As if their forced cheerfulness now could affect his success tomorrow. So, they danced and sang, cheered and jeered at each other with jokes, laughing too hard. Women even asked St. Kalwain to dance, but only the drunk ones. The smell of alcohol on their breath sickened him, and the whispers he heard after their mad whirls in his arms stung. *"It's like dancing with a dog!"* *"He looked like he was* leering *at me the whole dance."—"Oh, that's just his wolf snout; horrible, isn't it?"*

St. Kalwain would show them. He'd kill their dragon, and the faerie queen would return him to his proper form. Then they'd see who he really was. Unfortunately, St. Kalwain feared he'd already seen who they really were, and he couldn't imagine forgiving their cruel jibes. The only woman in the hall who'd been kind to him in his cursed form was Uta. Perhaps, the only woman in the world.

The lady Uta had come to the feast, transformed. She wore a simple white dress that draped to the floor, with sleeves that widened and hung from her arms like the wings that faeries don't have. Her hair was down, and in the warm lamplight, it glowed with auburn highlights. She didn't dance or laugh raucously. She separated from the others, and settled herself demurely on the floor with the hounds that guarded the hall's entrance. The hounds were a pair of bassets, trained to bay at the first sign of trouble. The lady Uta fed them table scraps and stroked their long ears.

Gathering his courage, St. Kalwain broke away from the frenetic whirl of drunken dancing. He approached the lady who had been his companion through many days' travel in the snow. He felt his claws click on the stone floor as he walked toward her, and his ears flicked nervously. He wished they didn't show his emotions so brazenly. He wished they weren't wolf's ears at all.

"My lady," he said, kneeling down beside Uta and the bassets. He reached a hand to join her in stroking them, but it looked too wrong. His paw on the basset's back.

One dog stroking another. He pulled the offending appendage back and wrapped his arms tight around himself, burying his paw-hands in the folds of his cloak.

They sat together for a while, listening to the noise in the hall. St. Kalwain's keen ears let him make out much of the drunken conversation, but he wasn't sure how much the lady Uta could distinguish. Most of it was village gossip. Of little interest to anyone and none to a traveler, new to the town. Then, St. Kalwain heard a man speaking with the mayor say, "Do you think he'll win? This dog-man? Do you really think he'll kill the dragon?"

The mayor's answer was slurred with drink, but the sentiment was clear enough: "If not, then thish shaint should 'ave enough meat on 'im to keep that ol' lizard fat an' happy for a week or more. Better'n no shaint, if you ask me. Better'n feeding the lizard more sheep."

The lady Uta met St. Kalwain's eyes, but then she turned away. Her cheeks grew faintly pink, and she breathed the words, "I'm sorry."

"There's no need to be sorry," St. Kalwain said boldly, surprising the lady by having heard her whispered words. "I will slay that dragon." His words were brave, but, in that moment, St. Kalwain was not. He'd slain many dragons, but it never got easier. Each dragon was a new battle to the death, and the death could easily be his.

Then, the lady Uta turned her face back and smiled at him. Suddenly St. Kalwain felt much more sure of his words. "Yes, I'll slay the dragon, and then the faerie queen has promised to free me from this curse. I'll be a normal man again."

The lady Uta's smile faded, and her face turned away.

"Perhaps not a handsome man," St. Kalwain faltered, wishing he knew what to say to please the woman before him. He had no guile. Only honesty. "But a man, and one that has done many great things."

"Will you be done doing great things, then?" the lady Uta asked. Her voice was low. "There are many villages in need of saving. Many other dragons."

"Haven't I done enough?" St. Kalwain asked, his voice beginning in honest inquiry but turning bitter by the end. "Will it never be enough?"

The lady Uta turned to face him again. She didn't smile, but her eyes searched his. Then, she touched his face—his muzzle—with her delicate, human hand. She traced her fingers along the bridge of his snout, over his brow, and then stroked his ear, much as she'd stroked the bassets. "Poor, tired saint," she said. "I suppose you'll want to settle here. Pick one of my fellow maidens, and make a life." The lady Uta turned to watch the drunken dancers, swaying dreamily. There were fewer now. Many of them had collapsed into chairs, slumped over the long table. St. Kalwain wanted none of them.

"What of you?" he asked. "Once your village is safe, will you go back to roaming the forests, searching out nomadic saints?" St. Kalwain meant his suggestion to be ridiculous. He expected that the lady Uta would want a quiet cottage with a good man caring for her. He would have liked to be that good man.

However, the lady Uta's eyes shone at the question, and her answer surprised him utterly. "Not exactly," she said. "I mean, how many nomadic saints are there? But, yes, I will return to traveling. Maybe I will be a nomadic saint myself some day."

"Truly?" St. Kalwain asked. "You'll return to wandering the forests alone with Jescha?"

"As I said," she answered, "There are many villages still in need of saving."

The lady Uta's attitude was strange and foreign to St. Kalwain. *She would willingly choose the life he'd had thrust on him?* He couldn't understand it, but he was intrigued. "Don't you want your own life? A family? Children?"

The lady Uta looked at St. Kalwain steadily. Her eyes held a seriousness beyond her years. "I do not care to risk my life in childbirth. If I'm to risk my life, I'll do it for a whole village of lives. Not merely one who may awake motherless with a useless, distraught father, too busy mourning to care properly for a child." The lady Uta's voice turned hollow, and she said, "My own mother made that mistake. I will not follow her. I will never marry."

For a moment, St. Kalwain saw years of loneliness stretching out behind those clear blue eyes: an only child of a distant man, with only her faerie-touched horse to befriend her. Then, the lady Uta turned away, and St. Kalwain felt that same loneliness turn into a gulf between them.

It was only a few inches from his hand to the bend of her knee, articulated under the white folds of her dress as they sat on the floor. He wanted to put his hand out and touch her comfortingly. But, he knew he couldn't. His hand was a deformed claw, a wolf's paw not meant to rake a lady's knee. And, yet, if it were a gentleman's hand, as he hoped it soon would be, he knew she would not welcome it.

The music ended and the villagers began to leave. "Good luck on the morrow," the lady Uta wished him. Then, she too stood, graced him with a sad smile, and took her leave.

The mayor of the village found St. Kalwain still sitting with the hounds, his head in a daze. The activity and noise of the feast would have been enough to dizzy him after months in the forest alone. The headiness of the lady Uta's blue-eyed gaze and the unattainable smoothness of her fair skin left St. Kalwain in a complete swoon.

"Come along, good knight," the mayor said, seeming to have sobered up. "The dragon comes early when it comes. And, after hearing our merriment tonight, oh, ho, ho. Tomorrow, it *will* come." So, the mayor showed St. Kalwain to a cot in the back of the church. "You can stay here. Get your rest while you can. Is there anything you'll be needing from us on the morrow?"

St. Kalwain looked at the mayor and wondered what it would be like to live out the rest of his life in this town. This pudgy, self-important man would be his alpha here. But, then, maybe if he settled in this town, St. Kalwain would become the mayor himself. He wasn't sure he wanted the job, but he knew he'd have trouble respecting a man who'd equated his own life to that of a sacrificial sheep the night before battle.

"No, thank you," he said. "I have everything I need." He gestured with his paw to the sword he'd dropped on the cot. "I'll try to do better tomorrow than one of your sheep. I think the sword and claws—", he raised his hands and showed his long, curved claws, "—will help."

The mayor staggered backward as if St. Kalwain had threatened him with a blow. His chubby face flushed purple and then red, but he didn't apologize for his earlier words. He merely stumbled out of the church hall as quickly as his awkward, drunken legs would carry him, muttering inchoately all the while.

Lying on the cot that night, St. Kalwain considered abandoning the village, but he didn't think the faerie queen would tolerate him returning to his hermitage in the forest. He would have to face the dragon, even if he didn't feel this village was worth saving. Nor humanity worth rejoining.

He would do it for Uta. But, in his heart, he formed a wish: he hoped the dragon would strike a fatal blow before the end. As he slew the dragon, let the dragon slay him as well. Rob the faerie queen of her last condescension. Save him from a life with accolades from cowards and love from women too shallow to see his worth beneath a little fur and a few claws.

Yet, part of him knew, when the snout was gone and

the keen sense of smell with it; the wolf's ears and their uncanny hearing; then, he could finally belong again. He'd no longer smell cowardice like a brand on a man or hear jibes whispered about him behind closed doors. Over time, he'd forget the cowardice and jibes existed. Surely, he would.

Wouldn't he?

St. Kalwain agonized between dreading and coveting the return of his purely human form all night. A tired, frightened man with the haggard appearance of an unkempt, bipedal wolf, fur scraggly and disarrayed, was greeted by the light of dawn shining through the church hall window. Moments after his eyes opened, St. Kalwain heard the many-tongued shriek of the dragon outside.

He rose, took up his sword, and went to greet his destiny. The stained glass glowed upon him, casting merry, dancing pools of colored light on his cloak and fur, as he strode through the church. He didn't notice. His eyes were filled with memories of Uta in her long white dress, sitting beside him on the cobbled floor. Perhaps as he died, she would cool his fevered brow. Perhaps, if he was indeed dying, that chaste lady would let him steal a final kiss.

The morning air outside the church was chilled. The wind carried the dragon's shrieks—a cacophony of voices, rising together into catcalls, challenges, and yet more jeers. St. Kalwain didn't mind them from the dragon as much as from his supposed peers at his own honorary feast the night before.

"Show yourssself puny knight!"

"I sssee your tracksss riding into town!"

"I heard your death-feassst last night!"

"And I can sssssmell your *fear!*"

The voices made sense when St. Kalwain saw the dragon's long shadow, stretched out by the early morning angle of the sun. It fell on the frost-bitten ground in front of the church—a dark sketch of a beast with one massive body and two broadly arching wings, branching at the shoulders into a veritable snakes' nest of long necks and spade-shaped heads.

The dragon dropped from the sky, landing on its shadow in front of the church. It stood nearly as tall as the church's steeple, and its wings would have spanned the entire width of the church's great hall. Iridescent scales covered the dragon's body, black with a shimmer of blue and green when hit by the light. Red eyes glowed demonically from the many reptilian faces. And forked tongues, ironically silver, flickered in and out of the many sharp-toothed mouths.

St. Kalwain drew his sword. He'd faced dragons before, and he usually went for the neck. A clean slice with his blade or a ragged tearing with his teeth, either way it stopped the putrid, sulfur-smelling breath. That wouldn't work here, so St. Kalwain aimed for another mark. His blunt claws curled around the hilt of his sword as he held the blade straight out before him, pointing like a deadly arrow at the dragon's breast. "Do you have a heart beast!?" St. Kalwain shouted up for the snaking heads to hear.

The dragon flapped its wings, and then folded them along its back. The heads moved in unison one moment, swaying one way together, then they'd change directions and move as if completely independent. As if they were all parts of separate beasts. It was mesmerizing to watch. Terrifying with all the teeth.

"Do *I* have a heart?" one head hissed. Another answered, "I'll have yoursss in a minute!" Others rasped a cackling laugh; others still echoed the first, repeating its words until they lost all sense. A few heads even seemed to babble incoherently, repeating the word *heart* like a chant. But all the eyes looked at St. Kalwain, burning with hunger and hatred.

To avoid the mouths, St. Kalwain dropped to the ground, rolling forward over his shoulder with his sword still gripped in his paw. The roll brought him closer to the dragon while keeping him low. He ran three-pawed, charging the dragon, then feinting to the side. He had to get behind those toothy mouths.

The dragon's back was broad and smooth with scales. St. Kalwain jumped for it and tried to get a purchase with the claws of his free paw. His claws scraped against the scales with a sickening screech, but he didn't get a hold. Meanwhile, the long necks turned, bringing those demon eyes and sharp teeth around to face him. St. Kalwain swung at the dragon's back, and the sharp edge of his sword sliced through the air. It struck hard and came away black with blood, but he couldn't stay for another swing. The heads were too close; the dragon's necks were so long, they could easily snake around to reach him. St. Kalwain loped three-pawed to a safer distance, but before he was out of reach, he took a painful bite to his sword arm.

The dragon's heads laughed and gnashed their teeth. The body turned, and the ropy muscled legs, each much wider than St. Kalwain's torso, carried the dragon after him. Its steps shook the ground.

St. Kalwain charged, feinted, and slashed at the dragon's flank again, but this time he kept a greater distance. He was able to dart out of reach before the vicious mouths reached him. He repeated the tactic until he was out of breath and panting. The dragon's mouths still laughed at him. Although St. Kalwain's strikes drew blood, the dragon seemed hardly injured. St. Kalwain couldn't get close enough for a reasonable swing without risking injury himself.

Snow began to fall from the sky. Great fluffy drops of white clouded the air between St. Kalwain and the dragon laughing at him. A few of the dragon's heads spat bursts of flame that sputtered in the cold air. Other heads hissed. A few still chanted, *"heart, heart!"*

The point of St. Kalwain's blade fell to the ground, and he leaned his weight against the sword like a crutch. The dragon watched him. It was taunting him. Playing with him. Snow gathered on St. Kalwain's muzzle; he licked it off with his long canine tongue. It was wet and soothing. Snow fell on his ears, and he flicked them to throw it off.

St. Kalwain realized that he could not reach the dragon's heart. It was buried too deep beneath the protective mire of necks and heads. He would have to fight the dragon head on. With a final breath to steel himself, St. Kalwain raised his sword again.

This time he charged the dragon, expecting the mouths to bite him and the bursts of flame to burn him. He charged onward anyway, and he brought the sword down with all the strength in his arms. Those cursed arms deformed by the faerie queen's touch were inhumanly, blessedly strong.

One slash after another shed the dragon of its heads. They fell to the ground with heavy thumps. St. Kalwain counted the falls to distract himself from the pain. His hands were slick with his own blood; it ran down his arms, matting his fur. He turned from the fight, fleeing the dragon before the blood could compromise his grip on his sword. He loped away, limping pitifully this time. But, this time, he also knew he'd robbed the dragon of at least fourteen heads.

To get a break from the battle—one he felt he'd more than earned—St. Kalwain continued his flight around the corner of the church and down the street. He headed away from the heart of town, aiming for the forest. He meant to draw the dragon away from the village he'd come to protect, but he also meant to escape to a world where he felt safer. One filled with trees and solitude, instead of with buildings hiding cowering people. All of them were merely waiting, watching, wondering about the outcome of his fight. None of them cared whether he survived, so long as the dragon died. Except maybe Uta.

St. Kalwain collapsed on the frost-broken grass under a sheltering tree. He touched the wounds on his sides lightly, gingerly testing them. He was badly bitten; gashes from the dragon's teeth covered much of his body. But it wasn't time to lick his wounds yet. St. Kalwain estimated that half or more of the dragon's heads were still left. Besides, he could hear the dragon's laughter coming toward him. St. Kalwain could hardly imagine subjecting himself to those horrible mouths again. The pain was so great...

He touched the locket at his breast and knew he was close to completing the faerie queen's service. His paw pads fingered the smooth metal, and he cracked the locket open. Not wide enough to look into: he didn't want to see his reflection, and he didn't want to see the faerie queen. No, he simply whispered into it the poem the faerie queen had given him. He hoped it was for the last time. Then, he made his wish: "Take the pain away. Let the dragon kill me, but take the pain away. That's all the reward I want from you."

St. Kalwain didn't know if the faerie queen was listening, and he didn't know what she would think of his wish. But he pretended to believe that she would grant it, and that was enough for him to raise his sword again and be ready when the great dragon with flapping wings, landed in front of his tree.

The red demon eyes looked at him, and St. Kalwain

saw with horror that there were as many as before. The heads had grown back. In these few minutes of respite, they'd all grown back.

It made no difference, though. St. Kalwain already meant to fight to the death. If the dragon went down with him, all the better. If he was finally bested in battle, so be it. He only hoped the faerie queen would grant his wish and let him die. He did not want to be a hound in her court. He would never see that as a fair price.

St. Kalwain thought of the mistake that had brought him here—one well-aimed arrow, and one terribly unfortunate mark. He hadn't known the creature was anything more than an unusual fox-like animal (and a very tasty one it turned out) until the faerie queen and her courtiers came to him later that night, long ago. The faerie queen informed him that he'd slain her favorite hound and would have to pay a price.

Even so, he felt that he should have been allowed to pay the price while remaining a man. Instead, he'd been cursed with that faerie hound's visage—a muzzle, paws, and fur—and had been constantly threatened with being forced to take its place at the faerie queen's feet. Well, no more. He raised his sword and met the hydra dragon.

The steel blade flashed and serpentine mouths danced fore and back, biting St. Kalwain from all sides. The dragon's front arms came up, and the large, scaly claws grasped St. Kalwain around the middle, lifting him and pulling him into the medusa's hair of necks and heads. The dragon's claws dug deep into St. Kalwain's waist, crushing him tightly, and he began to feel weary from all the blood loss and seemingly endless bites.

Heads continued to fall, but they also continued to grow. St. Kalwain gave up counting them. He swung the sword senselessly, waiting for unconsciousness or a gift from the faerie queen to take away his pain. Then, he noticed the gleam of golden eyes. Not red. Yellow eyes, like his own. The head hosting them disappeared into the fray of other heads, all black with scales and glinting with silver tongues and teeth. Had St. Kalwain imagined it? He wasn't sure, at first, but then he caught sight of that yellow gleam again. And he knew what he had to do.

St. Kalwain struggled against the massive claws gripping his body. He fought his way in deeper to the nexus of necks. He dropped his sword; it was only hindering him. When he saw the gleam of golden eyes next, he traced the path of that neck back. He waited for that particular cord of black, scaly flesh to come into reach, and then he flung out both arms and grasped with all the desperation of impending death. He would not let that neck go. Not until his teeth and claws had sunk into it, rent it apart, and left the golden-eyed head at the end of it rasping, ineffectively for breath.

The dragon's blood ran black, and its flesh tasted pungent on St. Kalwain's tongue. His teeth and claws pierced the scales and ripped satisfyingly into the meat of the dragon's throat. He would have preferred the final taste on his lips to be a kiss from the lady Uta, but St. Kalwain would have to settle for a final meal of raw dragon meat instead. At least, he wouldn't fail at his final task.

As St. Kalwain struggled, he felt the vise-like grip of the dragon's claws on his middle lessen. The bites slowed down; blinding pain decreased to stabbing, then to dull and throbbing as the bites stopped altogether. St. Kalwain kept his teeth lodged in the golden-eye's throat, but he could see the necks and heads swaying around him. They swooned and began to wilt, as if the dragon was fainting. The entire building-sized body toppled, and St. Kalwain felt a new pressure as half of the necks collapsed on top of him, slamming down like trees falling in the forest.

St. Kalwain closed his eyes and whispered, "Now, my queen. Grant my wish now, or you won't have the chance." Then, he laughed or sobbed; it was a strangled expression. He expected to die, alone and in pain. But that's not what the faerie queen wanted.

"I heard your wish," said a voice like dry leaves, blowing in the wind.

St. Kalwain opened his eyes, but all he saw was black flesh and the clouded sky above. Yet, he knew the faerie queen was near. "You've come," he said. He'd spent most of his life working in the service of the faerie queen. He thought he hated her. He certainly feared her. But, he couldn't have been more relieved and grateful to hear her terrifying voice. He didn't know what she'd do, but he no longer seemed to know how to live in a world without her running it. "Help me," he said.

"I won't grant your wish," she said, taking an edge to

her voice that would have made a dragon cringe. "But I will give you what you truly want."

The pain in St. Kalwain's body—already a fire, burning throughout every inch of him—burst into roaring flame. He cried out; the scream tore through his body, shredding his vocal cords. The sound ascended and then fell away, like a wolf's howl ending in a final whimper.

Slowly the pain ebbed. St. Kalwain's body transformed from a glaring beacon of pain to a physical vessel. He felt he could move again, and he lifted an arm. It bent differently than he expected. His elbow was higher; his wrist lower; and his fingers unresponsive. He was startled by the change and jumped, his legs pushing him out from under the weight of dragon necks. He moved quickly, fluidly, but he found his hands on the ground as if they belonged there. He looked at them, wondering what was wrong. But as he stared down at his paws, he realized he couldn't remember.

Then he heard the sweetest sound in the world. It was a voice singing, and it was a voice he knew well. St. Kalwain wagged his new tail for the first time, not even realizing the strangeness of having a tail now. For it wasn't strange. He was no longer a horrible half-beast. St. Kalwain had been reformed as a single whole: a sleek, beautiful wolf with gray-brown fur and majestic ears.

"This is what you were always meant to be," the faerie queen said, looking at the wolf her magic had made of him. "You are not free, but you are free from me. You will wander the forest in obscurity, at the side of your true love, providing the companionship she needs to be a hero herself. She will call you Saint. Go to her," she said.

The lady Uta was singing a ballad in honor of the fallen St. Kalwain in the distance, a song written by the town's bard as he had watched, safe inside his home, while the noble, tortured beast-man had slain the dragon.

The wolf Kalwain looked at the faerie queen and flicked one of his ears. He didn't like the smell of her, and he growled deep in his throat. Then, he backed away several paces, turned and trotted toward the sound of his new master's song.

38

SPOILER WARNING

SPOILER WARNING: Denise is not the killer.

When a series of people are brutally murdered and gnawed on, inconveniently one full moon after Denise is first bitten by that wolf, it will LOOK like she's the killer. And it will be heartbreaking, because she's just so awkward, nerdy, and sweet. But don't give up. Keep watching. It's not her.

SPOILER WARNING: the wolf who bit Denise is actually the girl in glee club with her.

If you watch carefully, Monica is in the background of every scene set at the high school during the first eight episodes of season one, and she's CLEARLY in love with Denise. Though, she still shouldn't have bitten her while in wolf form, even if she thought it would increase her chances of Denise going to prom with her. It's not cool to turn someone into a werewolf without consent. That goes without saying.

SPOILER WARNING: Monica isn't the killer either, unfortunately she dies in episode eight.

I LEARNED Monica wouldn't be in season two when I saw a trending article about the actor getting a big movie deal and cancelling her contract with *Moon Howlers*. So, obviously, the writers had to kill her off. Disappointing... but still, I'm excited to see the vampire movie she'll be headlining. She has a bright career in front of her. So talented!

SPOILER WARNING: the werewolf commune turns out to be a bunch of flowers-in-their-hair, tree-hugging hippies. None of them are behind the killings.

BASED on the previous shows from this show runner, as soon as we learn about the werewolves' socialistic nature, it's a dead giveaway that none of them are gonna be the killers. I mean, get real. The twin sister team behind *Blood*

Bonded where the vampires start a union? It's never gonna be the socialists in one of their shows. Much more likely to be the gun-toting, pro-fascism cops.

SPOILER WARNING: normal dogs can become infected with the virus and turn into werewolves too. And that one cop who yells at everyone has several dogs.

I COULDN'T BELIEVE how brave Denise was sneaking into the cop's backyard to rescue his dogs from where he'd chained them up. That man did not deserve to have dogs! Even werewolf dogs! Maybe ESPECIALLY not werewolf dogs! Those poor things would never have committed any murders without him beating them! Dogs are too good for cops!

SPOILER WARNING: Denise can communicate with the dogs telepathically when they're all in werewolf form!!!

THE FINALE of season one sets the next season of *Moon Howlers* up to be amazing! The secrets revealed by that Golden Retriever werewolf after Denise bribes him with a squeaky bone? Unbelievable! And to think the community on the /r/MoonHowlers subreddit had it all figured out by episode five from Morse code clues hidden in the twinkling lights decorating Denise's room!

SPOILER WARNING: Netshows cancelled *Moon Howlers,* just like they seem to do with all their shows that have a liberal bent. So we won't get to see what would have happened in season two :(

BUT YOU CAN READ what I think would have happened if you subscribe to my fan fiction, *Moon Howling.* I'll be posting new chapters every Monday.

SPOILER WARNING: in my version, Monica didn't die, and she definitely goes to prom with Denise.

39

SISTER GHOST

THEY SAY that Hot Lake Hotel is haunted, but the shimmer of bluish light in the corner of my room wasn't waiting for me when I arrived. She came with me. She's been following me all of my life. Almost all of my life.

I close the door to my room—lucky number 113—behind me and gratefully pull off the face mask I still wear everywhere. I know that most people have moved on from the pandemic, but between my rattly joints and asthmatic breathing, the last thing I need is to roll the dice on long Covid. So, I still mask up when I go out.

I wonder if Polly would still be masking up after all these years if she were still alive. I like to imagine that she would be. That we'd both be so careful about our exposure and so close, talking all the time, that she'd be the one person I really felt safe letting my guard down around. We'd meet up for dinners once a week, or maybe every other week, and we'd get take-out to share either in my house or her apartment. Or maybe she'd even live in my spare room. We wouldn't have to mask around each other, so we'd chat and laugh, eating chow fun and playing Bananagrams. I can picture it all so vividly.

Instead, Polly drifts through the closed door after me, looking lost and oh so small. She never grew up. She never grew up because of me.

I roll my suitcase into a corner, throw my jacket onto the wide, white bed, and then sit down beside it. Polly kneels down on the floor. There's a vagueness in her eyes like maybe the rest of the world looks as shimmery and translucent to her as she looks to me. She huddles on the floor shivering, always cold, in spite of the stuffy warmth of this hot summer day in eastern Oregon.

I'd hoped Polly wouldn't be cold here like she always has been in the valley, but also, I knew better. We get our hot days in the valley too—especially since the summers started heating up—and I've never seen Polly stop shivering. Not once since she died.

"What do you want to do first?" I ask. If anyone else were here, it would look like I were talking to an empty room. I've never met anyone else who could see Polly. Not even our parents. Not even Mom. And Polly almost never answers me anyway, so I learned a long time ago not to bother most of the time. But this trip is special. This trip is for her.

I wait a little longer than usual for Polly to answer, but then I start listing off the options—soaking pools, pub, sun room. "There's even a theater right inside the hotel, but they're only playing *Edward Scissorhands*," I say, tracing my fingers around the edges of the rectangular paper ticket that came complimentary upon checking in.

It's only one ticket, but a place like this won't have a full house. I'm sure I could find a seat with an empty seat next to me for Polly. Still, it feels wrong to do something that excludes her like that when I came here especially for her. "I don't think you'd like *Edward Scissorhands*. Too scary."

Polly may be a ghost, and she may have been walking this earth beside me for nearly forty years... But she's also the same five-year-old girl she was when she died. Unchanging. Untouched by time. She may not talk much, but she looks bored when I watch lawyer dramas, and I catch her smiling if I turn on Disney musicals.

There was a time when I tried to convince myself I'd done Polly a favor. I'd been a bitter, cynical teenager, angry at the world and tired of being angry at myself because she was gone, and I thought, maybe, being an eternal five-year-old, walking through the world unnoticed would be a better way to live. Ironic, since she's not living.

I'm not always sure what Polly is—a shadow of the past? My own guilt manifested? One of those squiggles that shows up in your eyes for an hour, and when you go to the doctor, they tell you it was a migraine episode, caused by wonky blood flow or something? Maybe I've been having some sort of unusual migraine headache ever since I was seven years old and made a fatal mistake, thinking I was just playing a game with my cousins.

"Right," I say, standing up from the bed, making an executive decision. "Let's start by exploring."

I put my mask back on and head back out into the eerie, long hallways of the hotel with their patches of exposed brick, high ceilings, and pipes of electrical wiring that were clearly added on long after it was originally built. This place has a long history: it was an asylum, a hospital, an orphanage. It's been about everything creepy that an old building could possibly be, and now it's a hotel. Lucky for me. Lucky for Polly, I hope.

There are large, old photographs hung in the hallway that show how the hotel used to look—not that different, really. So, there's a weird recursive quality to the photographs hanging like they're somehow fine art in their overly fancy frames. The carpeting sports a faded floral pattern, and I don't know what kind of flooring it's covering, but it's uneven and bumpy as hell.

Polly and I make our way back to the lobby with its windows made up from so many smaller panes of glass. Then we continue on to the pub. It's closed and empty, but overnight guests of the hotel can still wander through the darkened space. There's an eerie quality to a room cheerfully, optimistically filled with chairs and tables, clearly wishing to be occupied, but all of them empty. It's the perfect place for ghosts, and of course, that's the idea.

I brought Polly here to see if I can find her friends. Friends who can see her, maybe talk to her, and make it so she's not entirely alone except for me. She didn't get to live a life, but maybe, I can find a way to give her a better afterlife than she's been having so far, following around a disinterested sister living an unremarkable, very quiet life.

I keep exploring the hotel for a while—there's an old safe the size of a small closet that they've got propped open, and guests have left funny notes taped up inside. There's a courtyard out back with a fountain in it. A couple of other guests are hanging out smoking in the dark back there. I head upstairs to the sun room, despite it being well after sunset. It's really just another space like the various lounging and lobby-like areas around the pub downstairs. Maybe the sun room is more spectacular with sunlight pouring in through the windows, but mostly, this whole place is a funny, old, rickety hotel, and I can see why people would think it's haunted. Although, except for Polly, I haven't seen any ghosts yet.

Maybe after my visit, the Hot Lake Hotel really will be haunted. I think somewhat guiltily that I'm treating Polly like a stray cat who I didn't mean to take in—looking for anyone else who will take her off my hands.

But why shouldn't I? I never signed on to spend my entire life haunted by a little sister who didn't get to grow up. I was a stupid kid who didn't know what I was doing when I told her to hide in Grandpa's old chest from WWII. My cousins and I just thought we'd get to play together a little longer if our parents couldn't find all of us, and well, Polly was the smallest. She fit best in the chest. No one told us it was airtight.

Grandpa should've drilled holes in it. He should've thrown it away.

My cousins and I got more than we bargained for. After Polly was found—as blue as she still is to this day, but as solid as she used to be before I closed the chest with her inside—all of our plans for heading home were forgotten, obliterated by police and hospitals and mortuaries. It's blurred together over the years, but a few moments stand out as bright and sharp as they were when they were happening. I remember staring at an exit sign, bright red with clean, simple lines. I don't remember why or what else was happening while I stared at it, but I remember how it looked. Like any other exit sign, but that was the one that stuck in my mind. Exit signs still make me think of that day.

I don't know when I realized that Polly was a ghost. I was seven, and I understood that she was dead. I knew no one else could see her, and she didn't act the same anymore. She didn't fight with me over toys. She didn't complain when I told Mom that I'd rather go to a Chinese restaurant or a Mexican restaurant rather than some fast food burger place yet again. In some ways, she was easier to get along with—just a quiet shadow, never asking for full consideration anymore, because she wasn't really a person anymore. Just a memory. But a memory I couldn't let go of.

Having finished our tour of the grounds, I swing back by my room and change into my swimming suit, throwing one of the complimentary robes over the top of it and tucking a rolled up towel under my arm.

"Come on, let's check out the soaking pools," I say to Polly, trying to talk to her like a person. It feels weird and awkward after all of the years I've spent ignoring her, letting her be a smudge of blue seen out of the corner of my eye. She's sat through so many office meetings, rode quietly in the backseat of my car while I've listened to podcasts, wandered aimlessly through so many grocery trips. I had to learn to ignore her. It was self-defense. But now, I'm trying to open that wound back up, maybe dig out the piece of shrapnel that lodged in my heart, keeping the scar from ever fully closing.

The soaking pools are between the hotel and the lake, under the open sky. There are five of them in a row, each of them filled with hot water piped directly from the lake. The lake water is scalding hot. There are danger signs posted all around it, warning people to stay out if they want to stay alive. I wonder how many children have died trying to play in this lake. I wonder how long ago. I wonder if any of them are still around, lonely ghosts, waiting to meet a new friend.

I settle into one of the round concrete tubs. There's a bench under the water, and sitting on it, the water comes up to my shoulders. Warm and cozy. I can look out on the lake, surrounded by grassy reeds, with steam rising from its surface. Even if there weren't a history of insane asylums and orphanages associated with the hotel here, I can easily see how someone could look out at the amorphous forms hovering over the lake and imagine ghosts instead of simple steam.

A small figure flies by above in the darkness, and at first, I imagine it's a songbird because of the size. But it's too late at night by now for a songbird to fly by. Maybe a small owl? But when it flies by again, I can make out the wings better, and then it chirps and squeaks in that distinctive voice that can only belong to one thing—it's a bat. I'm soaking in a pool by a haunted lake, watching bats fly by overhead.

"What do you think, Polly?" I ask, trying not to let my tongue stumble over her name. None of us liked saying her name after she died. It was like the entirety of her life, her whole self, got tied up in the way she'd ended, and her name didn't mean her anymore. It meant death. It meant shame. It meant loss. It meant heartache. "Do you like the bats?"

Polly loved animals when she'd been alive. I don't remember a lot about her, not really. You'd think I would, since she's been following me all this time. But I don't. Like I said, it all starts to blur together when you're looking at it through the rear-view mirror of time. But I know Polly loved animals, especially cats.

That's when I notice that Polly has found a cat—a grumpy-looking tuxedo cat with a scar across his nose and paws so big that it almost looks like he has thumbs. This must be Rocky, the cat who has signs all over the outside of the hotel warning not to let him inside.

Polly is crouched down in front of Rocky, who's lying

on his side, tail twitching behind him. I've seen animals react to Polly before, not often, but often enough to seem significant. If Rocky can see Polly, I wonder if he can see other ghosts around here. Maybe if Polly and I follow him around, I could find clues as to whether there really are other ghosts here, simply hiding from me the way that Polly hides from everyone but me.

I soak in the hot water beside the lake for a long while. I don't know how long, because I left my phone back in the hotel room. All I brought out with me was the rolled up towel and the brass key to room 113 tucked into the pocket of my robe. As I watch, Polly strokes Rocky's side and scritches his ears. The gruff-looking cat seems to like it. Reality and daydreams blend together as I imagine a balrog storming about in the lake, heating the water with the fire under its rocklike skin. Kelpies prance along the scalding shoreline, luring children to their doom, but then, letting those same children ride on their backs, clinging to their kelp-like manes, once they've transformed from warm bodies into shivering ghosts—trading their lives for a chance to play with the dangerous, murder-ponies.

Once my fragile, living body has soaked up as much heat as it can take from the hot water, I get out, dry off with the towel, and put the robe back on. "I'm going to bed," I tell Polly, but she's too busy following Rocky around as he struts across the carefully manicured lawns to answer me. Or maybe she's playing tag with some of those other ghost children, the ones I can't see but have been imagining so vividly. "You stay out as long as you want, okay?"

"Okay," Polly says. If she were a real, living five-year-old, I couldn't leave her out here, alone, beside a scalding hot lake in the middle of the night.

But she's not real, is she? She's just a memory. No more real than the version of her I like to imagine sometimes who has an apartment across town from me and comes over every week for dinner. The version who grew up, got a job, and made a life for herself. The version who would have been free to fight with me over Mom and Dad paying off my college debt and how unfair it was that they didn't spend as much on her, while I argue back that it's not my fault I got into a more expensive college than she did. The version who lectures me on animal cruelty every time I eat meat or even put honey in my tea. The version who bikes everywhere and judges me for ruining the environment by driving a car. The version who hasn't talked to me for seven years, and neither of us seems to care at all about fixing it.

I don't know who Polly would have become if she'd gotten to grow up. I don't know if we'd even still be talking, but at least, she'd be out there, alive, and I would know she was out there. I could pick up my phone and call her, push aside all the trivial differences, and just find out how she's doing. Hear her voice. Know that the person I shared my earliest years with is still carrying those memories through the world, no matter how differently she saw those years. Maybe between us, we could triangulate the reality of what our childhood was really like, or maybe, we'd just argue over and over again, never really knowing which one of us was right.

There's an entire world of difference between having a living sister and having lost my sister to a terrible, heartbreakingly avoidable accident when she was five. But right now, in this moment, I go back into my hotel room, lay down on the wide, white bed, and I think about the clean, red lines of a glowing exit sign. And I know, Polly is going to stay here.

I'm done being followed by her ghost.

40

SEVEN RIDERS AND SIX HORSES

SEVEN RIDERS on six horsebacks and one mechanical contraption, each of the seven blessed with wings, flew toward the sea.

The horses' wings were made of tawny feathers, golden when the sun hit them right, downy and angelic. The mechanical contraption's wings were less wings and more of a spinning rotor in a tarnished shade of silver, held above the rider by a jointed, metal arm, heavy with bolts. It didn't look air-worthy, but it was.

None of them looked air-worthy. Horses don't usually take to the air. But these six did.

All seven riders flew toward the sea, summoned by the queen.

Her castle rose from the water, surrounded by pounding waves on all sides, centered on a tiny island, completely filling the tiny patch of land right up to its edges. Turrets and spires rose toward the sky, topped with sea-blue pennants and flags waving in the coastal wind. Built from warm, golden granite, the castle could have been a sand castle, mere moments from melting into the waves. And yet it stood, strong, having lasted for generations.

Salt filled the air as the winged horses landed on a flat patch of granite, the highest rampart of the castle. The mechanical contraption followed, whipping the salty air into a frenzy with its whirling helicopter blades. The horses pawed at the granite with their hooves, knackering and whinnying, shifting weight from hoof to hoof, ever moving, ever impatient to fly again.

The helicopter-device, though, once its blades stopped spinning, stood perfectly still. A strange statue, covered in gears and bolts. Nothing more.

One of the horses approached the closest of the blades, nostrils wide, sniffing the metallic flavor of the material in the salt air, sneezed, and backed away with skepticism in its dark eyes.

The riders dismounted, all seven.

The riders knelt, the rough fabric of their pantaloons wetted by the slick granite under each bended knee. But each rider stayed low, head held at a respectful forward tilt, until the queen walked by, nodded, and tapped each one on the shoulder with her fan.

"You may rise," the queen said as she tapped the final rider on her shoulder, the one who had flown in on a mechanical abomination instead of a trusty equine steed. "You may make your case."

"My horse died," the rider said. Simple and plain, three words. But the crack in her voice said more than mere words could communicate.

"I know," the queen said. "Your captain sent word ahead by carrier dove."

The captain of the guard—the rider of the tallest, proudest of the horses—nodded to their queen, acknowledging the statement and its truth. She added, "We tried to provide another, a perfectly good foal on the verge of adulthood. Smart, strong, and ready for bonding. Jyan refused."

Jyan shook her head. The riding goggles dangling about her neck bounced with the vehement suddenness of her gesture. "I cannot bond to a new horse. I cannot." She had loved her horse with all of her heart. She didn't need to say so. All the riders felt the same love for their own horses, and the queen, who would never be a rider or bond with a winged horse, would never understand.

The queen could imagine.

The queen could sympathize.

But she could never truly understand what it was to blend one's purpose and being with the steadfast might of a winged horse, bending the rest of your life to riding with one through the skies, moving together, sharing the world and a duty to defend the queen and her castle. Some experiences transcend words.

And yet, perhaps the queen's failure to fully understand the magic and power of bonding with a winged horse was exactly why she was able to look at the seventh rider's face, see the emotion in her eyes, and feel an empathy founded not on understanding but on simple compassion.

Where the other six riders saw a wound that could be healed—Jyan needed only to bond to a new foal and feel new contentment—the queen saw simply a wound.

"Show me this device you've made." The queen gestured at the seventh rider's contraption, and weariness fled from Jyan's face, chased away by joy.

"I learned the machine-crafting from a village of elves," Jyan said, putting her hands protectively, possessively on her contraption. She touched each part, explaining each part and its purpose, as proud of the hunk of metal as any rider could be of their newly bonded foal. But this bond came with no baggage. The mechanical contraption would never die. As pieces broke, they could be replaced. If the whole thing rusted into an unmoving block, each piece could be replicated and reconstructed into an identical, new copter. It would carry Jyan through the air without asking anything. It would neither share joy nor bring pain.

And right now, that was what Jyan needed. Not another foal to love and someday mourn. Or worse, leave to mourn her after she died.

Winged horses did not live long without their riders.

The metal contraption, though, could be passed down through the generations.

"What do you think?" Jyan asked her queen, trepidation shoving its way into the corners of her eyes, shadowing the joy and pride living there. "It's a powerful machine, and it lets me do everything I could do before—" Her voice broke. She could not say the name of her horse who had died. Not yet. "—before I needed to build it."

"Yes," the queen said. She did not keep Jyan waiting. "You are still a member of my guard. Your oath does not require you to bond to a new horse."

The other riders gasped. They had not expected Jyan's petition to succeed. Not a one of them. They were used to the old queen's stolid defense of tradition and had not expected the new, younger queen to be swayed to change so easily.

And yet, perhaps one or two of the other riders felt a sense of relief. They could choose whether to bond again to a new foal when their beloved horses died. There was a new choice, and even if it was strange and mechanical, there was a peacefulness to riding the skies in a device without a heart and mind of its own.

Sometimes, the greatest joy in life is to share. Sometimes, the greatest peace comes from being allowed to be alone.

Jyan would continue to ride the skies, and when other riders asked—and they would ask—she would teach them to make their own mechanical copters.

And maybe, someday, she would bond to a horse again. But if it ever happened, it wouldn't be for a long, long time. And it would be because she chose to, not because she was forced into an impossible decision between her calling and the tenderness of her healing heart.

41

DEALERSHIP WITH THE DEVIL

THE SALESMAN, Devin, shows me another junker—dented fender, bald tires, and a crack in the windshield.

"These cars look like death traps," I say. "You don't seriously expect anyone to buy them?"

Devin laughs, a hollow, plastic sound. "They're all bargains!" He looks over his shoulder, back at the dealership building with a half-burned out neon sign, *Bob Reaper's Autos*, over a window with venetian blinds. A gaunt man, probably Bob himself at a place this small, stares at us through the blinds.

Devin says, "Look, Mr. Reaper has a quota to meet, so he wants me to push these... uh... well-loved classics."

I frown at the gray Honda Civic in front of us. I wouldn't call it classic.

"We do have a car that you might like better."

Devin takes me to the end of the line of junkers. The

car he shows me is white, plain, but not obviously beat-up. "What's the catch?" I ask.

"No catch. This is the best car you'll ever buy, a dream to drive. Go as fast as you like, and you'll never hit anything, never get pulled over."

I roll my eyes, wondering why I even bothered to ask. But this one does look more promising. "I guess I could give it a test drive."

Devin gets the keys for me, and I settle into the driver's seat. He sits down beside me. I turn the key in the ignition, and the engine roars to life. It feels surprisingly powerful, like the car wants me to drive fast.

I drive us out to the freeway, pulled along by the car's hunger to fly. Damn, it feels good. Without realizing it, I'm already over the speed limit. I try to slow down, but I don't want to.

Sirens blare at the side of the highway. I glare at Devin. "I thought you said I'd never get pulled over?" Out of the corner of my eye, I see a car shift into the fast lane in front of me—it must be going the speed limit, because compared to me it's crawling along like an inchworm. I swerve, suddenly, to avoid rear-ending it. The car behind me isn't so lucky. In my rearview, I see the two cars collide, spin out. The cop is blocked and pulls off to deal with them.

"Damn," I say. "That was my fault."

"Does it matter?" Devin asks. "You didn't get pulled over. You didn't hit anyone. Sounds to me like the other drivers should have been more careful."

I press my foot into the accelerator and the engine roars again. I zoom along, thinking hard. If I drive carefully, then I'm not doing anything wrong. Is it my fault if other drivers have trouble staying out of my way? Hell, if I wasn't in such a maneuverable car, those careless drivers back there might have slammed into me.

I need this car. "Devin, you've got yourself a deal."

He grins. "I'll have Bob draw up the contract."

42

THE DRAGON IN MY TOE

A TINY DRAGON burrowed into the big toe on my right foot, curled up around the joint, and lives in there now. Well, sleeps there. It seems to sleep all day long, like a cat in a sunbeam. Except, a dragon. In my toe.

Most of the time, I don't notice it at all. But sometimes, the dragon shifts in its sleep, writhing and rearranging, and I feel all the spines along its back and long, coiling tail scrape and screech against my bones, brightening my foot with pain like lightning forks across the sky.

Surely, the sky would be a better place for a dragon than my toe? Even if it is a very tiny dragon.

I went to the doctor. To see if anything could be done. About the dragon, you know? I waited in the office with all the other tired-looking, patiently impatient people, and when my turn came, I wore the gauze slipper on my foot, got it X-rayed, and then waited in a different room for the doctor to come to me with news.

"It's a dragon all right," the doctor says as she shows me the black-and-white picture of the inside of my foot. The bones are white. The spaces between them black. And the dragon? A beautiful charcoal gray, coiled up around my toe like one of those earring cuffs girls wear when they want to feel like fairies.

I'd so much rather wear a fake dragon on my ear than have a real one hiding out in my toe. At least, when earring cuffs start to hurt and chafe, you can take them off.

"Is there anything I can do?" I ask to the doctor. "To make it go away? Like I could make a nice little nest for it in one of my shoes with some sparkly rocks like the ones they use to decorate aquariums... Maybe it would rather live there?"

The doctor stares at me like I'm some kind of blithering fool. "You've been chosen as the beloved treasure of a dragon," she says, "and you want to make it go away?"

"It hurts," I complain, pathetically.

The doctor frowns at me, shakes her head, and prescribes a special lotion. I pick it up from the pharmacy on my way home.

Later that night, I search the internet—desperately looking for alternatives. But there aren't any. When a dragon picks you, that's it. You're a dragon's home now, and there's not really anything anyone can do. Except, I guess, spread some lotion on it.

So, I settle down on my bed, one leg bent and the leg

with the dragon-toe stretched out in front of me. I read the instructions on the lotion bottle—they're in a tiny font and full of scary warnings about overuse or accidental swallowing. I definitely shouldn't get the lotion in my eyes. Anything strong enough to lull a dragon into a deeper, sounder sleep could do real damage to a delicate retina.

I sit there, holding the bottle of lotion, and stare at my toe. I imagine taking a knife to it—digging the sharp point of a kitchen knife into my toe, rooting around in my own flesh, trying to slice the offending creature out. It would hurt, and based on everything I've read—everything the doctor said, and the internet, and even the AI chat program I asked for advice—it wouldn't work anyway. At best, I'd leave my toe impossibly mangled by the time the dragon gave up and flew away. Then I'd have pain anyway, but no dragon. Is that better?

At worst—and as I understand it, this is much more likely—the dragon would crawl higher in my leg, perhaps wrapping around my ankle or slithering its way all the way up into my knee. Up there, it would have more room to grow. It would get bigger. There'd be more pain.

Right now, the dragon is small, and if I lull it into a deeper sleep with daily applications of lotion, it'll stay that way. It'll dream its way through my life.

I wonder what it's dreaming about.

Visions of butcher knives and amputations drift away as my mind fills with ponderings—do dragons dream about piles of gold? Soaring through the sky? Growing big enough to breathe fire and terrorize villages instead of just one person with a painful toe?

I unscrew the lid on the lotion bottle, squeeze some of the glistening paste onto my toe, and then rub it in, letting it soak through my skin to the sleeping dragon beneath. The lotion smells strongly of chemicals, a smell I'll probably get very used to over the years.

I can't see the dragon, but I keep thinking about how pretty it looked in the X-ray in black and white. What color are its scales for real—emerald green? As blood red as rubies? I'll never know.

There's something beautiful inside my toe.

And yes, sometimes, I'll jostle the dragon too much, and it will shift positions in its sleep, and my toe will scream with pain. That's part of my life now, for the rest of my life.

I hate pain.

But I hope...

I hope the dragon is having sweet dreams.

43

WHEN THE GHOST OF THE FUTURE CATCHES UP

THE HARSH BLUE light of Astralis II shone over the horizon, casting long shadows at an acute angle to the shorter shadows cast by the tawny, warm light of Astralis I, nearly overhead at this hour of noon-night. The longest, sharpest shadow pointed towards the volcanic cone of Mount Kiyaro; it was cast by the pearlescent, spiraling horn that rose from Elliae's snowy-furred equine brow. She faced the mountain; she faced her destiny.

"Giddyap!" the demon-imp on the unicorn's back shouted, digging his heels into her side.

Elliae reared and whinnied, but Karoon clung to her, fists wrapped in the unicorn's flowing mane, tight as a tick. He'd ridden her across solar systems, through the vacuum of space and the glittering darkness of nebulae. She'd spent eons lost in the void with only his telepathic whispers in her ear to remind her of who she was, where she was going. But now they were here, and the mountain loomed before them.

"The spirits will catch up to us!" Karoon dug his sharp heels deeper into the unicorn's heaving sides.

Elliae knew they had at least a lunar month's lead on the spirts chasing them. She had sliced through the folds of space with her horn, cutting across the empty blackness faster than any spirit could. Her horn had been designed by the All-Deity to carve through spatial dimensions, and her hooves had been designed to spring off the surface tension of reality. No mere ghost could fly as fast as a unicorn. The spirits' ectoplasmic structure was written onto the surface of reality and must fold with it. Only a unicorn could transcend the layers.

Yet Karoon dug his pointy demon heels into her side, and Elliae broke into a tired trot with a sigh. She had been made for better than this. She had been designed for spreading beauty and love across the universe—from brightening a single moment with the sudden appearance of a colorful butterfly (transported through a deftly cut portal in space-time) to adjusting the orbit of entire planets into the habitable zones around their stars (again by slicing space-time into a cooperative shape with her powerful horn). But ever since Karoon's master—Zilther the Corruption of Universes—had captured her, saddled her with his minor demon as a slaver, and held her beloved home of Lunaie hostage, Elliae had been little more than a carthorse, dragging Karoon from one planet to the next, ensuring none of them would grow into beautiful inhabited homes.

One wasteland after another.

Dead red planets.

Dusty gray orbs.

No life.

No love.

No beauty.

Not a world for unicorns.

Not a single one.

The peak of Mount Kiyaro grew closer as Elliae plodded across the desolate plains of this young world. Bits of green moss squished under her hooves, and tiny insects buzzed in the air, but once she delivered Karoon to the volcanic mountaintop, it would all end. This world would never develop to its full potential, never know the beauty of teeming with kingdoms and phyla of life.

The last few steps were always the hardest. While flying across the universe, Elliae could forget the corruption she was helping to spread. But when she set her hooves upon the ground that Karoon would soon cover with lava and riddle with extremophile bacteria, rendering the planet toxic to any other life form, Elliae could not avoid seeing the shades of the lifeforms to come, the creatures who would exist if it were not for her complicity. Voices spoke in her pointed ears, and shapes danced before her eyes as she trotted across the plains and up the mountainside.

These were the ghosts who would follow them to the

next world, joining the fleet of spirits chasing them down from all the worlds they'd already visited. Some day, those spirits would indeed catch up to them, but half the universe would already be destroyed by then.

"The day could be today," a voice whispered in her ear. Not Karoon's voice. Not scratchy and demonic. But soft and fluting, like a strain of music carried on the wind from the past. Or the future.

A ghost of this world's future was speaking to her.

"Not this world," the voice said. "Your future."

Elliae whipped her head to the side, flicked her ears, and felt Karoon yank on her mane in response, urging her to keep trotting. Still, she caught sight of an equine figure like herself painted on the air like a fading water-color—a ghostly vision of another unicorn.

"Lunaie is already lost. Do you trust the Corruption to release your home? Ever? Fight back now. Save every world you can, and that means starting with this one." The ghostly unicorn washed away in the hot, dry wind.

Leaving Elliae alone with her demon and her thoughts.

"Too slow, you stupid pointy horse!" Karoon screeched, kicking her repeatedly.

And suddenly, it was one kick too many. Elliae swung her head, swishing her mane, and slicing her horn through the air, cut a portal through the folds of space on the mountainside. Then she reared, stomped down her front feet, and galloped away from the new portal, toward the volcanic mountaintop.

Behind the unicorn and her demon-rider, the portal

poured forth spirits and ghosts who'd been chasing them for eons across the vastness of space. All of them displaced. All of them homeless.

At the lip of Mount Kiyaro's volcanic cone, Karoon leapt off the unicorn's back and screamed at her. "They'll catch us now! We'll never escape this world!" He took the obsidian amulet from his neck, but before he could uncork the black-glass vial to release Corruption's extremophile bacterial presence on this virgin world, Elliae sliced through the air with her horn again. She didn't cut through the dimensions. She only cut through soft demon-skin; she pierced Karoon through, as if he was nothing more than melting butter.

She should have done it long ago.

She unsheathed her horn from his limp body and flicked the still-unopened amulet into the sky, flying so fast, so high it escaped the planet's gravity. The dark amulet flew true, on course for the closer of the world's two suns: Astralis II's blue light would fry the dangerous bacteria inside. Even lava-loving extremophiles couldn't survive a blue star's super-heated plasma.

Elliae's attention returned to the world around her.

The spirits rushed toward her, spiraling around the mountain and stretching across the sky like smears of paint on an empty canvas. Elliae was ready for the ghosts of those she'd betrayed into never-existing to devour her, but then the ghostly unicorn reappeared in front of her like a mirror of herself in the shimmering volcanic air.

"Make this world into their home. Give it to the

ghosts." As the ghostly unicorn said the words to Elliae, she also said them herself. The ghost was her. It was her future to become the ghost.

With a final triumphant whinny, Elliae leapt from the lip of the mountain cone towards the roiling lava inside. As she fell, she speared her way through the air, pearlescent horn slicing a complicated portal into the mountain's volcanic mouth, connecting this planet with as many planets rich with life as she could find. Life would bleed through the folds of the portal, flowing into this world for centuries. In her final act, Elliae made Mount Kiyaro a cornucopia of life and left it to the ghosts, so they could finally realize themselves and create a future.

44

GINGER TEA FOR THE DRAGON

Ever since my fortieth birthday, I've been thinking a lot about mortality. What happens when we die? Is there anything waiting for us on the other side of the veil, or is this life all we have? The thoughts catch me when I'm alone; when it's late at night; or even sometimes right in the middle of a chaotic day, rushing around with my kids on errands.

Once as I was trying to fall asleep, I wondered what it would feel like to be dead—would it be like a dreamless sleep? And suddenly, it felt like my mind—which is far too good at imagining things for its own good sometimes—stepped backwards off a cliff. It felt like falling—not being dead, that is, but trying to imagine something that I literally can't imagine. Like trying to see the back of your own eyes.

I don't often face things I can't imagine.

* * *

MY SISTER INVITED me and my family to join her and her husband at the beach house. One of our aunts own it, and we've both gone there off and on since we were kids. But not at the same time, not for years anyway. We haven't even spoken in years, not until today when we all arrived, parked on the grassy turf between salal bushes in front of the house and started unpacking.

My kids are old enough now that they can mostly take care of themselves on a trip like this—pack a bag, claim a bed in one of the drafty bedrooms, and then either hit the beach or hang out in the living room playing one of the beat up old board games. Maybe reading a really old paperback. There's such an eclectic collection, sporadically updated when visitors to the house leave a new book behind. I don't know if I'd have ever read Steve Martin's memoir if I hadn't happened upon a copy here, and it was a really good read. On the other hand, some of the books are downright cringe-worthy, like the book of sanctimonious parables my dad used to insist on reading out loud to us when we were little. That book is simply awful, and of course, it's still here. This whole place is like a time capsule.

My sister and I play Bananagrams on the kitchen table, each solitarily building our little castles out of words, barely speaking, and I wonder: doesn't she want to catch up? Doesn't she want to hear anything and everything about my life from the years we've been estranged? But she doesn't ask questions. She doesn't volunteer stories from her own life. Instead, we laugh lightly about the silly words we can spell with our Bananagram tiles and keep it polite. Everything is polite and distanced.

I guess, it's better than feeling like I have no sister at all. But it's strange to me that this seems to be all she wants, getting noticeably uncomfortable whenever I gently try for more.

I WAITED seven years for our paths to come together again. I always knew my story and my sister's story weren't done with each other yet. We grew apart—violently, angrily, resentfully, both feeling like the other one was too much like our dad, who neither of us can trust. And it took this long for us to come together again, for us to each want the other one back enough that we're willing to spend our time together in a sort of quasi-silence, biting our tongues, trying to enjoy each other's company in a physical way—each of us is a warm animal in a room near the other, and we're not fighting. But we aren't talking either, not really. Like two cats sitting with their backs to each other, each with their ears skewed in annoyance, keenly aware of the other cat's presence and mad about it, yet doing nothing to change the situation. That's a kind of love, isn't it?

Maybe this is as good as we can do now. Maybe it's the

best we'll be able to do for the rest of our lives, and maybe, I can be okay with that.

But while we walk together on the beach, commenting only on simple things like the weather, I find my mind wandering, screaming to talk to someone, to truly connect...

...and I begin to see flashes of friends who I remember from a long time ago. Friends who I haven't needed in a while, as my life has been too busy, too chaotic to allow them space:

A bright white Unicorn prancing in the foamy edge of the surf, his cloven hooves dancing through thinned out waves. And a dragon as dark as obsidian curled up in the hot sand, sunning like a lizard on a rock, only so much bigger, so much grander.

AFTER EVERYONE else has gone to bed, I sit at the kitchen table, staring at the jumble of Bananagram tiles and holding a warm mug of lemon tea. I've laid two more mugs out in front of me. Both empty. All the mugs here are shades of brown with a mottled texture, almost like they'd been made by a novice at working with clay. I think they're older than I am. One of the empty mugs is filled with hot chocolate, topped with whipped cream and mini-marshmallows. The other is filled with ginger tea that's as real as any tea that ever graced a child's tea party with her stuffed animals and dolls.

I'm casting a summoning spell. Bringing my friends back to me. But they're more distant now than they used to be. Even with their mugs here, waiting for them, they don't come to the table to sit down. They keep walking beside the ocean, too far away to see through a darkened window. But I can hear them.

I close my eyes and listen to the voices in my head. Tonight, they're talking about me.

* * *

THE DRAGON PLACES one curved talon in front of the other, strolling along beside the waves in a steady line while the Unicorn dances beside him, in and out of the rolling waves, back and forth between the water and sand, along an ever-shifting scalloped path.

"You're the stories she tells," the Dragon rumbles, "and I'm the story telling her. I'm the darkness she sees when she closes her eyes, and you're the pictures she draws on it. The last time her eyes close, I'll be there for her, waiting to enfold her in my wings forever."

"What about me? What happens to me then?"

"Maybe she'll bring you with her."

"I'll be enclosed inside a dragon's wings? Forever?"

"*My* wings. Would that be so bad?"

The Unicorn looks at the Dragon, stilling his frenetic dance. The underside of the Dragon's wings are as dark as a starless night. "No," he says. "But maybe..." The Unicorn tries to imagine the world going on without him. Without *her*. (Without me.)

I'm the best thing in the Unicorn's world, and that's not arrogance on my part. I'm what imagined him into being, what made the world worthwhile and anchored him to it. Without me, the Unicorn wouldn't exist at all.

Without me, though, the world will continue to exist, but it will be missing something necessary. Something that makes it better. More worthwhile. (At least, I'd like to think so.)

And the Unicorn is part of me. The best part of me. That isn't arrogance on the Unicorn's part—it's what I believe about myself.

"No," the Unicorn says. "I think I'll have to stay behind. It's what she would want me to do." He'd have to find a way to prance through other people's minds and be seen by other people's eyes.

"You'd abandon her?" the Dragon asks pointedly, superciliously, almost angrily. Definitely aggressively. "Stay in a world she can't be in anymore?"

The Unicorn lowers his head until his horn almost touches the ground. The magic from his horn pushes the grains of sand aside around its glowing point, drawing a line along the beach as they walk side by side. He whickers in his softest voice: "She'll still have you."

"And what will you do here, all alone?" the Dragon asks, almost gently. They are best friends after all. "I won't be here anymore. Not without her."

"I'll do my best," the Unicorn says bravely, "to make sure she's remembered."

* * *

I shove the Bananagrams tiles aside, arrange my laptop on the kitchen table between the three mugs—two empty and one with a single sugary sip of lemon tea left at the bottom—open up a Word document and begin to type.

I write down everything. Every thought crossing my mind, every thought I've been collecting like shiny pebbles from the beach since arriving here, or maybe just the ones I can still remember. And then I begin to write down the echoing words of the voices I still hear. The voices of my friends as they continue to walk—silky soft and milky white beside glass hard and night sky black—along the beach. I can almost see them now, even though I'm not looking through the window anymore.

The Dragon's scales reflect the stars from the sky, and the Unicorn glows with his own gentle light. The Unicorn is innocence; the Dragon world-weariness. They've both been with me for almost as long as I can remember.

That's right; I was a world-weary child, and underneath all the shells I've learned to build around myself, all the times I've had to harden my heart, deep inside, I'm still innocent as a grown-up. I still believe that if I pour my heart out—regardless of all the times my cries have gone unanswered—someone will hear me. Someone will understand.

Maybe it won't be my sister or even my husband and children when we all unwind from this trip. Maybe it will be someone who reads these words long after I'm gone and the words on this page are all that's left of me. Maybe it's you, and maybe, even though we've never met, you can see from these words that I would understand you too. Two waves, separated by the wall of time, washing across the same shore.

Can you see them? Can you see the Unicorn and the Dragon walking together beside the sea?

* * *

"Can we keep doing this when she's gone?" the Unicorn asks.

"You mean, keep walking on the beach together?" The Dragon grows translucent, like a reflection on a window, completely at the mercy of the angle of the light. Like a quantum particle whose state depends on being observed or Tinker Bell in *Peter Pan* who needs children to clap for her, he only exists when someone looks at him. "As long as you stay," the Dragon answers, "we may keep doing it forever."

The Unicorn nods his head, trying to understand what the Dragon has said. But he is only a simple Unicorn. Sweet, good, and hopeful. Like a reflection on the glassy surface of a still pond—only as deep as the pond itself, and completely at the mercy of ripples—he only understands enough to be charming, to ask questions, to draw out the stories in me that will only be told if I know someone is listening.

The Unicorn will always listen. He loves stories, and he's one of my favorite stories to tell.

Some ponds are mere puddles, fated to dry up when the sun comes out or be splashed into incoherent chaos by rubber boots and tire treads. But some ponds might as well be oceans. Everlasting. Longer lived than those who play beside them.

This moment—as the Dragon and Unicorn walk together beside the crashing and ebbing waves, leaving neither hoof prints nor talon prints in the sand—is only a moment. And like every moment, it is an eternity unto itself for as long as it is happening.

The Unicorn draws in a deep breath. The coastal air smells sweet.

* * *

THE WAVES CRASH against the shore, one after another, like the pages of a book turning. They'll keep turning, long after I'm no longer here to listen to them. Long after the Dragon has folded me up in his wings and the Unicorn has left me behind, the waves will still crash. And other people will turn pages.

Maybe these pages.

The Dragon is mortality. The Unicorn is a dream of immortality. The Dragon is reality. But the Unicorn... is the hope for something better.

Maybe someday, after the last one of my pages has turned, while the waves still crash, the Unicorn will become yours.

ABOUT THE AUTHOR

Mary E. Lowd is a prolific science-fiction and furry writer in Oregon. She's had more than 200 short stories and a dozen novels published, always with more on the way. Her work has won four Ursa Major Awards, ten Leo Literary Awards, and four Cóyotl Awards. She edited FurPlanet's ROAR anthology series for five years, and she is now the editor and founder of the furry e-zine *Zooscape*. She lives in a crashed spaceship, disguised as a house and hidden behind a rose garden, with an extensive menagerie of animals, some real and some imaginary.

For more information:
marylowd.com

To read Mary's short stories:
deepskyanchor.com

For news, updates, discounts, and deals:
marylowd.com/newsletter

ALSO BY MARY E. LOWD

Otters In Space

Otters In Space

Otters In Space 2: Jupiter, Deadly

Otters In Space 3: Octopus Ascending

Otters In Space 4: First Moustronaut

Otters In Space Spinoffs

In a Dog's World

When A Cat Loves A Dog

Jove Deadly's Lunar Detective Agency (with Garrett Marco)

Paw Prints Beyond the Moon

The Entangled Universe

Entanglement Bound

The Entropy Fountain

Starwhal in Flight

Entangled Universe Spinoffs

You're Cordially Invited to Crossroads Station

Welcome to Wespirtech

Beyond Wespirtech

Brunch at the All Alien Cafe

Xeno-Spectre

Hell Moon

The Ancient Egg

The Celestial Fragments (A Labyrinth of Souls Trilogy)

The Snake's Song

The Bee's Waltz

The Otter's Wings

Tri-Galactic Trek

Tri-Galactic Trek

Nexus Nine: A Tri-Galactic Trek Novel

Voyage of the Wanderlust: A Tri-Galactic Trek Novel

Labrador Lieutenant: Chronicles of Tri-Galactic Trek

Collie Commander: Chronicles of Tri-Galactic Trek

Other Collections

The Necromouser and Other Magical Cats

The Opposite of Memory

Commander Annie and Other Adventures

Animal Voices, Unicorn Whispers

Hot Chocolate for the Unicorn and Other Flights of Fancy

Queen Hazel and Beloved Beverly

Some Words Burn Brightly: An Illuminated Collection of Poetry

Furry Fiction Is Everywhere (with Ian Madison Keller)

www.ingramcontent.com/pod-product-compliance
Lightning Source LLC
Chambersburg PA
CBHW021418150726
47989CB00001B/26